PENURY

A bizarre death tests Scotland's finest

PETE BRASSETT

THE BOOK FOLKS

Paperback published by The Book Folks

London, 2021

This book is a work of fiction. Names, characters, businesses, organizations, places and events are either the product of the author's imagination or are used fictitiously. Any resemblance to actual persons, living or dead, events or locales is entirely coincidental. The spelling is British English.

ISBN 978-1-913516-15-4

www.thebookfolks.com

PENURY is the twelfth novel by Pete Brassett to feature detectives Munro and West. Details about the other books can be found at the end of this one. All of these books can be enjoyed on their own, or as a series.

Prologue

Alan 'Duffy' MacDuff, an unassuming forty-nine-year-old with a penchant for tight T-shirts and a gleaming array of what his father referred to as 'dead man's teeth', lived under the constraints of a lengthy non-harassment order issued for the prolonged persecution of his estranged wife, a sentence which had inadvertently spawned a fruitful career as a security consultant, a vocation which, aside from the installation of intruder alarms, afforded him the opportunity to secrete micro motion-activated digicams in the bathrooms and bedrooms of his single, female clients which he accessed via an app on his mobile phone.

Despite being forced from the marital home, Duffy – whose appearance switched from that of a jaded hipster by day to a homeless jakey by night – bore no grudge against his wife, on the contrary he thanked her for releasing him from the shackles of a loveless marriage, for being the catalyst that sparked a burgeoning career, and for affording him the opportunity to go about his business without being lambasted about his intake of alcohol, his slovenly behaviour, or his tardy timekeeping. He did, however, resent the fact that she'd described him as a manipulative misogynist with a temper as volatile as Vesuvius in order to secure a divorce on the grounds of unreasonable behaviour, an aspersion which fuelled his desire to track her every move.

Unfazed by the prospect of having to keep a ledger and file a tax return, as one of the nation's self-employed he enjoyed instead being at liberty to do as he pleased, when he pleased, and so remained beneath the sheets with the curtains pulled against a harsh winter sun to browse his phone and ogle, in particular, a lissom, young blonde as she readied herself for work in a state of undress. The salacious grin was wiped from his face as the sound of his inbox pinged with another enquiry about the cost of his services, an email he would have returned to later had it not been signed by a Miss Rebecca Barlow, a thirty-six-year-old property developer who, according to her Facebook page, harboured a passion for fine wine and silk sheets.

Replying with an assurance that the sixty-minute drive from his home on Taylor Street in Ayr to the village of Auchencairn in rural Kirkcudbrightshire would not impact upon his pledge to provide free estimates *anytime, anyplace, anywhere*, he readily accepted her invitation to survey her latest acquisition; the old Commercial Hotel on Main Street where, he was certain, the fiery redhead like all his other clients, would find him positively irresistible.

* * *

With the snow-capped summits of Screel and Bengairn to the north and a view across the bay to Hestan Island in the south, the centuries-old village of Auchencairn – riddled with folklore and built largely on the proceeds of contraband smuggled across the Firth from the Isle of Man – had, with the passage of time, seen its once-thriving shops and pubs packed with sailors and crofters transformed into second homes by wealthy middle classes making it a seasonal destination for holiday-makers and day-trippers alike.

Having closed its doors to paying guests decades earlier, the Commercial Hotel – a small and unimposing stone-built affair located on the village square – was, in the absence of any signage, identifiable only by the presence of an overflowing skip placed precariously on the kerb outside, a clear indication that refurbishment was all but complete.

Aware that his arrival had caught the attention of a shadowy figure in an upstairs window, Duffy stepped from his van and smiled lecherously as a youthful-looking lady clad in woollen tights, a plaid mini skirt, and a quilted bomber jacket, emerged from behind the faded timber door.

* * *

Armed with a grammar school education, Rebecca Barlow – the only child of a general practitioner and a nursery school teacher – was lured from the family home in Penrith on the edge of Cumbria's Lake District by the bright lights of Carlisle and the prospect of a well-paid but unchallenging role within a firm of solicitors, a position she endured until a cocksure entrepreneur who was of the opinion that no woman should be drinking alone in his local bar at seven o'clock in the evening, invited her to join his chain of estate agents for a meagre salary, a healthy commission, and the opportunity to mooch around other folks' houses.

As a frontline member of staff she soon discovered a hitherto untapped skill for negotiating and with it the realisation that buying and selling property was probably the quickest way to amass a small fortune, an epiphany which drove her to embark on the renovation of a city-centre flat before moving on to more adventurous projects in sought-after locations, a calculated ploy to attract an altogether wealthier clientele, her swelling coffers helped in no small way by her ability to broker knock-down rates with the contractors she employed, a feat she achieved not by plying them with endless mugs of tea and chocolate biscuits but by smiling coyly, praising their skills and, wherever possible, bending seductively over a kitchen counter.

'Mr MacDuff?' she said, proffering her hand as if she were royalty.

'Miss Barlow. Your photo doesn't do you justice.'

'Photo?'

'Aye,' said MacDuff, 'on Facebook.'

'So you've been Googling me?'

'I like to call it research. There's lot of time-wasters out there.'

'Do I look like a waste of time?'

'Time well spent, I'd say,' said MacDuff with a wink. 'So, it's cameras you're after, is it?'

Barlow turned and waved her arm in the direction of the hotel.

'The Hass,' she said, 'or The Hass Burn Hotel, I haven't decided yet.'

'I'm not with you.'

'The Hass, it's the river which runs at the back.'

'So you do your research too?'

'The devil is in the detail,' said Barlow, 'especially if I'm going to haul in the rich and the famous.'

'So, that's your plan?'

'Indeed. A boutique hotel with–'

'With tiny rooms, fancy soap and exorbitant rates.'

'Something like that.'

'Why not stick with Commercial? Sounds right up your street.'

'Cheeky!' said Barlow with a smile. 'Come on, I'll show you around.'

* * *

Whilst some were blessed with an eye for aesthetics, others with a flair for oils and acrylics, and a few with the ability to carve a lifelike sculpture from a piece of driftwood, there were those who deluded themselves into believing they had the God-given talent of Charles Rennie-Mackintosh and although Duffy's own creativity was limited to his book-keeping skills, he couldn't help but cringe as he eyed a refurbishment that had more in common with a souvenir shop than an upmarket hotel.

Appalled by the fact that every original feature had been hidden behind plasterboard, he nonetheless smiled politely as he eyed the plethora of cultural icons filling every nook and cranny, from the prevalence of tartan curtains and tablecloths to the abundance of portraits featuring Bonnie Prince Charlie, William Wallace, and Robert Burns, a Saltire draped from the ceiling, crockery emblazoned with purple thistles, and a glossy reproduction of *The Monarch of the Glen* hanging behind the bar.

'So, what do you think?' said Barlow, proudly. 'I was going for *traditional Scottish*.'

'Aye, well, you're not far off. I'll give you that.'

'Is there anything missing?'

'Just a wee snap of the Loch Ness monster.'

'The monster!' said Barlow. 'How could I be so stupid! Where would I get one of those?'

'You could try Fort William,' said Duffy, incredulously. 'Just make sure you've a camera with you. Right, so it's wireless HD units you'll be needing, a couple by the doors front and back, a few more in all the public spaces, and two monitors; one in the office and one behind the bar. I can pick up the necessary this afternoon and start wiring up tomorrow if you like.'

'Perfect!' said Barlow, smiling as she slowly unzipped her jacket. 'So, how much are we talking about?'

Duffy took a deep breath, plucked a figure out of the air and vowed to return the following morning, 8am sharp, his mind already awash with fantasies of finding her wrapped beneath the sheets of an upstairs bedroom.

* * *

The next day, having left home without so much as a swig of coffee, Duffy – driven by the misguided belief that an enthusiastic show of diligence might procure a cashless bonus from his alluring new client – approached the square ahead of schedule and, enticed by the glow of the village shop, opted to defer his arrival to search for sustenance, his shoulders twitching as the gauge on the dashboard registered an external temperature of minus nine.

'Alright?' he said, puffing as he opened the door. 'It's absolutely freezing out there!'

A small, wiry woman stacking tins of beans turned around, peered over her glasses, and eyed him suspiciously.

'It's January,' she said, bluntly. 'What can I get you?'

'I don't suppose you've any food on the go? Just a sandwich, maybe?'

'I can do you a bacon roll.'

'Spot on,' said Duffy. 'Red sauce, and a coffee please.'

'So, are you on your way somewhere? Kirkcudbright, is it? Or Castle Douglas?'

'No, no. I'm stopping here,' said Duffy. 'I've some work to do, up on the square.'

The woman frowned as she contemplated his answer, dropped a couple of rashers into a pan, and waited for the sizzle to die down.

'The square?' she said. 'That'll be Barlow's place. Am I right?'

'Aye, that's it. Rebecca Barlow. Do you know her?'

The lady huffed and flipped the bacon.

'No,' she said. 'She's not one for mixing with the likes of us.'

'I'm surprised,' said Duffy. 'I'd have thought if she lived here in the village she'd be–'

'She doesn't live here. She stays in the town, twenty miles away.'

Duffy, ruffled by the palpable air of animosity, attempted to lighten the situation.

'So,' he said, grinning, 'I suppose she's not what you'd call *community spirited*, then.'

'The only thing that woman knows about community is how to tear it apart.'

'Oh? How so?'

'I'm saying nothing. I'm not one for gossip.'

'Fair enough.'

'The Commercial. That's her fourth.'

'Sorry, hen, you've lost me. Fourth what?'

'Her fourth property!' said the woman, scowling as she bagged up the buttie. 'She's had three already and sold them on at a profit. A huge profit.'

'Well, that's not such a bad thing, is it?' said Duffy. 'If she does a house up?'

'No,' said the woman. 'You're right. It's not a bad thing if she was selling them on to folk who could afford them, but no-one here can, so that's three houses gone to folk south of the border who we see for two weeks of the year, and even then they don't come to the shop.'

'Oh well,' said Duffy, 'maybe the hotel will bring–'

'See here, mister whatever-your-name-is, she's not welcome here! I'll tell you something about the Commercial, shall I? Do you know who used to live there? Jack Muir and his wife, eighty-nine years old, the pair of them, both born and bred in Auchencairn, and she didn't even wait for them to get planted. She offered them next to nothing to get out of the building and they took it.'

'Well, I'm not across the details,' said Duffy, 'but it seems to me that if they had a choice and if they–'

The woman plucked a spatula from the frying pan and waved it in Duffy's face.

'Do you know where they are now?' she said. 'Jack and his wife?'

'No. I'm guessing a nice wee flat, maybe. Or a retirement home.'

'The cemetery. They're in the cemetery.'

Rankled by the ensuing silence and the lady's unwavering stare, Duffy fumbled for his wallet.

'Well, maybe once she's finished the hotel she'll be on her way.'

'She'll not last that long.'

'Sorry?'

'The garden. She's decimated the garden and chopped down a sacred tree. So that's her humped.'

* * *

Dismissing the shop-keeper's anxieties surrounding Barlow's expanding property portfolio as nothing more than idle tittle-tattle and superstitious claptrap, Duffy demolished his breakfast, pulled his toolbox and a reel of cable from the back of the van and crunched his way across the frost-laden street to the Commercial which, much to his disappointment, was swathed in darkness.

Nudging the door with his foot he called for Barlow and, with no reply, seized the opportunity to engage in a more leisurely tour of the building pondering, as he went, the possibility of concealing a few undetectable cameras within the fixtures and fittings of the bedrooms on the upper level.

Declaring the master chamber, replete with four-poster bed and chaise longue, the most likely setting for any amorous activity, he stepped inside, sniggered at the plastic stag's head mounted on the wall and, distracted by the glare of the morning sun, turned to enjoy the vista from the rear window which, overlooking the grounds, offered a magnificent view of the burn and beyond.

Whilst work in restoring the garden to its former glory had clearly been hindered by the cold snap, some progress had been made: the high, dry-stone walls stripped of ivy, the limbs of a felled tree lying next to its stump, and the border shrubs hacked back to ground level. However, it was the variety of novelty knick-knacks scattered about the lawn which drew him outside.

Although the garden gnomes, complete with pipes and sporrans, were nothing less than he'd come to expect, he had to concede that a six-feet-tall effigy of the Wicker Man and the large metal signs extolling the virtues of Scotch whisky, chocolate-covered teacakes, and the Great Western Railway did exude a touch of class. However, it was the scarecrow sporting a tweed trilby which he found to be the most bizarre, not because the clothes appeared to be relatively new, nor because it was short in stature, but because it was facing the wall.

Expecting to find a kilt beneath the oversized stockman coat, he wandered to the front, raised the brim of the hat with his forefinger and gagged at the sight of Barlow's anaemic-looking face.

Chapter 1

Despite an irrational belief that hospitals were designed for the exclusive use of forensic pathologists and that the word 'consent' was actually a euphemism for 'do not resuscitate', James Munro – whose arteries were as clogged as a Glasgow sewer – had succumbed to his doctor's advice, drafted a last will and testament and, in the hope of achieving a degree of longevity, put his faith in the skills of a faceless surgeon.

Relieved to find that upon awakening he was neither hovering above the operating table nor possessed by a compulsion to walk towards the light, he thanked the team for their dedication and tenacity during the arduous bypass procedure and, after a brief period in the cardiac ward, hastened towards the door.

Dismissing the protracted programme of recovery prescribed by the consultant cardiologist as positively pedestrian, he devised an alternative plan which, based on the premise that the operation had been a success, involved restoring the status quo by taking vigorous exercise, reacquainting his taste buds with the finest sirloin steak, and indulging in the occasional Balvenie.

Twelve months on and accompanied by Murdo, the ageing Scottish terrier whose companionship and dogged determination to walk for miles had played no small part in his return to physical fitness, a rejuvenated Munro – filling his retirement as a voluntary advisor to his old team of detectives in Ayrshire – had decided to put his pension and savings to good use in order that the fruits of his labours could be enjoyed by others whilst he was in the land of the living rather than wait for his inevitable demise.

Ignoring the minor roof repairs, the need for a new boiler, and the installation of a central heating system, the selling point of the cosy one-bedroom cottage was, for Munro, not the wood-burning stove, the quarry-tiled floors, nor the whitewashed granite walls but the large, lawned garden which, at almost one hundred feet in length, had space enough for a healthy crop of home-grown tatties as well as providing the perfect setting for a relaxing dram or two on a warm summer's evening.

The agent, waiting patiently by the door, smiled as Munro ambled down the stairs with Murdo at his heels.

'That's your second viewing now,' she said. 'So tell me, Mr Munro, what do you think?'

'Ideal. In fact, I'd say it's perfect.'

'Does that mean you'll be making an offer?'

'I will,' said Munro, 'but not for the asking price, not with the amount of work it needs to bring it up to scratch.'

'Well, that's your call,' said the agent, 'all I can do is forward your offer to the vendor and see what they say.'

'Much obliged,' said Munro, 'and I'll be blunt, I'll not go a penny more, so if they're of a mind to haggle, then you can tell them I'm not interested.'

'I'll let them know but if they do accept your offer, does that mean you'll be moving here from Carsethorn?'

Of the opinion that to leave the house he'd shared with his late wife would be nothing less than an act of betrayal, he smiled wistfully and shook his head.

'No,' he said. 'I could never leave Carsethorn.'

'I see. So it's an investment, is it? Or a holiday let?'

'Neither. Let's call it a legacy and leave it at that.'

Caught off-guard by the icy blast blowing up the street, Munro, reaching for his cap, thanked the young lady as Murdo, refusing the sanctuary of his antiquated Peugeot, dragged him towards the village square where, much to his surprise, he was greeted by the sight of a cordoned-off building and a police officer huddled on a bench.

'No doubt this will give the village something to talk about,' he said, as he sat beside him.

'Aye, and not just the village.'

'Oh, how so?'

'I can't say,' said the officer. 'Listen to the radio, it'll be on the news, I'm sure.'

Often described as inquisitive by some and meddlesome by others, Munro, his curiosity roused at the merest hint of a misdemeanour, seized the opportunity to delve a little deeper.

'Far be it for me to tell you your job,' he said, 'but should you not be standing over there? By the door?'

The constable cast him a sideways glance and shook his head.

'No point,' he said. 'There's no-one about, I've missed my lunch, and I'm chilled to the bone. I deserve a wee sit down.'

'I'm sure you do. The name's Munro by the way.'

'Pleasure, I'm sure.'

'Detective Inspector James Munro.'

The officer, his eyes widening in much the same way an absent-minded pensioner might suddenly remember they'd left a pan of milk on the boil, dashed towards the door and stood bolt upright with his hands behind his back.

Munro turned to his dog and smiled.

'Did I forget to mention I'd retired?'

'I owe you an apology,' said the officer as Munro strolled towards him, 'I was out of order, I just didn't realise you were–'

'Och, wheesht! Who's the SIO here?'

'DI Byrne, sir. He's around the back. Will I fetch him for you?'

'No, you're alright,' said Munro. 'I'm sure I can find him.'

* * *

Perched on a picnic bench with his head in his hands, the young Greg Byrne – a fledgling DI whose workload to date had involved two cases of sexual assault, one of theft, and an ongoing game of cat and mouse with a gang of teenage drug dealers – had had the case foisted upon him by superiors sceptical of his ability to lead and co-ordinate such an investigation, their suspicions, he concurred, being well-founded; and whilst confronting a corpse with skin as white as the driven snow held no fear, finding one lashed to a couple of six-feet poles dressed in an overcoat with a frozen look of astonishment on its face, gave him the heebie-jeebies.

He turned and raised his head as the side gate creaked open.

'Ho! You!' he said, leaping to his feet. 'That's far enough! There's nothing to see here, it's not a peep show!'

'DI Byrne, I presume?'

'Aye, and you are?'

'Munro. James Munro.'

'Good for you, sir. Now like I say, there's…'

Byrne paused and cocked his head.

'Just a moment,' he said, with a frown. 'Munro? *DI James Munro*?'

'The very same.'

'I thought you were dead.'

'You're not alone, although for many it's just a case of wishful thinking.'

'Sorry, sir, no offence, it's the way they talk about you back at The Mount, it's like you're some kind of a legend.'

'I'm flattered but I can assure you, I am nothing of the sort.'

'Do you stay here, then? In Auchencairn?'

'Not exactly,' said Munro. 'That is to say, I might be. Possibly. Now, the fella out front says you've a body on your hands.'

'Aye,' said Byrne, scratching the back of his head. 'I certainly have.'

'Then why are you on your own?'

'My DS has gone to fetch some coffee and I'm still waiting on SOCOs and a pathologist.'

'Would it not make sense to wait inside with the victim? At least you'd be warm.'

'The victim's not inside,' said Byrne, with a flick of the head. 'She's right here.'

Munro looked towards the scarecrow and smiled.

'Are you joking me?' he said. 'You mean...?'

'Aye, in one.'

'That would explain the look on your face, then.'

'What look's that?'

'One of complete and utter consternation.'

'Aye, maybe.'

'Would it help if I–'

'Sorry, no offence, sir, but as you know, I'm not at liberty to discuss the case with anyone other than–'

'Of course,' said Munro, 'you're quite right. Well, I'll leave you to it then.'

'On second thoughts.'

'What is it?'

Byrne, riddled with anxiety, looked sheepishly at Munro and scratched his head again.

'It's just that, well, I feel a bit... you know, out on a limb. This is my first murder as a DI and...'

'And it's a baptism of fire?'

'Aye,' said Byrne, mustering a smile, 'although if I'm honest, it feels more like an inferno.'

'There's no shame in asking for help,' said Munro. 'Remember, every expert was once a beginner.'

'Thanks,' said Byrne. 'I appreciate it. I'll fetch you some boot socks from the car.'

* * *

Unwilling to sit tethered to a table when there was new territory to explore, Murdo slipped his harness and headed for the patio while Munro, donning his spectacles, leaned into Barlow's body for a closer look.

'I have to say, this is a first for me. Do we know who she is?'

'I think so,' said Byrne. 'We found a coat and a bag on the bar inside and she seems to match the photo on a driving licence, her name's Rebecca Barlow.'

'And do you know what she was doing here?'

'Not yet,' said Byrne, 'we're running a check on her now and my DC's on his way over to her place, maybe there's someone else at her address.'

'Good.'

'There is one thing, though.'

'Go on.'

'Like I say, I've searched her belongings but I couldn't find a phone. Everyone has a phone.'

'Is there a landline here?'

'Aye. Well, there's sockets on the walls but nothing's connected.'

'In that case,' said Munro, 'I'm inclined to agree. That is odd. Have you looked about the place? Perhaps she left it somewhere else?'

'I have,' said Byrne. 'Nothing.'

'What about her motor car?'

'Car?'

'Come, come, laddie, I think it's safe to assume she didnae arrive on public transport. Get your brain in gear, have you contacted DVLA?'

'No.'

'Why not?'

'Sorry, my head's mince.'

'Well do it!' said Munro. 'You've got her licence, find out what she's driving. It must be parked here, somewhere! I'll not be surprised if that's where you'll find her phone.'

'I'll do it right away,' said Byrne. 'The thing is, Mr Munro, what I don't get is why? Why do this? I mean, not just kill someone but dress them up like a...?'

'There's always a reason,' said Munro, 'and it's your job to find out what it is. Right, let's start at the beginning. First question, how did you enter the building?'

'Front door. It was open.'

'And the back?'

'Closed but not locked.'

'And the side gate?'

'Bolted from the inside.'

'And I take it you've had a look around the house?'

'Aye, we have,' said Byrne, 'nothing untoward, I mean, no sign of a disturbance or anything like that.'

'So what does that tell you?'

'That whoever did this was likely someone she knew?'

'Possibly,' said Munro. 'Possibly. What else?'

'That the perp must have left by the front door?'

'Excellent. Go on.'

Byrne looked blankly at Munro.

'Och, come, come. Look at her clothes, laddie. Her shoes in particular.'

'What about them?'

'Look around you! Tell me what you see!'

Byrne slowly turned through 180 degrees surveying the garden and commenting as he went.

'It's frosty,' he said, 'has been for a couple of days. Oh, except by the walls, it looks damp and a wee bit muddy where all the plants have been cut back. Same for the path that's been trodden from the back door.'

'So?'

Byrne turned his attention to Barlow's attire and pondered for a moment.

'Got it! Her shoes are clean, spotless in fact, so she didn't walk here. She must've been killed indoors and carried out by the perp.'

'Hallelujah. Now, the picnic table.'

'What of it?' said Byrne.

'You have the gift of sight, laddie. Use it.'

'Hold on, it's clear! There's no frost! So maybe that's where she was laid to get strapped to the poles.'

'Let's move on,' said Munro. 'The body, her posture, what can you glean from that?'

'Sorry,' said Byrne with a sigh. 'I've no idea, apart from the fact it looks like a mock crucifixion.'

'Dear God, and you were doing so well.'

'Sorry.'

'The arms,' said Munro. 'Her arms, they're sagging, bent at the elbow and her head's fallen forward but she's as stiff as a post, which means?'

Byrne shrugged his shoulders apologetically.

'Which means she must have been strapped to the poles before rigor set in. At least, that's what I think. Unfortunately, I cannae see any obvious injuries, not without undressing her so you'll have to wait for the pathologist to confirm a cause of death. Does that help?'

'Like you wouldn't believe,' said Byrne. 'Like you would not believe.'

'Then it's time I took my dog to lunch. Before I go, who actually called this in?'

'It was an anonymous call,' said Byrne. 'Yesterday, early afternoon. The handler thought it was a prank at first.'

'I'm not surprised.'

'Once uniform got here and realised it wasn't, the call was easy enough to trace. A mobile number, a fella by the name of MacDuff. He stays in Ayr.'

'Ayr? What on earth was he doing down here?'

'Search me, we're still in the process of finding out.'

'So you've not spoken to him?'

'Not yet, sir. No. It's a cross-border issue, we're waiting on the lads up there to give us the nod.'

'But you've an address?'

'Aye. Taylor Street.'

'And have you any idea when she, that is Miss Barlow, was last seen alive?'

'No. Door-to-doors are next on my list.'

'Well, I may be wrong,' said Munro, 'but I think the answer to that question may lie with a local gardener. You'd do well to contact every one in the area.'

'How so?'

Munro walked towards the scarecrow pointing at the boundary as he went.

'All those border shrubs,' he said, bending to retrieve a branch, 'they're evergreens and they've only just been pruned. And this tree, it's not long been felled. As a keen gardener I'd say that happened in the last day or two.'

Byrne lowered his head and smiled.

'I don't know what to say,' he said. 'If you hadn't shown up I think I might have–'

'Och, nonsense,' said Munro, 'you'd have got there in the end. Best of luck, laddie. If you've any more questions, I'll be in the office. I'm sure someone you know has my number.'

'So, you're still working, then?'

'In a manner of speaking.'

'Then I might just give you a call,' said Byrne. 'Are you taking that wee branch as a souvenir?'

'It's a rowan tree,' said Munro. 'They're lucky. For some.'

Chapter 2

Ranking Barlow's demise as possibly one of the most intriguing investigations he'd had the good fortune to come across – second only to a bagful of body parts stashed beneath a bathtub in an abandoned orphan asylum – Munro, proclaiming it an opportunity too good to miss, fastened his safety belt, cranked the heating up to full, and pulled his phone from his pocket.

As one of Munro's protégés, DS Dougal McCrae – an erudite introvert with a technological bent who, unlike his mentor, preferred to base his inquiries on hard facts rather than instinct – had a propensity to work the back shift thereby assuring himself a degree of solitude whilst simultaneously avoiding the harrowing task of having to socialise with friends or colleagues.

'Boss! Are you okay?'

'Never better,' said Munro. 'I'm on my way in.'

'Is it not a bit late for that?'

'Ordinarily, aye, but there's something I need you to do.'

'Fire away.'

'Have you heard anything from Dumfries?'

'Dumfries?'

'Aye, the lads at The Mount should be getting in touch about questioning a witness to a wee incident.'

'Well I've not heard anything,' said Dougal. 'Not yet.'

'Good, then a favour if you will. A gentleman by the name of MacDuff, he stays on Taylor Street. See what you can find out.'

'No problem. Is he something to do with the incident you mentioned?'

'He is, aye.'

'Oh. Is that allowed?' said Dougal. 'I mean, should we not wait for Dumfries to get in touch?'

Adept at ignoring regulations and bending the rules like a freshly stripped length of willow, Munro rolled his eyes and sighed.

'Dougal,' he said, 'how long have you known me?'

'Three years. Three years and nine months to be exact.'

'And in all that time, have you ever known me to be bothered by a wee piece of red tape?'

'Aye, okay. I get the message.'

'I'm obliged. Now, is Charlie there?'

'No, boss. She's on a shout with Duncan.'

'Then I'll not disturb her but if she calls in, tell her I'll be needing a bed for the night.'

* * *

Not one to begrudge anyone anything, even people from backgrounds more privileged than his own, Duncan Reid – raised on a run-down housing scheme, spurned by his tutors, and rejected by every prospective employer for even the most menial of jobs – enlisted with Police Scotland as a last resort, graduated with the minimum of effort and, despite a minor reprimand for his somewhat maverick approach to policing, rapidly rose to the rank of DS where he relished his role as a latter-day Frank Serpico.

Uniquely aware of how easy it was for youngsters without the proper guidance to fall by the wayside and turn to a life of crime as a means of supplementing their meagre welfare pay-outs, he could, to an extent, empathise with the plight of the delinquents dealing and stealing on his patch. However, a lack of willingness on their behalf to heed the warnings of the courts and the advice of their counsellors denied them any sympathy.

Emma Riley, a habitual reoffender who'd rendered herself ineligible for any kind of support by refusing every offer of employment from the Jobcentre, emerged from the supermarket looking more Burberry than Primark oblivious to the fact that her ostentatious display of wealth had made her the subject of further surveillance.

Duncan, hidden amongst a sea of nondescript four-door saloons in the overflowing car park, watched as she placed her groceries on the ground, opened her purse, and handed a twenty pound note to a bearded beggar squatting beneath the ATM.

'Not bad for someone who's not earning,' he said as Charlie West shifted uncomfortably in her seat.

'My backside's killing me,' she said. 'What did you say?'

'Emma Riley, miss.'

'Sorry, you'll have to remind me, I'm not with it today.'

'Rough night?'

'You could say that.'

'Not on the ale, surely?'

'Only after he left.'

'Uh-oh, say no more.'

'So, this Riley girl?'

'Released two days ago. She was done for possession. Eighteen months and a hefty fine.'

'Blimey, she must've got on the wrong side of the judge to get that.'

'She did,' said Duncan. 'Not only was it the second time she'd been caught carrying khat, which would've been enough to send her down anyway, but she claimed she was looking after it for a friend who'd told her it was basil and when she refused to name him, or her, that was it, game over.'

'Well I doubt she'll find any in the fruit and veg aisle here,' said West. 'I wonder what she's waiting for.'

'I'm guessing a taxi to take her back to Belmont.'

'Does she live alone?'

'Apparently. Though how she pays the rent is anyone's guess.'

Bemused by the sight of a gleaming white coupé with tinted windows crawling towards the entrance, Duncan reached for his phone and called the office as it drew to a halt by the ATM.

'I don't know about you, miss,' he said as Riley popped her bags in the boot, 'but that's not the kind of minicab I'm used to seeing around here. Dougal, I've got an index for you, quick as you can please, pal.'

'I'm all ears.'

'Papa, X-ray, two-zero, Yankee, Tango, Delta.'

'Give me a minute.'

Duncan, geared up for a discreet pursuit, turned to West and smiled.

'Will we follow?'

West pondered for moment.

'No,' she said. 'I don't want to spook them. Let's do our research first. We can pay them a visit once we know who the owner is.'

'Are you there?' said Dougal.

'Aye, you're on speaker, fire away.'

'It's a Lexus RC. The registered keeper stays in Belmont. Burnside Road.'

'But that's Riley's address,' said Duncan. 'Are you sure about that?'

'That's what is says here.'

'Who's the owner?'

'A Mr Daniel McIntyre.'

'Run a check please,' said West. 'I want everything you can find on him. Who knows, he might be the bloke she refused to name.'

'No bother,' said Dougal. 'Listen, are you two heading back here?'

'Not if I can help it, it's getting late. Why?'

'The boss has been in touch, he'll be here any minute.'

'Jimbo? What's he doing coming over at this time of day?'

'I think he's got a wee sniff of something, miss. I had to do some digging for him. Oh, and he says he'll be needing a bed for the night.'

Duncan flipped the key in the ignition and laughed.

'I get the feeling we're about to get roped into something we know nothing about.'

'You and me both,' said West. 'Okay, tell him to meet me at mine, and if he hasn't got wine, he's not getting in.'

Chapter 3

Following the untimely passing of his beloved wife some years earlier, Munro – keen to maintain a sense of purpose in his life – had flatly refused the offer of compassionate leave in favour of relocating, albeit temporarily, to London where, secure in his anonymity, a serendipitous meeting with a young Charlotte West had provided a much needed diversion from the anguish of having to deal with the commiserations and condolences of neighbours, friends, and fellow officers.

Thrown together to investigate the case of a missing person, West – desperately trying to survive the emotional trauma of a broken engagement to a philandering fiancé whilst failing to cope with sexist colleagues who harangued her ruthlessly with erroneous claims of incompetence – would have suffered an irreversible breakdown were it not for Munro's timely intervention.

Detecting a resilience beneath her crumbling exterior, he exercised his right as her superior to administer a well-aimed kick in the pants, a course of action which, though repetitive, boosted her confidence and set her on the way to fulfilling her potential.

However, fearful that his departure might invoke a return to her former vodka-dependant self, he'd cajoled her into joining him on secondment north of the border where, upon accepting the offer of a permanent position, she grafted relentlessly before filling his shoes as a no-nonsense if not headstrong DI.

* * *

Enticed by the tantalising aroma of two twenty-eight-day dry-aged cuts of sirloin, Murdo, suffering from a sudden bout of selective hearing, ignored the call to heel, dashed through the open door, and headed straight for the kitchen leaving Munro cursing in his wake.

'Just what I need,' said West, grinning as she eyed the bottle.

'A disobedient puppy?' said Munro.

'A hair of the dog. You're looking well.'

'And you're looking tired, Charlie.'

'Charming,' said West, as she handed him a corkscrew. 'I've been stuck in the car all day.'

'How so?'

'Keeping tabs on some no-mark with a taste for life's little luxuries.'

'And why is he of interest?'

'She,' said West. 'Because she's done time for possession, more than once I might add, and it seems she just can't kick the habit.'

'Dear, dear,' said Munro, handing her a glass. 'The thing about easy street, Charlie, is it's not easy at all. Your very good health.'

'We know that, but they never learn, do they? Cheers.'

West, whose repertoire in the kitchen was limited to anything involving protein and the minimum amount of washing-up, slipped the steaks under the grill, joined Munro at the table, and gave him a knowing look.

'Come on, then,' she said, sipping the wine. 'Let's have it.'

'Have what, Charlie?'

'You were on the blower to Dougal earlier. What's going on?'

'Just a body,' said Munro.

'You should be used to that by now.'

'Not one done up like a scarecrow, I'm not.'

'Come again?'

'A lassie by the name of Rebecca Barlow, found dead in a garden strapped to a couple of poles with her arms outstretched.'

West leaned back in her seat, her cheeks billowing as she heaved a sigh.

'Now that,' she said, 'sounds creepy. What did she do to deserve that?'

'I've no idea. At this stage all we have is an address. As yet, her background, marital status, and occupation remain unknown.'

'Cause of death?'

'Also unknown. But I'll tell you this,' said Munro, 'it's not the fact that she was made to look like a dress rehearsal for events at Golgotha that intrigues me. It's the fact that she was staked on the site of a rowan.'

'You've lost me,' said West. 'What's a rowan?'

'A tree.'

'And that's important?'

'It could be,' said Munro, 'if you believe in folklore, that is.'

'Go on.'

Munro swigged his wine, placed his hands palm down on the table, and settled back as if regaling a book at bedtime.

'As far as we Celts are concerned, the rowan is regarded as, shall we say, *special*. Sacred, if you will. It can live for as long as two hundred years and thrive at an altitude where nothing else will grow.'

'Fascinating,' said West, facetiously. 'Is that it?'

'It will be if you interrupt again.'

'Sorry.'

'They're said to protect the living from the dead and as such, they've been planted for centuries to ward off changelings and to keep evil spirits at bay. The wood itself was used to fashion coffins, crucifixes, and amulets. To use it for any other purpose was, and still is, frowned upon to say the least.'

'So where is this leading us?'

'Luck,' said Munro. 'Or the lack of it. To cut down a rowan is considered extremely bad luck. The belief is that such an action could unleash a barrage of catastrophic events, even death.'

'So you're telling me this girl died because she chopped down a rowan?'

'I'm saying nothing of the sort, Charlie, but instinct tells me that the felling of that tree is somehow related to her death, in a symbolic way perhaps, but related all the same.'

'I'm surprised,' said West, grinning as she turned the steaks, 'you're normally so rational. I'd dig out that rabbit's foot if I were you. So, what was Dougal looking for?'

'I asked him to run a wee check on the gentleman who found the body. He stays here, in Ayr. I'm of a mind to have a wee chat before the chaps at The Mount get their hands on him.'

'Good luck with that,' said West. 'You'll have to get it past The Bear first.'

'You're forgetting, Charlie, DCI Elliot and myself go way back, I'm sure he'll be most accommodating.'

'Well, I hope you're right, because if the boys in Dumfries find out you've been meddling in their inquiry without their approval then your days as a volunteer are well and truly numbered.'

'I've already met the senior investigating officer,' said Munro. 'We got along famously.'

'Maybe, but what makes you so sure he won't go ballistic when you start treading on his toes?'

'Because he's in much the same boat you were, Charlie, when we met. Only without the alcohol. Or the fiancé.'

'Thanks for reminding me.'

'He's a novice. Keen but inexperienced. He'll appreciate all the help he can get.'

'Well just don't expect any help from me,' said West, 'or Duncan, or Dougal, we've got enough on our plates and… just a bloomin' moment! What the hell do you mean; *the lads at The Mount?* Just where exactly was this body?'

'Auchencairn.'

'Auchencairn? What the hell were you doing in Auchencairn?'

'Viewing a house.'

West paused as a look of enlightenment crossed her face, reached for her wine, and scowled at Munro.

'You went to see that house, didn't you?' she said accusingly. 'The one we looked at together months and months ago.'

'If you're referring to the one you were hankering after but couldnae afford, then aye, I was.'

'Why?'

'To see if it was up to scratch. And it is. So I've made an offer.'

'Oh that's nice!' said West. 'Here am I looking for a cottage with a garden and you go and snap it up!'

'You said yourself you couldnae afford it. But I can.'

'I don't believe I'm hearing this.'

'By my reckoning, once the sale has gone through, it'll only take a month or so to see to the roof and have the boiler installed so you should be able to move in by the spring.'

'That's all very well for you to say but… hang on, *me*? *Me* move in?'

'Aye,' said Munro, '*you*. See here, Charlie, as you know, I've nae family and without wanting to sound morbid, who knows how long I've got. I'd rather my money was put to use now rather than have it squandered when I'm gone.'

West – confused, surprised, and uncharacteristically speechless – stared blankly at Munro and drained her glass.

'I don't know what to say,' she said. 'No. Sorry, Jimbo, it's a lovely offer but no. It doesn't seem right.'

'Well if I dinnae sign it over to you, Charlie, the taxman will take it and sell it on to someone who doesnae deserve it.'

'It still doesn't seem right. It's like… it's like charity.'

'Och, you'll not be getting it for nothing,' said Munro. 'I propose you pay some rent until all the paperwork is done.'

'Here we go.'

'A peppercorn rent. I was thinking twenty-five pounds.'

'A week?'

'No, no. A year.'

'Are you mad?'

'A question that's been levelled at me several times and the answer is no. You need a house of your own, Charlie. This place has gone downhill since you moved in.'

'Thanks very much.'

'You know what I mean.'

'Can I think about it?'

'Take as long as you like,' said Munro, 'you'll be getting it anyway, the only difference is, if you wait until I'm gone, then you'll have inheritance tax to pay. By the way, there is just one condition.'

'I knew there'd be a catch.'

'If they should plant me before wee Murdo here, then he's not to go to a home. You're to look after him. The proceeds from the sale of my house in Carsethorn will pay for his keep.'

'I'm glad you came over, Jimbo. Cheered me right up, you have.'

'I do my best. And who knows, once you've settled into a place of your own, you might feel more inclined to settle down.'

West topped up their glasses and took a large slug.

'That,' she said, 'is not going to happen anytime soon.'

'Oh? How so?'

'I took your advice and invited Andy over.'

'Mr McLeod, our favourite pathologist? Good for you, lassie, I'm glad. He's had the hots for you for quite some time.'

'I know,' said West, 'and last night I realised his feelings for me were unrequited.'

'That,' said Munro, 'is a shame. I hope things didn't get too… out of hand.'

'They didn't get anywhere. I kicked him out after dinner and now I feel guilty. Bottom line is, Jimbo, I just couldn't bear it, him being here, anyone being here, all lovey-dovey that is. I think I like being on my own too much.'

'It's no surprise,' said Munro. 'After what you've been through, you're just protecting yourself. Perhaps you should buy yourself a rowan to plant in your new garden, just to be sure.'

Chapter 4

Surrounded by the gloom of a darkened room with the cool, eerie glow of two computers illuminating the gaunt features of his sun-starved face, Dougal – on to his second litre of Irn-Bru and last slice of cold pizza – squinted at the screen and groaned as he tried in vain to identify the pixelated image of a woven trademark, his frustration peaking as the sound of footsteps along the corridor broke his concentration.

'Is it that time already?' he said as Duncan, balancing four takeaway coffees and a paper carrier bag edged his way through the door.

'It's the back of seven. Have you been here all night?'

'Aye.'

'How so?'

'This came in yesterday,' said Dougal as he rewound the footage from a CCTV camera. 'See this roofless fella? It's 11:40pm and he's cooried down in a doorway having a wee kip. He's not doing anyone any harm.'

'I feel for him,' said Duncan. 'I'm surprised he didn't freeze to death.'

'Aye, now watch. Suddenly he's set upon by some ned who's using him for target practice.'

'Oh! That's out of order! What kind of twisted pleasure can anyone get from kicking some defenceless fella in the back!'

'Search me,' said Dougal.

'Well something's wound him up, that's for sure. What's the betting that dobber just lost all his dole on the horses. Or just split up with his girlfriend. Or got barred from the pub. Or all three. In that order. Is the homeless fella alright?'

'I think so,' said Dougal. 'When the ned takes off, he just curls up and goes to sleep. Come the morning he's gone. I checked with the infirmary and no-one matching his description's been admitted to A&E.'

'I despair. So you're trying to identify the assailant, is that it?'

'Aye. The problem is, Duncan, what with the weather and all, he's done up like a ninja and he's got his back to the camera. All I've got to go on so far is this bleary image of a logo on his jacket. It looks like "FIR" or "FIRL".'

Duncan took a step back and narrowed his eyes as he focused on the screen.

'That's not a fancy coat like the ones you're used to wearing,' he said. 'Firetrap. That logo, it says "FIRETRAP".'

'I've not heard of it.'

'Budget clothing, pal. The only place I know that sells those is the big sports retailer in the town. Where did this happen?'

'Braehead.'

'There you go. The lad's a local. Any other cameras along the way?'

'Aye, a couple,' said Dougal, 'but I've not secured the footage yet.'

'There's some council houses nearby; Glenmuir Road and Ferguson Street. I'm not one to cast aspersions but I'd not be surprised if he lives round there.'

Duncan plucked a toastie from the carrier bag and placed it on the desk.

'Here,' he said, 'I reckon you've earned this. Sausage, red sauce, and your favourite caramel cappuccino.'

'Oh, you're alright,' said Dougal. 'I've still some pizza left.'

'You're unbelievable, pal. How you've not caught scurvy or salmonella by now is beyond me.'

'I think it's what they call a cast-iron constitution. Are you stopping long?'

'We need to visit the Riley girl but I'm not going yet, I'll wait until it's light outside, you know what folk are like, if the neighbours hear me chapping her door when it's still as black as night, the curtains will be twitching the length of the street.'

'Right enough,' said Dougal, 'and the way you're dressed they'll probably think you've come to collect a debt or break somebody's kneecaps.'

'I'll take that as a compliment.'

* * *

Although Dougal, a keen fisherman and all-round nature lover had been fortunate enough to witness the majesty of a golden eagle gliding on the thermals above Kirriereoch Hill and pouting brown trout nibbling his bait on the surface of a moonlit loch, face-to-face encounters with even the most docile of dogs left him quaking in his boots.

Terrified his ankles might make an appetising alternative to his usual bowl of dried kibble, he discreetly lifted his legs from the floor as Murdo, nose to the ground, scampered around the office in search of something edible.

'You're in early,' said West, pulling up a chair. 'What's going on?'

'He's not been home, miss,' said Duncan. 'The man's pure frazzled. Chief, nice to see you! Are you okay?'

'Couldn't be better,' said Munro. 'And yourself?'

'Aye, all good. Okay for Murdo to have a wee piece of sausage?'

'Aye, but I'd toss it to the ground if I were you or he'll have your fingers off as well. Incidentally, I could go one of those myself.'

'In the bag, chief.'

Munro helped himself to a toastie, glanced at Duncan, and smiled.

'Forgive me for saying so,' he said, 'I know you like working in plain clothes, Duncan, but could you not wear some that are clean?'

'They are clean, chief. It's called *the power of deception.* You should know by now, never judge a book by its cover.'

'If you were a book, young man, you'd be in the bargain bin at Waterstones.'

'Now, now,' said West, grabbing a coffee, 'it's too early for squabbles. So, Dougal, what kept you up all night?'

'Assault on a vagrant, miss, it came in yesterday. I'm trying to identify the perp but it's a wee bit of a struggle.'

'Fill me in later, right now I need to know about the bloke who's living with Emma Riley, or should I say, the bloke *we think* is living with Emma Riley.'

'Daniel McIntyre? That won't take long. He's what you might call a bit of an enigma.'

'Oh?'

'The vehicle we traced, that Lexus, is registered to Riley's address but he isn't. He's not on the open register or the electoral roll so he's clearly not voted, not around here, and he's not paying council tax or anything else for that matter. I'm working my way through all the McIntyres in the county to see if I can find one with the same date of birth but it's taking time.'

'How far have you got?'

'I'm on number 6. Only another 138 to go.'

'Well, keep at it,' said West. 'And get onto the DVLA, ask for a copy of the picture he's used on his licence, at least then we'll have a likeness. Okay, next – Emma Riley. Has she applied for Jobseeker's or housing benefit since she got out?'

'I've not checked but if her track record's anything to go by, I doubt she'd bother.'

'Have a look anyway. If she has put in a claim, I want to know if she's told them she's living alone.'

'Okay, but why?'

'Because,' said West, 'if she has, and it turns out she's living with this McIntyre bloke, then we'll do her for benefit fraud.'

'Nice one,' said Duncan. 'A good night's sleep seems to have cleared your head, miss.'

'It has. That and a decent bottle of red. So, are we good to go?'

'We should wait until sunrise,' said Duncan. 'We don't want to cause a ruckus, do we?'

'No, fair enough. Right, let's finish breakfast while Dougal tells us what he's been doing for Jimbo.'

'Aye,' said Munro, 'and I'm hoping you've had more success with my Mr MacDuff than you did with that McIntyre fellow.'

'I did, boss. Alan MacDuff. He's forty-nine years old and he rents a flat here, in Ayr. He's recently divorced and get this, he's got a restraining order hanging over his head.'

Munro, excited at the prospect of dealing with someone whose slate was less than clean, pushed his coffee to one side and listened intently.

'Tell me,' he said, 'what exactly did he do to deserve that?'

'I'm not across on the "whys",' said Dougal, 'jealousy maybe, but it appears that once he'd separated from his wife he felt obliged to keep an eye on her. He'd pop up unexpectedly when she was out shopping, or getting her hair done, or having a drink with her pals. On top of that he had a habit of pulling up outside her house and just sitting there. Watching. She finally reported him to the police when she found an air freshener on the dressing table of her bedroom, one she claims she never bought. It turns out the air freshener contained a wee camera and that instigated a search of the entire property during which they found two more cameras and a tracking device in her car.'

'So the man was obsessed?'

'To say the least.'

'Hang on,' said West. 'If he lives in Ayr then how come we didn't conduct the investigation?'

'The marital home was in Springburn, miss. Galloway Street. The lads in Glasgow handled it. MacDuff moved here when he was handed the order.'

'Fair enough.'

'He'd worked as a mechanic prior to their separation,' said Dougal, 'but the garage let him go on account of him intimidating the female clients.'

'And his wife?' said Munro. 'What do we know about her?'

'Very little. She goes by her maiden name now of Catherine Clark and she works as a sales assistant in the local pharmacy. It was MacDuff's behaviour at the garage that tipped her over the edge, that and the fact he'd been unemployed for a couple of months as a result, so she kicked him out and I can't say I blame her.'

'Nor I,' said Munro. 'And is he still unemployed?'

'No, no. He set himself up as a security consultant soon after he moved here.'

'What kind of security?'

'Cameras mostly. He's on all the social media and often posts a wee photo of the work he's done.'

'Is he listed as a limited company?'

'There's nothing on Companies House,' said Dougal, 'and he uses his own name on all his publicity so I'm guessing he's operating as a sole trader.'

'It's a bit of a change, isn't it?' said West. 'I mean, to go from a grease monkey to a techno-boffin?'

'It's not that different, really,' said Duncan with a smile. 'You should take a look under the bonnet of that Defender of yours, miss. You'd be surprised at the amount of wiring tucked away in there.'

'Watch it, you.'

'All I'm saying is putting a camera up is just some basic wiring, a few leads, and a plug. I reckon anyone who's trained as a mechanic could get his head around that, easy.'

Munro finished his coffee, tossed the sandwich wrapper in the bin, and scooped Murdo under his arm.

'I'm inclined to agree,' he said. 'Now, if you'll excuse me, I think it's time I was off.'

'Watch your back, Jimbo,' said West. 'You haven't cleared this with The Bear yet.'

'Och, dinnae fret about George, lassie. You leave him to me.'

'And don't let on to MacDuff that you know what you know or you'll back him into a corner and he'll clam up.'

'I shall be the soul of discretion, Charlie. Aye, that's the word. Discretion.'

Chapter 5

Lined with warehouses, workshops, light industrial units, and a cluster of low-rise tenement blocks, Taylor Street – a deserted cul-de-sac awash with well-worn tyres, wooden pallets, and piles of bin bags, appeared all the more foreboding in the dark before dawn.

Munro – no stranger to skulking around unsavoury housing estates in search of suspects – dipped the headlights, coasted to the end of the road and, ascertaining MacDuff's residence to be the corner flat with uninterrupted views of a builders' yard to the front and Griffin Dock to the west, stopped just short of the communal entrance.

Believing that anyone in gainful employ should by now have risen from their bed, he left Murdo wrapped in a tartan blanket, dashed across the street, and stabbed the entryphone, grimacing as a biting breeze whipped around his head.

'Mr MacDuff?'

'Who's asking?'

'James Munro. Police Scotland.'

Munro, expecting a sharp rebuff, frowned and cocked his head at the ensuing silence before allowing himself a satisfied smile.

'Hold on.'

Wary of anyone claiming to be a delivery driver, a meter reader, or even an MP canvassing for votes, MacDuff, dressed in jogging pants and a T-shirt, padded down the hall and inched open the main door, a grave look of suspicion on his face.

'Police?'

'Aye,' said Munro, disarming him with a gentle smile and a twinkle in his steely blue eyes. 'Accept my apologies for arriving unannounced. I hope I didnae drag you from your bed.'

'No. You're alright.'

'Would it be okay if we had a wee chat?'

'What about?'

'Your discovery.'

MacDuff thought for a moment, shuffled nervously on the spot, and shivered.

'Have you any ID?'

'No,' said Munro. 'I'll be perfectly frank, Mr MacDuff, I'm not here as part of an official inquiry. I'm retired. You're under no obligation to speak with me at all and if you prefer I can simply walk away and leave you in peace. The senior investigating officer, Detective Inspector Byrne, will be in touch soon.'

'I'm confused,' said MacDuff. 'If that's the case, then why are you here?'

'To help. You see, Mr MacDuff, I've dealt with cases like this before, more than I care to remember, and after an ordeal like yours I can assure you it's often better to talk things through with a friendly face before the real questioning starts. Trust me, it will help to get things straight in your head. Clarify the sequence of events, as it were.'

'I don't know about that,' said MacDuff. 'I mean, how can I be sure you are who you say you are?'

'You cannae,' said Munro. 'As I say, I'm retired and although I continue to work as a volunteer with the Ayrshire force, I no longer possess a warrant card so I suppose you'll just have to take me at my word.'

'Me, trust a policeman? That's a first.'

Munro, as if admitting defeat, raised a hand, turned to leave, and paused.

'How are you sleeping?' he said, glancing over his shoulder. 'Cannae be easy with an image of a scarecrow stuck in your head.'

MacDuff took a deep breath and exhaled slowly.

'Come away inside,' he said. 'It's pure Baltic out there.'

* * *

Comfortably furnished in the style of a house-bound pensioner with neither the funds nor the desire to decorate, MacDuff's ground floor flat was devoid of the mementos and worthless knick-knacks married couples have a habit of accumulating over the years.

Suffocating in the dry heat of the electric storage heaters, Munro, unimpressed with the lack of ventilation, unzipped his jacket, loosened his tie, and stood in the centre of the lounge with his hands clasped firmly behind his back.

'Kettle's just boiled,' said MacDuff. 'Will I fetch you a brew? You look like you could do with warming up.'

Never one to refuse hospitality when offered, Munro nodded and accepted the offer graciously.

'Much obliged,' he said. 'Milk and three.'

Without so much as a pot plant to capture his attention, he focused on a half-eaten slice of toast and the flickering laptop lying on the coffee table as he waited for MacDuff to return.

'How did you find me?' he said, handing Munro a mug. 'I didn't leave any details when I reported the body.'

'Tracing a number and identifying the caller is easier than you think,' said Munro. 'The fact that we have to do it is, I'm afraid to say, a sad reflection of the times we live in.'

'Everyone looking over their shoulder, you mean?'

'Aye, something like that. I understand you're in the security business, Mr MacDuff.'

'Who told you that?'

'You're all over the internet.'

'I suppose I am. Aye, security, that's what I do.'

'And if you dinnae mind me asking, what does that entail exactly? Arranging bouncers for nightclubs, is it?'

'No, no. It's not that kind of security,' said MacDuff, 'it's cameras, CCTV, that sort of thing.'

'Is that so? Sounds quite complicated to a Luddite like myself. You're obviously blessed with the technological know-how.'

'Anything but,' said MacDuff. 'It's easy really, no different to wiring a plug and sticking a wee telly on the end.'

'And is that why you were in Auchencairn?'

'Aye. Rebecca Barlow. She's doing up the old hotel and wanted a surveillance system installed, nothing fancy, just the usual.'

'I see. Don't take this the wrong way,' said Munro, 'but would it not have been easier if she'd got someone closer to home, in Dumfries maybe?'

'Probably,' said MacDuff, 'but she said I'd been recommended so she invited me to tender for the job. It was work and I wasn't going to turn it down.'

'No, of course not. Tell me, did you find out who it was that recommended you?'

'I never asked. Perhaps I should have. Although I did rack my brains trying to think whom I'd worked for recently that might have known her but I gave up.'

'Well that's by the by,' said Munro. 'So, you were saying Miss Barlow contacted you and was that by phone?'

'No. Email.'

'And you arranged to meet?'

'Aye.'

'And where was that?'

'At the hotel,' said MacDuff. 'I suggested it, after all I had to survey the property before I could quote on it.'

'And Miss Barlow, did she seem okay? I mean, not depressed, or pre-occupied, or anything like that?'

'No, no, quite the opposite,' said MacDuff. 'She was in good spirits, we had a wee laugh. If I'm honest, I thought she was a cracking lass, and not just to look at.'

'I'm sure. And then?'

'We agreed a price and I said I'd be back the following day to start laying some cable. She said if she wasn't there to let myself in, that the door would be open, and it was.'

'So, just to be clear,' said Munro, 'the morning you started the job, you left here and went straight to the hotel, is that correct?'

'Aye. No. Actually I stopped at the shop in the village. I'd not had my breakfast and I was hoping to get some food and something hot to drink.'

'And did you?'

'Aye, she fired me up a bacon roll and did me a coffee, too.'

'I bet they must have been curious,' said Munro. 'A stranger dropping by at that time of the morning.'

'You're not wrong there, it was like…'

'Like what, Mr MacDuff?'

'Sorry, I'm just thinking back. See here, the woman in the shop, she was nice enough, just small talk, you know? She thought I was passing through but when I mentioned I was working on the hotel it was like I'd touched a nerve.'

'How so?'

'Hard to say,' said MacDuff. 'She went cold. Angry. I got the distinct impression Miss Barlow was not well-liked in the village. No, actually I'd go so far as to say she wasn't welcome. At all.'

'And what gave you that impression?'

'Apparently the hotel's not the only property she's snapped up. She's had a few, given them a lick of paint, and sold them on but not to the locals. I think what annoyed them more than anything else is the fact she doesn't even live in Auchencairn.'

'Oh? So where does she stay?'

'About twenty miles away. I'm guessing Dumfries.'

'I'm not wanting to sound flippant,' said Munro, 'but it sounds like a case of sour grapes to me.'

'Aye, that's what I thought although, now I think of it, she did say one thing that was, well, odd.'

'Go on.'

'She said something like she'll get what she deserves because she's cut down a sacred tree.'

'A sacred tree?' said Munro, feigning a subtle laugh. 'What on earth did she mean by that?'

'I've no idea. No idea at all.'

'So, back to the house.'

'Hotel.'

'Aye, hotel. After the shop you went on to the hotel and started work, am I right?'

'Not quite,' said MacDuff. 'I fetched a reel and my tools from the van, I'll give you that, but I never started work. I had a second look around to see where I could hide the cable so it's not noticed, right?'

'And?'

'I was upstairs in the main bedroom and got distracted by the view. Smashing it is, you can see clear across to the burn running–'

Munro held a hand aloft and frowned.

'Sorry,' he said. 'You say you were in the main bedroom?'

'Aye.'

'Miss Barlow asked you to install cameras *in the bedrooms*?'

MacDuff glanced furtively at Munro, took a large swig of tea, and almost choked.

'No, no,' he said, spluttering. 'I was upstairs to see if I could run the cable above the ceiling. To the hallway. She wanted a camera in the hallway.'

'I see. Sorry, I shouldnae interrupt,' said Munro. 'You know your job better than I. Please go on.'

'Like I say, I was at the window and I saw some stuff in the garden.'

'What kind of stuff?'

'Interesting stuff. Unusual stuff, like a willow man sculpture, and some signs.'

'So you went outside?'

'Aye, just to take a look, mind, after all Miss Barlow's taste in décor is what you might call, unusual.'

'And that's when you found her?'

'Aye,' said MacDuff, sighing as he shook his head. 'At first I thought it was just another one of her wacky garden ornaments but then… but then I saw her face.'

'And?'

'And what? I was out of there like Usain Bolt. I didn't even stop to get my tools.'

'And then you called the police?'

'Aye. Eventually. When I'd calmed down, I mean it's not every day you find a dead body. I had to tell someone.'

'You did the right thing,' said Munro, 'in fact, you're to be congratulated for doing so. I take it you've been back to collect your tools?'

'Are you joking me? I've not even been out the house.'

'I cannae blame you,' said Munro, fastening his tie. 'It's not easy to overcome the shock of what you've seen, although for your sake, I wish it was.'

'As long as you catch the fella responsible,' said MacDuff. 'I'd not like to come across one of those again.'

'Rest assured,' said Munro, 'I think you've a better chance of seeing Brechin City lift the cup. Just one more thing, is there any particular reason why you didnae leave your name when you reported the body?'

'No reason, really,' said MacDuff, 'other than I don't like to get involved. I like a quiet life.'

'Don't we all. Well, I shall leave you in peace. I'm grateful for your time, Mr MacDuff. And for the tea, of course.'

'No bother, and you were right, it has helped to talk it through. A problem shared, right?'

'Indeed. You can tell DI Byrne I was asking for him when he arrives.'

* * *

Finding MacDuff to be an affable if not hospitable witness with a willingness to co-operate, an inexperienced Munro may have been satisfied with the outcome of their meeting, however, with a non-harassment order already compromising his integrity, a less than convincing explanation for his presence on the upper floor of the hotel, and an eagerness to divulge the details of his gruesome discovery with an unidentified member of the force, MacDuff left him rankled.

Surmising that anyone with the ability to successfully stalk their estranged spouse undetected might also possess the cunning to deceive even the most trusting of folk, Munro reversed down the street, parked on the corner, and called the office.

'Duncan,' he said, 'have you not left yet?'

'We're on our way now. How'd it go with you?'

'Aye, as planned. Can I have a word with Dougal?'

'He's away, chief. The fella needs to get some sleep.'

'Then a wee favour before you go,' said Munro. 'Call The Mount and ask for a DI Byrne. Tell him to ring me, would you? I dinnae have his number.'

'Roger that, chief.'

'And if you see George on your way out, tell him I'll be needing a word, as soon as possible.'

Fighting the urge to clamber into the back seat for a sly snooze, Munro – cynical of the benefits of what was widely referred to as a 'power nap' – took a newspaper from the glove compartment and perused the cryptic clues for the previous day's crossword while he waited for the call.

'Mr Munro,' said Byrne, excitedly. 'Are you okay?'

'It sounds like I should be asking you the same question.'

'Oh, you know what it's like. I can't afford to put a foot wrong at the moment.'

'Can you talk?'

'Aye, I'm outside. And I'm wishing I'd brought my hat.'

'Then I'll not keep you long,' said Munro. 'Are you making progress?'

'Of sorts. You were right about the trees behind the hotel. They were cut down the day before Barlow was found.'

'So you've spoken to the gardener?'

'Aye, but I'd not call him a gardener, more a handyman.'

'Have chainsaw, will travel?'

'Something like that. He's not from the village, he stays in Palnackie. I've no reason to suspect him of any involvement. He was in and out in three hours. He says Barlow paid him cash.'

'Good. And speaking of Miss Barlow, what have you found on her?'

'Nothing yet,' said Byrne. 'I've got someone on it but she's not a priority just now.'

'Jumping Jehoshaphat! What do you mean *not a priority*?'

'Well, I need to–'

'Listen to me, Mr Byrne,' said Munro, losing his patience, 'I'm not going to teach you how to suck eggs but you need to find every scrap of information you can on that girl! Go all the way back to her school days if you have to. You may find someone she crossed or someone who has a grudge against her, an ex-boyfriend or a business associate. You'd do well to look into her financial affairs while you're at it, make sure there's nothing awry there, too.'

'You think so?'

'I know so! Dear God, I'm willing to help you out, laddie, but you need to prove to me you're worthy of your rank, do I make myself clear?'

'Aye, point taken.'

'Good. Now, have you managed to cut through all that red tape yet?'

'I have,' said Byrne. 'We're away up to Ayr this afternoon. I just hope this MacDuff fella's not going to give us any grief.'

'I doubt that,' said Munro. 'Have you run a check on the chap?'

'Aye. It seems he moved from Springburn by order of the court.'

'So I understand,' said Munro. 'Listen, I've a wee confession to make. If you want to take it up with your superiors, then it's entirely up to you. I'll not mind.'

'I'm not with you.'

'MacDuff. I had a chat with him myself. In fact, I've not long left his house.'

'I see,' said Byrne. 'And?'

'And if you're offended by my interfering with your investigation then you must do as you see fit.'

'Don't be daft. I meant *and what did he say*?'

'He was friendly enough,' said Munro. 'I persuaded him to open up on the premise that he could get things straight in his head before he talked to you.'

'So he's expecting us?'

'Aye.'

'Brilliant,' said Byrne. 'That's one less thing for me to worry about. So what do you think? Do you reckon he's involved in any way?'

'On the face of it,' said Munro, 'I'd have to say no, but…'

'But what, Mr Munro?'

‘There’s something else.’

‘I’m listening.’

‘His computer was lying open when I arrived and there was something on the screen, a film of some sort.’

‘Oh?’

‘A young lady in what can only be described as a state of undress.’

‘So he was watching a porno movie?’

‘No,’ said Munro, ‘the movie was black and white, and it certainly wasn’t film quality. It was like the footage you see from these fancy doorbells some folk have.’

‘So, live-streaming, then?’

‘I wouldn’t know, but see here, Mr Byrne, if you’re not already aware of the fact, MacDuff has a history of installing cameras to keep an eye on the unsuspecting, if you know what I mean.’

‘I think I do, and if that’s the case then we should requisition his gear and take a closer look.’

‘And on what grounds would you do that?’

‘Suspicion.’

‘Of what?’

‘Christ, I don’t know!’

‘You’re not thinking hard enough! Come on, laddie, you’re halfway there!’

‘Maybe… maybe,’ said Byrne, ‘if we asked him to attend voluntarily we could sneak a peek while he was out.’

‘You’ve gone off the boil. You cannae do that, and you know it. Besides, if he does have something on his computer then it’s a separate investigation, it’s nothing to do with Rebecca Barlow. You’ll have to do better than that.’

‘I’m not sure I can,’ said Byrne. ‘Help me out here, Mr Munro, what would you do?’

‘I’m not at liberty to say,’ said Munro. ‘Unless it was strictly off the record.’

‘To be fair, Mr Munro, everything you’ve done since we met has been *off the record.*’

Munro glanced out of the window and smiled.

'How many suspects do you have, Mr Byrne?'

'Precisely none.'

'Wrong answer,' said Munro. 'You have one. MacDuff.'

'How?'

'You tell me.'

'Because he was the last one to see her alive?'

'So what's stopping you?'

'Bring him in on suspicion of murder?' said Byrne. 'But that doesn't make sense. No offence, but if he was anywhere near guilty then why would he talk to you?'

'Och, you've a lot to learn, but you'll get there. You have my number. Let me know what you decide.'

Chapter 6

Hailing from the milder climes of southern England there was, on her arrival some years earlier, an unspoken scepticism amongst her younger colleagues that a Sassenach like herself would cope with Caledonia's unforgiving winters. However, much to their surprise, West had proved herself to be as hardy as an Arctic fox.

Preferring the dour surroundings of her draughty old Defender to the comfort of Duncan's fully-functioning Audi, West – wearing her trademark waxed black jacket and matching jeans – drew to a halt behind the Lexus, killed the engine, and bundled her hair beneath a baker boy cap.

'Could you not at least get the heater fixed?' said Duncan, blowing into his hands.

'Stop complaining,' said West. 'I didn't think a hard nut like you would be bothered by a bit of cold.'

'There's cold, miss. And there's Siberia. And I'm currently experiencing the latter.'

'I'm surprised,' said West. 'I'd have thought a native like you would've been used to it by now. At least his car's here, that's a good start.'

'If you say so.'

'Dougal didn't find anything on McIntyre, did he?'

'Correction, miss. He's not even *found* McIntyre.'

'Stop being so pedantic. So, what's the connection between him and Riley? Any ideas?'

'Well, she's not long released,' said Duncan, 'and she's already spending like a sheik, so she must be dealing again. I'm guessing he's either her supplier or they're in it together.'

'Okay, but without the evidence we're scuppered so I'm thinking once we're in, you need to keep your eyes peeled for any man-stuff. If she has signed on and we can prove she's not living alone, then at least we can get her off the streets by doing her for benefit fraud.'

'You're assuming she's going to let us in.'

'God, you're in a negative mood this morning.'

'My brain's starved of oxygen, miss. It'll be the frostbite next.'

'When's your birthday?'

'Next month. Why?'

'I'll get you some gloves. Come on, time for a game of knock-knock.'

* * *

Of the options available for gaining entry to a house, Dougal, polite to a fault, would ring once, step back and wait, whilst Duncan, armed with a gift from the mentoring Munro, preferred to work under cover of darkness with his set of lock-picks. West, however, had the irritating habit of scaring the bejesus out of anyone in the building by hammering the door with the side of her fist whilst screaming at the top of her voice to 'open up'.

Duncan, wondering if he could possibly arrest his superior for breach of the peace, looked away and cringed.

'Emma Riley?' said West, grinning as she flashed her warrant card.

'Who's asking?'

'DI West. And this is DS Reid. Can we have a word?'

'Have as many as you like,' said Riley. 'But you'll not get any from me.'

'Off to a flying start,' said Duncan, muttering under his breath. 'How was life inside, Miss Riley?'

'Same as usual.'

'Must be like a second home to someone like yourself.'

'Actually, it's more like a hotel.'

'Did you by any chance win the lottery while you were locked up?'

Riley stared at Duncan, nonplussed.

'The Lexus,' he said, nodding towards the street. 'It's registered to this address.'

'Is it?'

'Aye. So it's not your car?'

'Never seen it before.'

'Oh, I think you have,' said West. 'You see, Miss Riley, we know for a fact it picked you up after you'd done your shopping at the supermarket. And we know for a fact you popped your bags in the boot. And we know for a fact you hopped on-board, presumably to get a lift home.'

Riley, as cool as the proverbial cucumber, forced a smile.

'Not me,' she said, shaking her head. 'You're confusing me with somebody else.'

'Oh, I doubt that,' said West. 'You're one of kind, you are. How are you coping since you got out? Financially, I mean. Have you signed on?'

'No.'

'So, you're living off your savings?'

Riley threw her head back and laughed.

'Savings? Are you joking me?'

'Well you must be surviving somehow.'

'My pals help me out.'

'You must be popular,' said West, 'you look like you've just come off the catwalk.'

'There's nothing wrong in taking pride in your appearance,' said Riley. 'You should try it sometime.'

'Touché.'

Realising that West's typically confrontational, if not aggressive approach was getting them nowhere fast, Duncan chose to deploy an alternative tactic.

'We appreciate your time, Miss Riley,' he said. 'Apologies for disturbing you.'

'What? Is that it?'

'Aye, as far as you're concerned it is. We'll be in that Land Rover until Mr McIntyre comes to collect his car.'

West smiled as Riley's thin veil of bravado slipped to reveal the vulnerability of a kitten in a dog pound.

'So, you know who owns it?'

'We know everything,' said Duncan. 'We even know what you had for your tea.'

Riley glanced up and down the street and gestured towards the open door.

'I'll give you five minutes,' she said. 'Five minutes. That's it.'

* * *

Expecting the interior of Riley's pebble-dashed maisonette to be typical of the other ex-council properties lining the street, West was amazed to find the lounge decorated as a shrine to gaudy opulence.

Repulsed by the gilt chandelier and matching mirror, the gargantuan TV and the blue, velvet Chesterfield, she declined the offer of a seat and opted to stand by the door rather than risk sullying the sofa or staining the shagpile while Duncan, still feeling the chill, thrust his hands deep into the pockets of his battered leather car coat and stared at Riley.

'Right,' he said, 'let's start again. Daniel McIntyre. What's the story?'

'We're pals,' said Riley as she perched on the couch.

'Just pals? So, he's not your partner?'

'No. He's not my partner.'

'Then what exactly is your relationship?' said Duncan. 'Is it business?'

'I'd not call it that.'

'Then what would you call it?'

Riley shrugged her shoulders.

'I scratch his back, and he scratches mine.'

'So you just help each other out?'

'Aye. If you like.'

'And how long have you two known each other?'

'Years,' said Riley. 'Several years, in fact.'

'How did you meet?'

'I worked in his office.'

'Doing what?' said Duncan. 'Were you a secretary? Or a receptionist? Or a colleague?'

'A dogsbody,' said Riley. 'Filling envelopes, answering the phone, making coffee. Six hours a day, five days a week.'

'Go on.'

'He was always behind me, hovering about like a lost puppy.'

'So he fancied his chances?'

'Aye. I think he fancied me,' said Riley, 'definitely, but I had my looks back then.'

'So what happened?'

Riley sat back on the sofa, thought for a moment, and smiled.

'I had a Cinderella moment,' she said. 'Danny said it couldn't be easy getting by on what I earned. He said I deserved better. He said he could make things better.'

'And did he?'

'Aye. For a while.'

'How?' said West. 'How exactly did McIntyre make things better?'

'He said if I made myself presentable, if I wore a skirt and some heels, he'd see me right.'

'He sounds like a pimp.'

'He is,' said Riley, 'but not in the way you're thinking.'

'How then?'

'It started easy enough. He'd give me a package, like a small Jiffy bag, then tell me where to go and who to give it to, then he'd slip me a few quid afterwards.'

'How much exactly?'

'Fifty. A hundred. Sometimes more.'

'You must have been raking it in. Had you any idea what is in these packages?'

'None,' said Riley. 'I could've guessed but I was enjoying myself too much.'

'So how did things progress?' said West.

'The drops got more frequent, the parcels got bigger.'

'And your earnings went up?'

Riley looked at West and nodded.

'Right up,' she said. 'To the point that I got used to it.'

'So Daniel McIntyre,' said Duncan, 'is he the fella you refused to name in court? Is he the one who landed you with a sackful of khat?'

Riley hesitated before answering.

'Might be,' she said.

'And it's not the first time he's landed you in it, am I right?'

'Maybe.'

'Am I missing something, here?' said West, frowning as she folded her arms. 'A minute ago you wouldn't let us in the house and now you're gassing like a guest on Oprah. Why the change of heart?'

Riley pulled a tissue from her pocket and slowly shredded it between her hands.

'I'm getting on,' she said. 'I want my life back.'

'My heart bleeds.'

'I've taken the fall for him once too often. I'm not doing it again.'

'But why now?' said West. 'Why didn't you do something about it before? Why didn't you speak up in court? Why didn't you tell them the gear you were carrying belonged to McIntyre? Were you scared?'

'Petrified,' said Riley. 'See Danny, he's clever. He covers his back. If I'd have said anything he'd have denied even knowing me. Then he'd have come after me when I got out.'

'How can you be so sure?' said Duncan. 'I mean, has he ever threatened you?'

'It's second nature to him.'

'Has he ever been physically abusive towards you?'

'No. He wouldn't dare do that. It'd be like leaving evidence.'

'It still doesn't answer the question though, does it?' said West. 'Why now?'

'It's an opportunity,' said Riley. 'I mean, I didn't come crawling to you begging for help, did I? You came to me, and right now I really don't care anymore. I really don't care. I'm fed up being at his beck and call seven days a week. I'm fed up keeping the curtains pulled day and night. I'm fed up not knowing who's chapping my door and if I should hide. I'm not even allowed out on my own.'

'How so?' said Duncan.

'He doesn't trust me to keep my mouth shut if I have a wee bevvy.'

'Charming,' said West, 'I think we'll add coercive control to the list of charges when we nick him. Right, Miss Riley, here's the thing, you do realise that if you want him out of your life, you're going to have to make a statement, don't you?'

'Oh,' said Riley, a look of trepidation on her face. 'Does that mean he'll know it's me who's blagged?'

'Possibly. Either way, you'll probably have to show your face in court, too.'

Riley, looking doubtful, stood and nibbled her fingernails as she paced the floor.

'Suddenly,' she said, 'I'm not so sure. I mean, what if he only gets a few months and a fine? He'll batter me like a fish supper when he gets out.'

'He'll be away a lot longer than that,' said West. 'A lot longer. And like you said, we came to you. You can always tell him *we twisted your arm*. A bit of police brutality always goes down well with the likes of him.'

'The thing is,' said Duncan, 'once we secure a conviction, you can kiss goodbye to all of this; the big TV and your fancy clothes.'

'I don't want fancy clothes,' said Riley. 'I want my sweats and trainers back. Okay. I've decided. You're on. Let's put him away.'

'Not so fast, hen. There's no guarantees on that score, not just yet anyway.'

'I'll take my chances,' said Riley. 'I think I'd rather be on your side than his.'

'Right, I'm not being funny,' said West, 'but that's probably the best five minutes of your entire life.'

'So what now? Are you going to wait for him to come back?'

'No. We've got some groundwork to do first, the worst thing we can do is scare him off. What I need to know right now, and you need to be straight with me, is if he's living here or not.'

'No. He is not.'

'So he's not down as a legal occupier of this flat?'

'No.'

'Then why is his motor registered here?'

'I didn't know it was,' said Riley. 'I thought that was illegal.'

'It is,' said West, 'unless he's got plans to move in, in the very near future.'

'No, he's certainly not doing that.'

'Then he's definitely committing an offence.'

'So can you not arrest him for that?'

'We could,' said Duncan, 'but there's a chance he could walk away with a hefty fine and you wouldn't want that. No, no, we need to wait until we can charge him with something more substantial, dealing or possession, and we need to gather evidence for that.'

'How long will that take?'

'Can't say, hen, but for now we'll be needing a phone number and an address. Does he stay nearby?'

'Not far,' said Riley. 'Taylor Street.'

'Okay, we'll be in touch. All you have to do in the meantime is keep your nose clean and act like you've never seen us, got that?'

'Aye.'

'And a word of advice,' said Duncan. 'If you've been winding us up, you'll be back inside before you know it.'

* * *

West, rattled by Riley's abrupt about-face, slipped the key into the ignition, turned to Duncan, and frowned.

'You're not convinced, are you?' he said.

'I'm in two minds,' said West. 'I mean, why the sudden change of tune?'

'It's a woman's prerogative to change her mind,' said Duncan with a smile. 'No offence, miss, but you've done it yourself.'

'Yeah, I know, but I was engaged to be married, she isn't.'

'It's like walking a maze,' said Duncan. 'It doesn't matter how miserable you feel, you can't do anything about it until you can find a way out. She just found hers.'

'Okay then, answer me this,' said West. 'If McIntyre lives on Taylor Street, why has he left his motor here?'

'Trust me, miss, you'd not leave a go-kart on Taylor Street, let alone a Lexus. So, will we pay him a visit?'

'No. I think we need to put a tail on him first, see what he gets up to. If we're going to put him away, then we need to catch him with his pants down.'

Chapter 7

As a young officer pounding the streets of a nostalgically nicer and altogether less troubled Ayr city centre, George Elliot – with his towering frame and innate sense of justice – achieved a certain notoriety amongst the criminal fraternity for his ability to apprehend the villains polluting his patch with nothing more than the promise of a week in the infirmary if they refused to *come quietly*, a universally successful proposition which not only spawned a fearsome reputation as The Bear but also kept his fellow officers in line.

However, keen to placate an anxious spouse who, with the prevalence of armed fanatics roaming the streets, had become increasingly concerned that she'd be drawing a widow's pension a little sooner than expected, he happily accepted a more sedentary position and duly ensconced himself behind a desk where he juggled rosters, penned performance reviews, and winced at budgets whilst supplementing his wife's healthy eating regime with a variety of calorie-laden snacks.

Startled by the unexpected knock on the door, he hurriedly swept the last of the teacakes into a drawer and adopted an appropriately studious expression as he tried to fathom a spreadsheet sitting on his screen.

'James!' he said, retrieving the packet. 'You scared the life out of me! Will you take a teacake?'

Munro smiled and pulled up a chair.

'You should watch yourself, George, or you'll end up in the diabetes hall of fame.'

'Well I need to keep my strength up.'

'I take it Mrs Elliot's still attacking your waistline, then?'

'Aye. And do you know what delights I have to look forward to this evening?'

'Enlighten me.'

'Couscous,' said Elliot. 'A vegetable stir-fry with *couscous*. I ask you, how's a man supposed to survive on that?'

'Well, at least eat something that's not covered in chocolate,' said Munro. 'A ham sandwich, perhaps?'

'You're right!' said Elliot. 'What I'm needing is a decent steak! I know; Cecchini's. They do a smashing *bistecca fiorentina*. What do you say?'

'I'd be inclined to go for something a little less exotic, myself.'

'Have what you like, James! You're retired and I've an expense account, let's go.'

'Hold on,' said Munro, 'I think you might lose your appetite once you've heard what I've got to say.'

'How so?'

'I was viewing a house yesterday. In Auchencairn.'

Elliot clasped his hands behind his head and looked to the ceiling.

'Ah, it's a beautiful part of the country,' he said, wistfully. 'I'd love a wee cottage down there. The problem is Mrs Elliot. She's not a fan of what you might call *rustic*. She likes modern. Modern and sterile. Sorry, I digress. You were saying; Auchencairn.'

'Aye. I was viewing a house and I happened to come across… an incident.'

Elliot lowered his arms and leaned on the desk.

'What kind of an incident?'

'A body,' said Munro. 'I'll keep it brief. The SIO is a DI Byrne.'

'Ho! Hold on! You've spoken to the SIO?'

'Aye. And he was grateful for my input. It's his first case and he was floundering, to say the least.'

'Dear God, so you took it upon yourself to help him out?'

'I thought I'd give him the benefit of my experience. Aye.'

'But he's not even on our patch! Still, I suppose if it was just a friendly chat, then no harm done.'

'I'm not finished,' said Munro. 'There's a witness. He stays here. In Ayr.'

'You didn't?'

'I did.'

'I'll be needing a dram with my lunch.'

'Byrne's not going to mention it, for obvious reasons, but it may come up in the witness statement.'

'And what happens then?' said Elliot, rubbing his forehead. 'At the very least you'll have done yourself out of a job! An unpaid job, I'll give you that, but a job all the same!'

'Och, that doesnae bother me,' said Munro. 'It means I'll have more time with Murdo. Anyway, I just thought I'd mention it, that's all.'

'Could you not apply your talents to something a wee bit closer to home?'

Munro, saying nothing, simply sat back and smiled.

'Well, James, I'll be frank. If something resembling a cowpat comes hurtling towards the fan, then you're on your own, do I make myself clear? And don't go asking the team for help, I simply don't have the resources just now, we're at breaking point.'

'I'll not need help,' said Munro. 'Not much anyway.'

Elliot gripped the desk with both hands, pushed himself back, and stood.

'I'd like to say I'm lost for words,' he said, reaching for his coat, 'but there's one in particular that springs to mind.'

'I'm guessing *discharge*.'

'Wrong. It's Cecchini's. You can give me the details over lunch.'

* * *

Nestled in the darkest recesses of the bustling restaurant, Elliot, wiring into his T-bone with the savage gusto of a ravenous wolf, listened intently as Munro fired his imagination with images of possessed villagers offering up a sacrifice to a pagan deity before finally relenting and, against his better judgement, agreeing to some limited and strictly unofficial assistance on the proviso that any request for help played second fiddle to the team's already full agenda.

Having satisfied his uneducated palate with an agreeably bland portion of deep-fried haddock and chips, Munro left Elliot to settle the bill and sought the privacy of his car to return one missed call from an unassigned number.

'Thanks for calling back, I appreciate it.'

'Och, it's you, Mr Byrne. I had no idea. Are you okay?'

'No. Aye. No. I'm on my way up to MacDuff's place.'

'There's nothing wrong with my hearing, do you have to shout?'

'Sorry,' said Byrne, 'I'm on speaker, do you mind?'

'I can cope. What's the problem?'

'It's all getting out of hand, Mr Munro, I need to talk it through with someone, is that okay?'

'Aye, go on,' said Munro. 'What's the story?'

'Well, the good news is we found Barlow's car, it was parked on the square, one of those wee Fiat 500 numbers.'

'And?'

'We've all but stripped it and still no sign of a phone.'

'Och, it's not the end of the world,' said Munro. 'Not yet anyway. What else?'

'We've traced her next of kin to Penrith. They'll be coming up to ID the body just as soon as the post-mortem's complete.'

'Well it sounds like you're on the ball,' said Munro, 'but experience tells me that whenever someone starts a sentence with *the good news is,* it invariably means there's bad to follow.'

'There is,' said Byrne. 'Barlow's house in Dumfries, it's been ransacked.'

Munro, thrilled at the prospect of having to unravel a case as complex as an ancient labyrinth, listened carefully.

'There's no sign of a forced entry and it's definitely not a burglary.'

'What makes you so sure?'

'There's plenty of valuable stuff about the place,' said Byrne, 'jewellery, a fancy watch, a drawer full of cash, all untouched.'

'So you think someone was looking for something?'

'Aye. Definitely,' said Byrne. 'There's a box room downstairs, like a wee office, that's the worst hit, there's all kinds of bank stuff and receipts and bills scattered all over the place.'

'So what does that tell you about the perpetrator?' said Munro. 'Assuming of course that he's not a locksmith.'

'That he must have had a key, which means he'd have been known to Barlow.'

'Good. And SOCOs?'

'They're on the scene just now. As soon as they've finished up we can do a more detailed search.'

'And in the meantime,' said Munro, 'I presume you've got someone running a background check on Miss Barlow?'

'Sort of,' said Byrne. 'Well, no. Not exactly.'

'Then you need to up your game, laddie! By jiminy, you've a whole team of officers at your disposal, why are you not using them?'

'I am! It's just that there's so much going on it's difficult to keep on top of things.'

'Well, you'd better get used to it,' said Munro, 'because that'll not change anytime soon. If you cannae stand the heat, I suggest you get out of the kitchen.'

'I can handle it,' said Byrne. 'I know I can. I just have to get used to the responsibility.'

'Right, listen to me,' said Munro. 'You need to pull over, take a deep breath, then call the office. I've told you before, if whoever trashed Barlow's place was known to her, the only way you'll find them is by digging up her past. Do I make myself clear?'

'Aye.'

'Then get on it! Start with old work colleagues, employees, and work your way back, all the way back to old school friends if you have to.'

'I'm trying and that's why I need to get my hands on her phone,' said Byrne. 'See here, Mr Munro, apart from her Facebook page which reveals nothing at all, it's like she doesn't exist, she's not even got an address book and her folks haven't seen her in a couple of years so they have no idea who she's mixing with.'

'Does she not have a computer?'

'We've not found one,' said Byrne. 'Which means her phone is my only hope. At least it'll have a list of contacts and maybe even her email, we can see exactly who she's been in touch with.'

'So you can think straight,' said Munro. 'Well done, but if you're going to make any progress, you need to start turning those thoughts into actions.'

'I will,' said Byrne. 'Honest, I will.'

'I'm glad to hear it. Now redeem yourself by telling me you've completed the door-to-door enquiries.'

Byrne hesitated and cringed before answering.

'Nearly,' he said. 'I mean, uniform are on it. They start tomorrow.'

'As I thought,' said Munro, sighing, 'more time wasted. You best get a move on, at least you'll not have a problem with MacDuff. I think you'll find him most accommodating.'

* * *

Frustrated by his failure to identify little more than a manufacturer's logo on the assailant's coat, Dougal, despite a restless night, rose early and returned to the office to view the footage afresh, his relief at finding the place devoid of colleagues short-lived as a carnivorous canine emerged from beneath a desk.

Erring on the side of caution, he raised his feet and sat cross-legged on the chair before scanning the video with his "Amped FIVE" image-enhancing software, his elation at capturing some unique markings on the attacker's left hand rapidly dissipating as Duncan and West breezed through the door.

'Don't you ever sleep?' said West. 'You'd be better off setting up a camp bed in the corner of the room.'

'This fella's been doing my nut in,' said Dougal, rubbing his eyes, 'but I've made some cracking progress.'

'What have you got?'

Dougal flipped the monitor to reveal an enlarged and remarkably sharp image of the perpetrator's hand pressed against the wall.

'There!' he said, triumphantly, 'a tattoo on the fingers of the left hand, the initials "L.I.F.E.".'

'He's probably got "roaster" inked across his forehead,' said Duncan. 'I've never seen the point of tattoos myself, and I never will. Anything else?'

'Aye, his trainers, they're Nike. I've matched the style, they're called Air Force 1.'

'Obviously the shoe of choice for high-flying presidents,' said West. 'Do you want some grub?'

'What have you got?'

'Chips for me, Duncan's having soup and a roll, so that leaves a pie or haggis in batter.'

'No, you're alright,' said Dougal, 'thanks for the offer but I need to crack on.'

'Well, we'll not disturb you,' said Duncan, 'although there is one thing I've been meaning to ask.'

'Oh, aye?'

Suppressing an almost irresistible urge to rib him about his tryst with the young Kay Grogan, an elfin scenes of crime officer who shared his passion for solving mysteries, Duncan, concerned that his timorous counterpart was gathering dust on the dating shelf, cut straight to the point.

'You've not told us how it went,' he said. 'Your first date with the adorable Kay.'

Dougal, his face flushed with embarrassment, swallowed hard and stared at Duncan in disbelief.

'Kay?'

'Aye, you remember Kay, the wee lassie who's fallen head over heels for some copper who's too daft to realise a good thing when he sees it.'

'Oh. Kay. It was okay.'

'Just okay? Don't tell me you dragged her for a wee walk in the woods with one of your packed lunches?'

'No, no,' said Dougal. 'Actually, I took your advice after all.'

'So you booked a restaurant?'

'No, I daren't. I get confused by all the cutlery. We grabbed a fish supper and went back to mine.'

'You sly old dog!' said West. 'I never knew you had it in you!'

'I haven't!' said Dougal, breaking into a sweat. 'No, I mean, we didn't! Jeez-oh! Look, it was very pleasant, that's all.'

'So what did you do?'

'We had dinner. And we listened to some music.'

'Let me guess,' said Duncan. 'Barry White. The Walrus of Love always gets the blood pumping! Then what?'

'We talked.'

'What about?'

'Oh leave him alone,' said West. 'Stop getting so personal.'

'It's just a question.'

'Forensics,' said Dougal. 'If you must know, we talked about forensics.'

'Are you joking me?' said Duncan. 'A first date with a gorgeous wee lassie, you get her back to your place, and you talk about *forensics*?'

'Aye.'

'You need a spell on the couch, pal. You're a gene short of a chromosome, you are.'

Murdo, having successfully filched a morsel of bread from Duncan's hand, jumped intuitively from his lap as the door swung open.

'I could hear your biology lesson down the hall,' said Munro. 'What's going on?'

'Boys' banter,' said West. 'Are you hungry, Jimbo? There's some haggis going begging if you fancy it.'

'I appreciate the offer, Charlie, but George beat you to it.'

'Let me guess; Cecchini's?'

'Aye.'

'Alright for some. How'd it go? Did he give you your marching orders?'

'On the contrary,' said Munro. 'He offered me some limited assistance–'

'There's a lot to be said for nepotism.'

'–so I'm limiting it to Dougal. When you have time, laddie – I'm under strict instructions not to encroach on your schedule – kindly crawl into the internet for me and see what you can find on one Rebecca Barlow, originally from Penrith, last domiciled in Dumfries.'

'No bother, boss. Leave it with me.'

Recognising the topical disfiguration of the human self as a centuries-old artistic means of expressing allegiance, offering protection, or denoting status with its roots firmly steeped in traditional symbolism, Munro was willing to accept the tattoo as an integral element of certain cultures, be they Native American, Māori peoples, or even the Yakuza, however, he regarded the tasteless desecration of body parts with trite statements, particularly by the younger generation, as nothing less than vulgar.

Catching sight of the image on Dougal's screen, he pulled his spectacles from his breast pocket and leaned in for a closer look.

'Dear God,' he said, shaking his head. 'What on earth possesses a person to do that?'

'They think it's cool,' said Dougal. 'It's what they call body art.'

'Well, you'll not see that in any gallery, I can assure you of that. Who is it?'

'That's what I'm trying to find out,' said Dougal. 'At the least the tattoo will make him easier to spot.'

'Well, when you do catch him,' said Munro, 'tell him he needs to see a doctor.'

'Oh? How so?'

'His hand! Can you not see it's infected?'

'Really?'

'Aye! The middle finger,' said Munro, pointing at the screen, 'it's the size of a sausage and if I'm not mistaken, there is a weeping scab.'

'I'd never have spotted that,' said Dougal. 'The problem is, boss, I've no idea where to look for him.'

'Well dinnae waste your time walking the streets, laddie. If I'm right about his hand, then that tattoo was done just two or three weeks ago. I'd visit all the parlours in the vicinity, if I were you. Whoever did that is bound to remember.'

'How is it you know everything about everything?' said West.

'Because, Charlie, I have experience on my side and an insatiable thirst for knowledge. The brain is the most powerful organ in the body but it's like a muscle, if you dinnae exercise it, it will wither away.'

'That reminds me, miss,' said Duncan, cheekily. '*University Challenge* is on the telly tonight, you might want to tune in.'

'Watch it, you. So, Jimbo, if The Bear's cut you some slack, I take it your unofficial interview must have gone according to plan?'

'You're referring to MacDuff, of course? Aye. Swimmingly, in fact he was most hospitable but I'm afraid to say the chap does have a dark side.'

'What do you mean?'

'First instinct tells me he's in the clear as far as Miss Barlow's concerned, but there's something not right about his personal habits.'

'Like what?'

'He had, shall we say, some dubious imagery on his computer but that's a separate matter and I shall have to leave it up to DI Byrne to sort out. Unfortunately he's not adept at multi-tasking so I'm away back to Auchencairn to chat with some of the locals. How about you? Did you succeed in your mission to clear the streets of druggies and dealers?'

'Not yet,' said West, 'but we're getting there. We managed to wheedle an address for McIntyre out of the Riley girl so we're going over there now to sit it out. We'll wait for him to show his face and see what he gets up to.'

'There's only one way in and out of the street,' said Duncan, 'but there's a plumbers' merchant on the corner. I'm going to hang out there in Westy's Defender while she lies low in the Audi across the street.'

Munro, struck by the vague recollection of a familiar scene, turned to the window and stood in quiet contemplation with hands clasped behind his back.

'What's up?' said Duncan. 'Is it something I said?'

'The location you describe, it sounds strangely familiar. Is it hereabouts?'

'Aye, not far, chief. Taylor Street.'

Munro spun on his heels and stared at West.

'Taylor Street?' he said softly. 'Jumping Jehoshaphat! That's where MacDuff stays!'

'MacDuff? Your witness?'

'Aye! DI Byrne's on his way there now, so for everybody's sake, be sure to keep your distance, Charlie, and if you see anything untoward, you're to phone me immediately, okay? I'm away to Auchencairn. I'll see you tonight.'

Chapter 8

Without the authorisation nor frankly the desire to knock on every door in the village with questions pertaining to the sighting of Rebecca Barlow or, for that matter, any visitors to the old Commercial Hotel, Munro – adjudging the only person of interest to be the proprietor of the village shop – stepped from the car and, without a wind as sharp as a sabre to cut him in two, found the temperature to be an agreeable if not positively balmy minus two degrees.

Donning his gloves, he crunched his way along the icy street pausing en route to marvel at a flock of barnacle geese honking ecstatically as they flew towards the firth before stepping gingerly through the door and assaulting the lady behind the counter with a mollifying smile.

'It's fair jeelit out there,' he said, unzipping his jacket. 'I'm after some milk.'

'In the chiller,' said the lady, warming to the sparkle of his cold, blue eyes. 'Is there anything else you're needing?'

'Aye, maybe,' said Munro. 'Some shortbread, perhaps. It's always handy to have in the cupboard.'

'Aye, you're not wrong, there. A wee nibble with a cup of tea, it's just the ticket. I'll fetch some for you.'

'Much obliged.'

'You're not here on your holidays, are you? Not at this time of year.'

'No, no.'

'On your own?'

'Aye.'

'So, you're just passing through, then?'

Delighted by the shopkeeper's blatant curiosity, Munro, maintaining an air of nonchalance, saw no harm in bending the truth in order to exploit her over-inquisitive nature.

'I'm not passing through,' he said as he perused the shelves, 'I'll be moving up the street. I'm James, by the way. James Munro.'

'Barbara. So we'll be seeing a lot of you, then?'

'I dare say you will. Aye.'

'What brings you to Auchencairn?'

'Peace,' said Munro. 'I like the peace.'

'Well, we've plenty of that.'

'Although,' said Munro, placing the milk on the counter, 'I must admit, I was surprised to see the police up the road.'

'Oh, that'll be the murder you're talking about.'

Committed to delivering as convincing a performance as possible, Munro took a step back with a look of horror etched on his face.

'*Murder?*' he said. 'Are you joking me?'

'No, no. Murder plain and simple.'

'Dear, dear, you're not telling me there's some lunatic on the run?'

'Aye, there is,' said Barbara, 'and as far as I know, they've not caught him yet.'

'So, what's the story?'

'Apparently some fella working on the Commercial–'

'Sorry, I'm not being rude but, *the Commercial?*'

'It's an old hotel, just up the street. Anyway, this fella, he's an electrician I think, apparently he's the one who killed her.'

'Who?'

'The woman who owns the building.'

'But what makes you think it was him?' said Munro, reaching for his wallet. 'And not somebody else?'

'Because he looked the type,' said Barbara. 'And he called her Miss Barlow. If he was a friend, he'd have called her Rebecca. And as far as I know, friends aren't in the habit of killing each other.'

'That's some cracking detective work,' said Munro, 'but tell me, why on earth do you think he killed her in the first place?'

'I have no idea,' said Barbara. 'Perhaps it's karma. As far as I'm concerned, she got what she deserved.'

'Oh? How so?'

Barbara placed the groceries in a bag and handed Munro his change.

'My da, Jack, he owned that hotel,' she said. 'Barlow pushed him and my mother into accepting a cash offer for the place then turfed them out before the ink was dry.'

'And where are they now?'

'I planted them a month after they moved.'

Munro offered an empathetic smile and shook his head.

'Dear, dear. I'm sorry,' he said. 'You have my condolences. A tragedy if ever there was one.'

'Aye. A tragedy, right enough.'

'Had the woman no morals? I mean, was that not a wee bit brash, to barge right in and offer to buy their house while they were still living there?'

'Brash?' said Barbara. 'It's not the word I'd use.'

'Well, she clearly ruffled your feathers. And understandably so.'

'Not just mine. The whole village was raging.'

'So, the electrician fellow, was he the only one to visit her?'

'Aye. I think so.'

'But surely if she was doing the place up,' said Munro, 'the place would have been riddled with workmen.'

'To start with, aye, but she was nearly done. There was only the electrician. Oh, and the gardener.'

'Gardener?'

'Aye. Well, odd-job man, really, but he's near enough a local and we've known him for years.'

'So, she's not had any other visitors? Recently I mean?'

'No. No strangers, anyhow. Just her pal.'

'Pal?'

'Aye. Boyfriend, I think. We'd met once before, when she first chapped the door to make my parents an offer. Nice fella.'

'I see. So, you got along okay?'

'I liked him for the simple reason that he was trying to put her off, get her to back down. I got the distinct impression that he thought what she was doing was wrong.'

'Indeed it was,' said Munro. 'And you're sure he was her boyfriend?'

'Boyfriend. Husband. Partner. Makes no difference. They were in some sort of relationship, that's for sure.'

'How could you tell?'

'I'm no fool,' said Barbara. 'It was the way they talked to each other. Contradicting each other. Arguing with each other. Only couples act like that.'

Munro smiled.

'I cannae argue with that,' he said. 'So, he came back?'

'Aye, he popped his head round the door and said, "Have you seen Becky about the place? I've got her keys." So I told him, she's at the hotel.'

'And what day was that?'

'The same day the electrician arrived.'

'And do you happen to recall what time it was?'

'About 10:00am, I'd say.'

'So he would have met the electrician, at the hotel?'

'Aye. Maybe. Who knows?'

'Who knows indeed,' said Munro. 'Well, it's a plot worthy of a TV show, Barbara. I'll say that for nothing.'

'Right enough. Who'd have thought something like that could happen in a place like this.'

'Tell me,' said Munro, 'this boyfriend of hers, do you remember what he looked like?'

Barbara took a step back, folded her arms, and hesitated before answering.

'I'll give you this, James,' she said, smiling as she wagged a finger. 'You're clever.'

'I'm not with you.'

'All these questions! You're a reporter, am I right? Are you looking for something for the papers?'

'I'm afraid I'm not a reporter,' he said. 'I dinnae even read the newspapers, but if I'm to be living here then I think I'm entitled to know who I should be looking out for.'

'Well, I can't blame you for that,' said Barbara. 'I'm sorry. Suspicious by nature, me. So, what does he look like? I'd say *average*. Average height. Average build. Grey hair. Smart though, I'll give him that. Well turned out.'

'And he's definitely not been back?'

'No.'

Munro zipped his jacket, pulled on his gloves, and grabbed his groceries.

'I've kept you long enough,' he said. 'And I've some packing to be getting on with.'

'Pop in next time you're up,' said Barbara, 'I'm always up for a blether. I can fill you in on all the gossip.'

* * *

Confused as to whether his prowess at drawing the short straw was a genetic fault, payback for something he'd done in a previous life, or sheer bad luck, Duncan, sitting in the Defender with his hands in his pockets, collar turned up, and his radio tucked beneath the side of his watch cap, stared enviously at West as she reclined in the five-star comfort of his car across the street.

'Warm enough?' he said, muttering into the radio.

'Toasty. You?'

'Positively tropical. How long are we going to wait?'

'As long as it takes,' said West. 'He has to come out to play sooner or later.'

'I suggest we give it half an hour, miss. Then swap.'

'Dream on. I've been thinking–'

'Dangerous.'

'–and I'm still not sure about Riley.'

'How so?'

'I'm wondering if she's given McIntyre the tip-off.'

'Well, if she has,' said Duncan, 'then we're wasting our time. He'd have left before we got here, picked up the Lexus, and legged it. But I have to disagree, miss. She's not stupid. She knows if she gives us the runaround she'll be back inside before she knows it.'

'You think so?'

'Aye. Trust me. I grew up with folk like her and when they want saving, there's that look in their eyes. A look of helpless desperation.'

'Probably the same look I've been carrying for years.'

'I'll fetch the violin from the boot,' said Duncan, 'but as we're talking doubts, I'm not convinced if McIntyre does show up, that we'll be able to recognise him.'

'Why not? We've got a photo.'

'Aye, my point exactly,' said Duncan. 'That wee photo off his driving licence is nine years old, miss. He could be a wee baldie with a weight problem by now.'

Aware of a car signalling a right turn into Taylor Street, West slid down in her seat and glanced across the street at Duncan.

'Watch out,' she said. 'Incoming. Can you see who's driving?'

'No chance, miss. Too much glare off the windscreen.'

'Well, whoever it is, they're on the mooch. It looks like they're trying to ID a building.'

With the car far enough away to avoid detection, Duncan leaned on the steering wheel and squinted down the street as the scruffy-looking occupant stepped from the car and surveyed the block of flats before striding confidently towards the door.

'That's not McIntyre,' said Duncan. 'He's completely different. Even with the aging process, that fella's completely different.'

'And he's not getting an answer,' said West. 'Whoever he's visiting is clearly out.'

'Aye, but he's not giving up,' said Duncan, 'he's punching that entryphone again and oh! Result! He's in!'

'Maybe he's a bailiff,' said West. 'Or someone from TV Licensing. He looks the type.'

'What do you mean?'

'Shifty.'

West sat up straight as the unidentified driver emerged from the block and glanced up and down the street whilst frantically reaching for his phone.

'Blimey, that was quick,' said West.

'And he's not looking happy,' said Duncan. 'In fact, he looks like he's about to wet himself.'

'I wonder who he's calling?' said West. 'I think we should have a word. Maybe we can help.'

* * *

As the street lamps flickered into life and the flurries of snow began to fall from a darkening sky, Munro, concerned for the welfare of his ageing canine companion, tossed him a treat and turned the heater up full, his departure delayed by an unexpected call.

'Mr Byrne,' he said, 'that didnae take long, is everything okay?'

'No, Mr Munro. It is not.'

'Why am I not surprised. So, tell me, what's the problem now? Is it Mr MacDuff?

'Aye.'

'Is he not co-operating?'

'He's not co-operating at all, Mr Munro. He's dead.'

Chapter 9

Although the benefits of living in an urban conurbation were deemed by many to outweigh the negatives, those who triumphed the pubs and clubs, the sprawling shopping malls, and the countless sports facilities were also keen to play down the inherent risk of falling victim to opportunistic muggers, racist thugs, and even dognappers which, as testimony to the failings of modern society, were a daily occurrence throughout the country.

Observing a shady pair of likely miscreants approaching at speed – a tall, unshaven male dressed like a docker from a fifties B-movie and his sidekick, slight of build and clad in black – one such individual, afraid of being on the receiving end of some gratuitous violence, pulled his keys from his pocket and hastened towards his car.

'Ho! You!' said Duncan, increasing his pace. 'Hold on, there!'

'You alright, sir?' said West, catching her breath. 'You look distressed.'

Byrne whipped his warrant card from his pocket and held it at arm's length like a petrified priest conducting an exorcism.

'That's far enough!' he said. 'Police! Back off!'

Duncan, amused by his reaction, smiled and produced his own.

'Snap!' he said. 'DS Reid, and this is DI West.'

West pulled a flashlight from her hip and directed the beam towards Byrne's badge.

'You're not one of us,' she said, bluntly.

'Dumfries!' said Byrne loudly, as if protesting his innocence. 'I'm stationed in Dumfries!'

'Then what the hell are you… oh, hold on, you're the bloke Jimbo's been talking about. I mean, DI Munro.'

'James Munro! Aye! Thank God for that! For a minute there I thought you two were a couple of–'

'Say no more,' said West, raising her hand and cutting him short, 'it happens a lot, especially with him. You're here to interview a witness, is that right?'

'Aye. Alan MacDuff. So Mr Munro's obviously filled you in then?'

'He gave us a few details,' said West. 'In confidence. Something about a fatality in Auchencairn, right?'

'Spot on.'

'So what's the problem?' said Duncan. 'Is this MacDuff fella giving you grief?'

'No, no. I never got the chance to speak to him.'

'How so? Has he legged it?'

'No,' said Byrne. 'He's dead. He's in the kitchen and he's dead.'

West glanced furtively at Duncan and fumbled in her pocket for a pair of latex gloves.

'How did you get in?' she said, snapping them on.

'The door's open.'

'In that case, we'll handle it from here. First you can show us exactly where he is, then you can wait in your car while we make a few calls.'

'With all due respect,' said Byrne, 'MacDuff is my witness and I–'

'*With all due respect*, Mr Byrne, I've got one word for you – jurisdiction. Now, lead on.'

* * *

Quietly content to have the case taken off his hands, DI Byrne led them into the building and waited as West, her brow furrowed with bewilderment, glared at Duncan.

'Flat 2!' she said, pointing out the numerals on the door. 'This is McIntyre's address!'

'I hope you've got that photo handy,' said Duncan, 'because it looks like our Mr McIntyre's been living under a pseudonym.'

With her blood pressure rising and the adrenalin pumping, West followed Byrne along the narrow hallway to the dingy lounge.

'Can we get some lights on, please? I can't see a flipping thing in here.'

'I'll pull the curtain,' said Duncan, flicking the switch. 'We'll not want folk queuing at the window for a wee swatch at what's going on.'

'It doesn't look like anything's been touched,' said West. 'Mind you, there isn't actually much *to* touch.'

'Aye, it's a bit like Barlow's place,' said Byrne.

'Barlow?'

'She's the girl in Auchencairn. Someone gained entry to her house and left everything untouched. Everything except her office, that is. It was a total mess.'

'In what way?'

'Completely trashed, paperwork, files, documents, they were all over the place.'

'Trashed?' said West. 'Or ransacked?'

'Sorry, you're right. Ransacked.'

'So they were looking for something?'

'Aye, I reckon so,' said Byrne. 'And there was no sign of a forced entry at her place either. Like I say, the door here was open.'

'So MacDuff might have known his attacker?'

'Aye, maybe, unless…'

'Unless what?'

'Well, I'm just thinking,' said Byrne, trying his best to sound proficient, 'unless it was some chancer. A courier maybe who bluffed his way in and–'

'Oh, give me a break!' said West, pointing at the coffee table, 'a couple of mobiles and a laptop. He'd have had it away with that lot for a start!'

'It was just a thought.'

'Not a very productive one.'

'He'd have had this lot too,' said Duncan, squatting by a pile of boxes stacked against the wall. 'You'd get a fair few quid for these on eBay.'

'What are they?'

'Security cameras, miss. Brand new. And an LCD monitor.'

West turned to Byrne and regarded him with a frown.

'This Barlow girl,' she said, 'have you ascertained a cause of death yet?'

'We're still waiting on results,' said Byrne. 'I'm hoping we'll have something by the morning.'

'But she definitely knew MacDuff?'

'Aye.'

Duncan stared at West and smiled.

'Are you thinking what I'm thinking?' he said.

'If you mean that Barlow's dead and she knew MacDuff and now he's dead so the perp could be the same person then, yeah. It's worth a shot. If we can find someone who's known to the pair of them, then we might be on to something. Mr Byrne, have you got a list of people that Barlow might have been mixing with? Workmates, friends, that sort of thing?'

Byrne, biting his lip, nodded a little too enthusiastically.

'Aye, of course,' he said. 'Actually, what I mean is, almost. We're working on it.'

'Good. Send it over as soon as it's available. Right, let's have a look at this MacDuff geezer, shall we?'

* * *

Untouched in decades, the kitchen – with its brown melamine units, speckled Formica worktop, antiquated gas cooker, and farmhouse style table – held a questionable appeal for lovers of retro-inspired interiors but for Duncan the most interesting feature was the rise and fall pendant, which lent a jaundiced tinge to the anaemic body lying prostrate on the floor.

'Well, I can tell you this for nothing,' he said, 'that's not Daniel McIntyre.'

'So, he's got two addresses and doesn't live at either of them.'

'Correction, he's got two that we know of. I'd not be surprised if he's got two more.'

'Right,' said West, 'we need another word with Riley. At this rate she'll be getting a loyalty card from Gateside.'

Duncan, crouching beside the corpse, stared into the lifeless eyes and, struck by the look of utter surprise frozen on the face, laid the back of his hand gently across the forehead.

'Still warm,' he said. 'Not roasting, but warm all the same. We'll need McLeod to confirm it but I'm guessing it may have been as little as two or three hours ago.'

'What? So we could've just missed him!'

'Sorry,' said Byrne, 'missed who?'

'Are you for real? The bloke who did this of course! Christ, this is so annoying!'

'Well we did have other fish to fry,' said Duncan, 'and to be honest, we could've missed him by a mile.'

'Yeah, yeah, I know,' said West. 'I'm over-reacting. Well, McIntyre's going to have to take a back seat for now, this is more important.'

'You've lost me,' said Byrne. 'If you don't mind me asking, who's McIntyre?'

'He's the reason we're here. Nothing for you to worry about.'

'There's no sign of blood,' said Duncan, 'and no weapon to be found, just a whopper of a bruise on his neck, just below the Adam's apple.'

'What does that mean? Did he choke?'

'I'm not Quincy, miss. That's another one for McLeod to sort out.'

Duncan stood aside as West, folding her arms, scrutinised the body before muttering out loud as she slowly paced her way around the kitchen commentating on all that lay before her.

'Black T-shirt, jeans, bare feet. Wrong position to have slipped and hit his head. Washing in the sink, one plate, one fork. Mug on the counter, teabag floating on the top, not stirred. Bread in the toaster, not pushed down. A side plate, knife, a jar of marmalade and a butter dish on the table–'

'I'm not normally one for interrupting,' said Byrne, 'but should we not be calling the SOCOs by now? I mean, all this talk of bare feet and toast, is that really relevant?'

'Aye. No offence, sir,' said Duncan, 'but it's incredibly relevant. See, what it means is that MacDuff wasn't entertaining, in fact he wasn't even expecting anyone and with no shoes he had no intention of going out. He was making himself a brew and something to eat when he was interrupted by someone chapping his door. More than likely, the same someone who killed him.'

'And there's no sign of struggle,' said West, 'which means that whoever did this took him by surprise, got straight down to business, and left.'

'Aye, one thing's for sure,' said Duncan, 'this fella was deliberately targeted.'

'So,' said West, 'have you got any pearls of wisdom to add to the mix, Mr Byrne? Anything that might help us on our way?'

'I think you've covered everything,' said Byrne. 'I'll wait in the car while you make your calls.'

West returned to the lounge and listened for the slam of a car door before speaking.

'He's not going to last long, is he?' she said. 'He's got his flipping head in the clouds.'

'You're not wrong there,' said Duncan. 'Even a twelve-year-old playing Cluedo shows more nous than him.'

'Right, I'll call McLeod, you take care of the rest.'

'Roger that.'

'We need uniform out front and SOCOs here asap, tell them to dust his personal gear first then bag it up and bring it back so Dougal can get cracking. I'm going to have a quick word with Poirot outside then I'm going to see Riley. I'll get you at the office.'

'No bother and, miss, be sure to take your Defender. If it's all the same with you I'd quite like my car back.'

* * *

Ignoring Byrne's invitation to chat through the open window, West, drawing on the compassionate side of her nature in an effort to ease the tension between them, walked around the front of the filthy Astra and hopped into the passenger seat.

'Talk through the window like that,' she said, 'and people will think you're propositioning me.'

'I should apologise,' said Byrne. 'I'm not thinking straight.'

'One of those days, eh? No worries, we all have them. Things are always a bit fraught at times like this.'

'Aye, right enough. It was a bit of a shock, that's all. I thought I'd get a wee interview under my belt and be on my way.'

'Well there's nothing like the odd body to keep us on our toes. So, tell me, how was MacDuff involved with the girl in Auchencairn? They were in a relationship, is that right?'

'No, no,' said Byrne, 'at least, I don't think they were. From what we can gather he was working for her. I'm just glad Mr Munro had a chat with him before he died or we probably wouldn't even know that.'

'And why is he of interest? Why him in particular?'

'Because,' said Byrne, 'there's every chance that he was the last one to see Barlow alive. I was hoping he might have given us a lead.'

'Well, it looks like him snuffing it has put the kybosh on that. Have you got a plan B?'

'Aye. I just have to think of it first.'

'That's the spirit. Now listen, if MacDuff was working for Barlow then I'm going to need everything you've got on her. Maybe then we can sort this mess out between us.'

'No bother,' said Byrne. 'I'll send it over this evening. And thanks.'

'What for?'

'Listening. Understanding.'

'Don't be daft. This is your first case, isn't it? At the helm, I mean.'

'Aye.'

'Well, we've all got to start somewhere but take it from me, it doesn't get any easier.'

* * *

Mindful of the fact that the rumble of her rattling Defender might arouse the suspicions of Riley's nosy neighbours, West, keen to arrive undetected, coasted to a halt some distance from the house, walked briskly along the darkened street and, with Riley keeping her profile as low as a limbo dancer, pressed her ear to the door and listened for any signs of movement as she gently rapped the letterbox.

'It's DI West,' she said, softly. 'Can you open up, please.'

Riley inched open the door and beckoned her inside.

'Back already,' she said, nervously. 'Is something wrong?'

'More than you'll ever know,' said West, 'but let's not worry about that now. I see McIntyre's motor's still outside.'

'Aye, Christ knows when he'll be back. It could be two in the morning, then again, he could be two minutes away.'

'Then I'll get out of your hair. I just need to verify a few things.'

'Oh, aye?'

'And listen, I'm putting my trust in you so you'd better be straight with me, have you got that?'

'Aye, of course.'

'Good. Now, McIntyre, the address you gave us, you're sure that's the right one?'

'Aye, positive.'

'Have you been there? To his house?'

'No. Never.'

'How come?'

'No need,' said Riley. 'He only told me where he lives in case of an emergency. He said that unless it was a matter of life or death then under no circumstances was I ever to go there.'

'Why?'

'He said it was for my own good,' said Riley. 'My own protection. He said he couldn't afford to leave a paper trail, whatever that is.'

'Do you know if he rents it, or owns it?'

'I honestly couldn't say,' said Riley.

'Okay,' said West, 'do you know if he has any other addresses? Another flat, or business premises, maybe?'

'No, not that I know of.'

'Right. Last question. Have you ever heard of someone called Alan MacDuff?'

Riley pursed her lips and shook her head.

'No,' she said. 'I once knew a MacAllister if that's any help.'

'None at all. What about McIntyre, has he ever mentioned a MacDuff? A drinking pal, maybe? Or someone he's bought gear off?'

'No, sorry. Not that I recall.'

'And you're sure about that?'

'Aye, positive. Why?'

'Let us worry the "whys",' said West. 'Just you keep your nose clean and we'll be in touch.'

* * *

With only two rooms left to inspect, Duncan – hoping to unearth a kilo of smack to justify the apparently motiveless murder – was surprised to find MacDuff's lack of personal possessions and high standards of hygiene to be the antithesis of the average person's perception of the single male.

Proclaiming the bathroom a health hazard due to the toxic stench of bleach and tiles white enough to incur a debilitating bout of snow-blindness he moved to the sparsely furnished bedroom where a chest of drawers revealed enough neatly pressed T-shirts to open a clothing store whilst the wardrobe held precisely two shirts, a full length overcoat, some bed linen, an expanding box file containing everything pertaining to his financial affairs, and a hand-written sales ledger detailing his business transactions to date.

Distracted by the sound of voices emanating from the street, he bagged up the book and the box file and made his way back to the lounge.

* * *

Whist many of those skilled in the art of forensic investigation considered the peace and relative isolation of a crime scene the ideal environment in which to work, the diminutive Kay Grogan – an experienced SOCO blessed with a contagious enthusiasm – preferred to share her discoveries in real time with anyone who cared to listen.

Clad in a Tyvek suit with a matching face mask strapped around her chin, she bounded into the flat with a fire in her eyes and an aluminium briefcase dangling from her left arm.

'Duncan!' she said, grinning wildly. 'This is exciting, isn't it!'

'Aye. I'm beside myself. Are you on happy pills?'

'Don't need them. So, what have we got?'

'Nothing special, hen. Not unless you want to give a body the once over.'

'I'd love to,' said Grogan, 'but I think the pathologist might have something to say about that. I'll take a few pics for posterity, though. Did they break in?'

'No,' said Duncan, 'it looks as though the fella in the kitchen let his killer in so we're looking for any dabs that don't belong to him.'

'It's not just fingerprints, though, is it?' said Grogan. 'There's fibres, latent footprints, dead skin cells, DNA swabs, everything! I'll be as thorough as I can.'

'I had a feeling you would but first,' said Duncan, pointing at the coffee table, 'I need that laptop and those mobile phones dusted as quick as you can. I need to take them with me.'

'No bother,' said Grogan, 'but there's no need to wait, I can drop them over later.'

Duncan smiled at Grogan and winked.

'Any excuse to see Dougal, eh?'

'Maybe.'

'Well, I hate to disappoint you, Kay, but you've got your hands full here and Dougal's going to be flat out once I get this lot back, so you'll have to make do with a Zoom call at bedtime.'

'Spoilsport. Give me twenty minutes and I'll be done.'

'Ho! Anyone home?'

Recognising the voice in the hall, Duncan threw his head back and sighed as the fatigue began to set in.

'It's like Piccadilly Circus,' he said. 'In here!'

With a mop of wavy red hair and a tangled mess of a beard, the willowy Dr Andy McLeod – half lumberjack, half Viking – possessed all the skills of a master butcher, a career he'd considered before excelling in his chosen profession as a forensic pathologist.

'Duncan,' he said, dryly. 'Another body?'

'Aye. You should be paying us a finder's fee, pal. We're keeping you in work. Follow me.'

As somebody used to staring death in the face, McLeod, unfazed by the sight of a cold cadaver, stood over MacDuff and made a cursory scan of the body with a forensic light source while Duncan watched from the door.

'He's not slipped,' he said with a yawn, 'or banged his head. And there's no blood.'

'No,' said McLeod, 'just the contusion on his neck.'

'Aye, it's a belter. What would cause a bruise like that? Is that what killed him?'

'I can't say for sure,' said McLeod, 'not yet, but it's certainly possible, aye. Have you got your snaps for the album yet?'

'No.'

'Then I'll wait until she's done before I take a closer look.'

'Is there not anything you can tell me right now?'

'Aye, plenty,' said McLeod. 'Are you needing notes?'

'Not unless you're using that fancy medical jargon.'

'Then I'll keep it simple. The contusion is located on what we call the *fossa jugularis sternalis*, or jugular notch for short. Directly behind it is the trachea, or windpipe. Enough pressure here could cause the victim to black out. Prolonged pressure could result in death. And a sharp blow could force the hyaline cartilage through the larynx which would result in blood drowning and obstruction of the airways, but as you know, Duncan, I can't confirm any of that until I get him on the slab.'

'Aye, I get that. How about a time of death?'

McLeod grasped a lifeless hand by the fingers and squeezed gently before repeating the process on the toes.

'No sign of rigor just yet,' he said, 'and the extremities are cooling nicely. It's not exactly cold in here so I'd say somewhere between three and five hours ago. I can give you a better idea once I get a thermometer on him.'

Grogan, carrying a camera in one hand, came prancing into the room like a personal shopper on a hefty commission and handed Duncan a collection of sealed plastic bags.

'That's you,' she said with a smile. 'Is he ready for his close-up?'

'Just about,' said McLeod. 'I'll get out your way. Duncan, are you heading back to the office?'

'I am, aye.'

'Tell Charlie I was asking for her, would you?'

Chapter 10

Although the harsh winter months had an adverse effect on those susceptible to seasonal affective disorder – the lack of daylight dragging them into the depths of depression and burdening them with a crippling sense of apathy – for others the short, dreich days offered the ideal excuse to hurry home and settle in front of a roaring fire with a large dram and a bar of chocolate, however, much to the annoyance of the over-stretched police departments it also sent the undesirables scurrying to the streets to conduct their business like a plague of cockroaches scavenging for scraps.

Stuck in a queue of slow-moving traffic, Duncan, keen to offload MacDuff's personal effects and reacquaint his taste buds with an ice cold beer, watched as a couple of scallies – either on the run with a pocketful of merchandise lifted from the convenience store or desperate to get their next fix – scrambled over the railings in the centre of the carriageway, dodged the oncoming traffic, and took shelter in the doorway of a boarded-up shop where one pulled a packet of doubtless stolen cigarettes from his jacket and tossed the cellophane to the ground.

More annoyed at the littering than the thieving, Duncan watched as he cupped his hands around the tip of the fag, the flame of the lighter illuminating the pasty face of a habitual user, and dismissed their antics with a silent '*there but for the grace of God*' before suddenly glancing in the rear-view mirror, leaving the lane of traffic, and mounting the kerb with his hazards flashing.

The two miscreants nudged each other with their elbows as he lowered the nearside window and leaned forward.

'Lost something, pal?' said one with a scowl.

The lad with the cigarette, ignoring his accomplice, swaggered confidently towards the car.

'Alright?' he said. 'Need some help?'

'Aye,' said Duncan, clutching a twenty pound note between his fingers.

'Not here,' said the lad. 'Drive around the corner. I'll get you there.'

Duncan turned down the dingy side street, stepped from the car, and perched on the bonnet with his hands in his pockets, his shoulders twitching against the cold as the young man sauntered towards him.

'What are you after?' he said, giggling as only an addict could. 'Speed? Benzos? Mary Jane?'

'Got any black?'

The junkie narrowed his eyes, stared at Duncan with a half-smile, and produced a small pellet of tin foil.

'You're in luck,' he said. 'Forty.'

Duncan looked to the ground, chuckling as he shook his head.

'Jog on,' he said. 'I'll give you twenty.'

The druggie, holding the nugget between his thumb and forefinger, held out his arm and nodded.

'Twenty, it is,' he said as he dropped it into Duncan's open palm.

'Nice,' said Duncan, squinting at the tattoos on his fingers. 'Can I see?'

The druggie clenched his fist and straightened his arm.

'Choose life,' he said, proudly. 'That's what I'm doing. Live for the moment, know what I'm saying?'

Taking advantage of the dazed dopehead's mild sense of euphoria, Duncan, acutely aware that his senses had slowed to that of a banana slug on the brink of hibernation, casually slipped a cuff around his wrist, spun him onto the bonnet of the car, and forced his arm halfway up his back.

'I'm arresting you under Section 1 of the Criminal Justice Act for possession of a class B drug,' he said as he fastened the other cuff. 'I believe that keeping you in custody is necessary before bringing you before a court or otherwise dealing with you in accordance with the law. Do you understand?'

The junkie stared back with a look of surprised bewilderment smeared across his face.

'I'll take that as a *yes*,' said Duncan as he bundled him into the back of the car. 'Play your cards right and I could do you for intent to supply as well.'

* * *

Astounded by Byrne's staggering inability to fulfil even the simplest of tasks, and Emma Riley's apparent amnesia regarding the whereabouts of Daniel McIntyre, West – her frustration heightened by a drop in sugar levels and the desire to demolish a three course meal with a bottle of red – stormed into the office, pulled up a chair, and flung her feet on the table.

Amused by her sullen expression, Munro glanced at Dougal and smiled as Murdo scampered across the floor to greet her.

'You won't believe what I've just been through,' she said, stroking the dog.

'Take a deep breath,' said Munro. 'You need to relax.'

'It's going to take more than a deep breath to do that, Jimbo. To start with, that Emma Riley, I still say something's not right about her. Her story's about as fishy as a tuna sandwich. She claims she's never been to McIntyre's house, which I simply cannot believe, and why after all these years she's suddenly decided to turn on him is beyond me.'

'Sounds like you've had quite a day of it.'

'I'm not finished yet,' said West. 'Your mate Byrne, blimey, I'll be surprised if he lasts a week in the job.'

'He's trying, Charlie.'

'You're telling me. Oh, and brace yourself for a shock,' said West. 'That MacDuff bloke you've been talking to…'

West paused as Munro raised his hands to the side of his head, pressed his fingers against his temples, and closed his eyes.

'I'm getting a picture,' he said.

'You what?'

'It's MacDuff. He's in a kitchen.'

'Are you kidding me?'

'He's on the floor,' said Munro, 'he's not looking well and… och! He's no longer with us. He's passed over to the other side.'

'How the hell…?'

'DI Byrne,' said Munro. 'He telephoned as soon as he found the body.'

'So it was you he was calling! Well I hate to say it but MacDuff snuffing it has put the spanner in the works as far as his investigation's concerned. The poor bloke doesn't know where to turn.'

'Then he's lucky MacDuff expired on our patch, Charlie. It's one less thing for him to worry about.'

'Yes,' said West, 'one less for him and one more for us.'

* * *

Duncan, clutching MacDuff's personal possessions, appeared in the doorway and glanced around the office before his eyes finally settled on West.

'You look as bad as I feel,' he said.

'Thanks very much,' said West. 'What took you so long?'

'I got side-tracked,' said Duncan as he placed the bags on Dougal's desk. 'Do you believe in fate?'

'You're asking me?' said Dougal.

'Aye.'

'I do. That's how I met Kay.'

'Good. Because apart from these I've got something else for you downstairs.'

'Oh?'

'The ned who assaulted the roofless fella. I've just nicked him for possession.'

'Are you joking me?'

'I'm not in a laughing mood just now, pal. He's wearing a Firetrap jacket and he's got that festering tattoo on his hand so listen, as we've only got twelve hours unless he's charged I suggest you get yourself down to the interview room as quick as you can. I've a meeting with a pint to go to.'

'I can't!' said Dougal. 'Not if you're wanting me to go through this lot! It's going to take a wee while to burrow through those phones, not to mention the laptop.'

'He's right,' said West. 'Sorry mate, but you'll have to do it. It's not late.'

'No offence, miss, but it's the back of six,' said Duncan. 'That's twelve hours I've been on the go already.'

'Well, one more won't hurt. Please. I'll make it worth your while.'

'I'll do it if you don't. Right, that's me away downstairs, then. I hope you all have a pleasant evening. Oh, and miss, McLeod's been asking for you.'

'Well, someone's not happy,' said West as Duncan left the room.

'I cannae blame him,' said Munro, 'I'd be raging too. Right, wee Murdo needs his supper, as do I. Will we go?'

* * *

Of the rag-tag bunch of guilty offenders ever to have graced the cramped confines of the interview room there had been those who'd regarded the likes of West as less qualified, less capable, and less threatening than her male counterparts whilst others, when confronted by Dougal, had considered it empowering to laugh in the face of the somewhat bookish detective. But only the foolish, invariably driven by the ignorance of youth, dared to cross the line with Duncan who, by appearance alone, was more likely to land a right hook than worry about answers to any questions.

Sitting with his legs splayed and his eyes still slightly glazed, the tattooed ned looked up and gave a fatuous grin as Duncan tossed a large, brown envelope onto the table, pulled up a chair, and glared unflinchingly across the desk until the smile dropped from his face.

'Are you just going to sit and stare?' he said. 'Or are you actually going to say something?'

Duncan reached forward and stabbed the voice recorder.

'The time,' he said, 'is 6:29pm. I am Detective Sergeant Reid. For the benefit of the tape would you please state your name.'

'No,' said the ned, smirking as he shook his head.

'Sorry?'

'No. I know my rights.'

'Well, see here, pal,' said Duncan with a sigh, 'I'm a wee bit rusty myself so perhaps you'd care to remind me.'

'Right. Well, for a start, I don't have to say anything. I don't have to say anything at all.'

Duncan leaned back and folded his arms.

'Actually,' he said quietly, 'that's where you're wrong. As you've been arrested on suspicion of committing an offence you are required by law to state your name, your address, your date of birth, and your nationality.'

'No.'

'Failure to do so means you'll be issued with a fine and detained until you do.'

'Okay then. Humpty Dumpty.'

'Providing a false name is also an offence. So, that's two fines you've got so far and by the way, unless you're one of those secret millionaires, you should know that failure to pay the fines will result in a custodial sentence. Now, I'm sure your mother's wondering where you are so let's go for third time lucky, shall we? Name?'

Ruffled by the fact that Duncan, unlike the other officers he'd encountered in recent years, failed to show the slightest signs of anger or even raise his voice, the ned glanced sheepishly around the room, dropped the bravado, and lowered his voice.

'John,' he said.

'John what?'

'Drennan.'

'Address?'

'Green Street.'

'Good. Now before we go any further,' said Duncan, 'someone as clever as you will no doubt be aware that you're entitled to legal representation, so would you like to call your solicitor?'

'I don't have one.'

'Would you like me to appoint a duty solicitor?'

'Waste of time,' said Drennan. 'I've done nothing wrong.'

'Well there's clearly something wrong with your memory,' said Duncan, 'because you were arrested less than an hour ago for carrying a class B drug which you then sold to me. That's supply as well as possession, two offences rolled into one.'

Drennan, reverting to form, locked his hands behind his head and laughed.

'That's not going to stick!' he said. 'You've no chance! See, the way you got me, that's called *entrapment.* You can't do that!'

'I can,' said Duncan, calmly, 'but that's not why you're here. I'm not interested in your drugs. I want to know why you knocked seven bells out of some poor homeless fella who was trying to get some kip in a doorway.'

Drennan, wearing a look normally reserved for eight-year-olds who'd just been told that Santa Claus did not exist, froze in his seat.

'Do you know what I think?' said Duncan. 'I think it's hard enough for fellas like that at the best of times but at this time of year, Christ it must be tough. So, why did you do it?'

Drennan hesitated as his mouth began to dry up.

'You've got the wrong fella,' he said. 'It wasn't me.'

'See here, Mr Drennan, I'll give you some advice. If you're going to do something like this then you have to be one hundred per cent sure you're not going to get caught. Now, dressing in black, keeping your back to the camera, and wearing a hood, that's good, I'll give you that, but you should have worn some gloves. Especially with a tattoo like yours. So, what was it? Were you angry? Had you argued with someone? Or was it just a bit of fun?'

Drennan wiped his mouth with the back of his hand and stared blankly at the desk.

'No comment,' he said.

'Let me spell things out for you,' said Duncan, as his patience wore thin, 'we have enough evidence to put you away for assault, that means anywhere from six months to a couple of years in the big house but I'm going to do you a favour. Tell me exactly why you did it and I'll see what I can do about getting you a lenient sentence, even a suspended, maybe.'

'No comment.'

Duncan grabbed the envelope, tipped the contents to the desk, and laid them out in a neat line.

'For the benefit of the tape,' he said, 'I am now showing Mr Drennan the items found about his person when arrested. One mobile phone. One packet of cigarettes. One lighter. One packet of cigarette papers. One set of house keys. One plastic pouch of what appears to be hashish, yet to be verified. Two foil pellets believed to contain cannabis resin, also yet to be verified. And exactly three hundred and fifty-seven pounds in cash. What do you do for a living, Mr Drennan?'

Drennan shrugged his shoulders.

'No comment,' he said.

'How did you come by this much cash?'

'No comment.'

'Well, as you've chosen to exercise your right to remain silent, I may as well leave you to it.'

'You're letting me go?'

'Don't be daft. You had a chance, pal, and you blew it. You'll be here for another twelve hours and when I come back in the morning if you still refuse to co-operate, I'll not waste my breath with any more questions, I'll simply charge you with assault and make a recommendation to the fiscal that you get the maximum sentence possible.'

'Then what?'

'Then,' said Duncan, 'you'll be in court before lunch and I can almost certainly guarantee you'll be in your cell by teatime.'

Drennan, squirming in his seat, frowned as he hastily weighed up his options.

'But you could get me off?' he said. 'With a suspended sentence?'

'No. I said I'd see what I could do. So, do you want to start again?'

'Aye.'

'Right. So what do you do for a living?'

'Nothing.'

'So, you're signing on?'

'Aye.'

'And where did you get this cash?'

'It's my dole money.'

'Oh, you must think I'm zipped up the back, pal! Jobseeker's Allowance is fifty-eight quid a week so I'll ask you once more, *where did the money come from?*'

'I did a job,' said Drennan. 'A wee job. Cash in hand.'

'What kind of job?'

Mindful of repercussions should he speak up, Drennan, wondering if there really was such a thing as honour amongst thieves, sat on his hands as he contemplated the hole he was in.

'Okay, I've had enough,' said Duncan. 'See here, Mr Drennan, I'm not like those snowflakes and councillors you see on the telly whining about the likes of you being victims of society. I've been there. We all have a choice and as far as I'm concerned you can either turn your life around or do a spell inside and right now, you're in line for the latter. I'll see you in the morning.'

'Wait!'

'What?'

Drennan stared at Duncan with a look of apprehension on his face.

'What's it like?' he said. 'Inside.'

'It's not pleasant. I'd not believe the stories you hear about inmates having mobile phones and TV sets. If your cellmate doesn't do you, the depression will.'

'The homeless fella,' said Drennan with a gulp. 'I was asked to put the frighteners on him.'

'Say that again.'

'I was paid to scare him off. Get him to do one. Scarper.'

'Who was he?'

'I've no idea.'

'Then how did you know you had the right fella?'

'She pointed him out to me.'

'Who pointed him out?'

'Emms,' said Drennan. 'Emma.'

'Emma who?'

'I don't know her last name.'

'Who is she?'

'My supplier.'

Duncan pulled his phone from his pocket and began typing.

'And why did she want him moved on?' he said as he sent a text.

'She said he needed to be taught a lesson. She said he'd scored off her and not paid up.'

'Can you describe her?'

'Flash,' said Drennan. 'Expensive clothes, always turned up in a fancy motor and…'

Drennan paused at the ping of the phone.

'For the benefit of the tape,' said Duncan, holding his phone aloft, 'I am now showing Mr Drennan a picture of Miss Emma Riley. Is this your supplier?'

'Aye. That's her.'

'When was the last time you saw her?'

'When she paid me,' said Drennan. 'The day before I clocked the homeless fella.'

'And you've not seen her since?'

'No. She's disappeared. And she's late with my gear.'

'How much did she pay you to assault that fella?'

'Five hundred,' said Drennan.

Duncan stood, picked up the envelope, and reached for the voice recorder.

'Interview terminated, the time is 7:03pm,' he said. 'You've done the right thing, pal. Someone will take you back to your cell now and you'll be in court tomorrow. Like I said, I'll ask for leniency on the grounds of your co-operation. Take it easy.'

* * *

Though not as experienced as the code-breakers of Bletchley Park or as proficient as the hackers who inhabited the dark side of the web, Dougal was nonetheless skilled enough to access any password-protected device without the loss of data by over-riding protocols with a few choice key commands and some simple coding.

Having successfully logged into MacDuff's computer as 'Administrator' he gleefully set about foraging through the files and folders of the largely unused laptop which, much to his disappointment, revealed little of interest whereas the hidden cache of the well-worn browser contained a history of links to locations risqué enough to make the prudish detective blush with embarrassment.

'You're looking pleased with yourself,' said Duncan.

'Aye, I'm rattling away. Not only that, Kay's on her way over and she's bringing supper.'

'Very good. There's nothing like dinner for two in the intimate surroundings of a freezing cold office. What are you having?'

'Pizza,' said Dougal. 'Pepperoni. And some garlic bread. And some buffalo wings. And–'

'That's plenty. You'll be done before I get home. I should have left ages ago.'

'I know,' said Dougal, 'that's probably my fault, I owe you. I'd have questioned him myself if I didn't have all this to do.'

'You're alright, pal, although, as you're offering, there is one way you can repay the favour.'

'Name it.'

'The report for the fiscal. We need to send it as soon as possible.'

'No bother,' said Dougal. 'I'll get a transcript of the interview and do it straight after supper. I take it the photo of Riley did the trick then?'

'Aye, spot on,' said Duncan. 'Emma Riley, would you believe, is his supplier and she paid him to attack the roofless fella.'

'Are you joking me? But why?'

'He reneged on a deal, apparently. Not that that's anything to do with us, what matters as far as we're concerned, is we can do him for assault. I need to call

Westy and let her know, she'll not be happy about Riley's involvement.'

'Right enough,' said Dougal, 'especially as she's probably halfway through a bottle of Merlot by now.'

'Well, that's not my problem, Dougal. I've done enough for one day. Either she has to have a word with Riley now or get uniform to pick her up and face her in the morning. Anyway, how are you getting on with MacDuff? Find anything interesting?'

'Oh aye,' said Dougal, 'but I'd not call it interesting. More *creepy*.'

'Go on.'

'He's got remote access on this laptop to a network of cameras all over town. Cameras he's installed.'

'So what's wrong with that? I mean, that's his job.'

'These are tiny wee cameras,' said Dougal. 'Spy cameras. And they're hidden in bathrooms and bedrooms. *Ladies'* bathrooms and bedrooms.'

'The dirty… so he's some kind of voyeur, then?'

'Aye. I'm going to trace the locations then we'll have to contact all the residents, tell them what's happened, and strip out the cameras.'

'Well, as MacDuff's not around to spy on those folk anymore, I'd say that's the least of our problems just now.'

* * *

Declining the offer of a biscuit, Murdo, shrewd enough to know that something more palatable was on the horizon, bided his time on the sofa while West, in a consummate display of effortless multi-tasking, swigged from a glass of red while pulling a steak and haggis pie from the oven.

'I'm glad to see you've got the hang of cooking again,' said Munro. 'Now if you could only master the art of washing-up, you'd make the perfect hostess.'

'Any more of that and you'll be queuing at the soup kitchen tomorrow, trust me.'

'Well, you'll not have to bother with the washing in your new house, Charlie. I'll make sure the plumbers install a dishwasher for you.'

'Hold on,' said West, 'I haven't said I'm taking it yet! Look, Jimbo, I don't want to seem as though I'm looking a gift horse in the mouth but…'

'But that's precisely it, lassie! It's a gift horse, not a Trojan one. There's nae catch, nae caveats. Think about it but dinnae dither or I shall leave it to the Dogs Trust.'

'You wouldn't. You would. Okay, I'll think about it but don't rush me, I've got too much going on right now.'

'Take your time,' said Munro, raising his glass. 'Your very good health. I wonder if Duncan's made his way home yet?'

'I hope so,' said West. 'I feel a bit guilty for leaving him to it.'

'It's one of the benefits of being the boss, Charlie. It's called delegation.'

'I'd call it a cop-out. So, what does tomorrow hold for you? Any more suspects you'd like to tell me about?'

'None,' said Munro. 'First I shall see what young Dougal has for me regarding the Barlow girl, then I shall visit The Mount and present his findings to DI Byrne. Lord knows, that chap's going to need all the help he can get.'

'You're telling me. He'd be lost without you.'

'And I'm sure you know how that feels.'

'Thanks for reminding me,' said West as the phone rang. 'It's Duncan, I'd better take it. Haven't you got a horse to feed or some armour to polish or something?'

Munro helped himself to a forkful of pie as Murdo, licking his lips, appeared silently by his side and gazed longingly at the plate.

'Sorry, Jimbo,' said West, struggling to put her coat on, 'I've really got to go.'

'At this time? What on earth's going on?'

'It's what they call karma. That scally with the tattoos who attacked the tramp? He was paid to do it by Emma Riley.'

'Well, I have to admit,' said Munro, 'I like a convoluted tale as much as the next man, but I never saw that coming.'

'No, nor I. Don't wait up.'

'A word to the wise before you go,' said Munro. 'I'd not drive if I were you.'

'What? Why?'

'I think you'll find the answer to that question lies in that half-empty bottle of wine.'

'Oh, crap.'

'Dinnae fret,' said Munro, 'I've only had a sip, I shall drive you myself but if you're about to arrest someone, I suggest you arrange for uniform to meet us there. You'll be needing some assistance to bring her back.'

* * *

Belying his appearance as a doddery old pensioner returning from a late-night shopping trip, Munro – despite the ageing Peugeot twitching erratically on the black ice – hurtled along the street and slew to a halt inches behind McIntyre's car.

'I didn't know you had it in you,' said West. 'I'm impressed.'

'There's more to me than meets the eye, Charlie. You should know that by now. I'll leave you to it.'

West bounded up the steps and, no longer concerned about being the centre of attention, hammered the door with her fist as Munro signalled the patrol car to pull up alongside.

'Is he here?' she said as Riley, still dressed to the nines, inched open the door. 'McIntyre?'

'No. I mean, this is a surprise. I wasn't expecting you.'

'Clearly not,' said West. 'Do you like keeping secrets, Miss Riley?'

'Sorry?'

'We just found a skeleton in your closet and his name's John Drennan.'

Riley, looking completely confused, frowned and raised a hand.

'Can you slow down a wee bit,' she said. 'Drennan?'

'He's a druggie. About five foot eight. Tattoos on the fingers of his left hand.'

'Oh.'

'Oh, indeed. So, let's cut to the chase,' said West. 'Who's the bloke you had beaten up?'

'Sorry, Inspector, but now I really am confused.'

'According to Drennan you paid him five hundred quid to give a fella a good kicking. So, who was he, and why?'

'No, no. It's not me,' said Riley. 'I'd not hurt a fly let alone have some smelly old tramp beaten up.'

West took half a step back and smiled as she pulled a pair of cuffs from her hip.

'Who said anything about a tramp? Emma Riley, I'm arresting you under Section 1 of the Criminal Justice Act on suspicion of art and part whereby you instructed one John Drennan to carry out an assault on an unidentified male. You do not have to say anything but anything you do say will be noted and may be used in evidence. Do you understand?'

Chapter 11

Born of an age when delving into a suspect's past would have involved weeks of scouring newspaper archives, countless door-to-door enquiries, and travelling to some far flung location for a five-minute conversation with somebody who'd died three weeks earlier, Munro – enthused by the wonders of the internet and Dougal's flawless ability to follow the smallest snippet of information to a veritable gold mine of pertinent data – watched in admiration as his fingers flashed like lightning across the keyboard.

'I'm beginning to think your talents are wasted here,' he said. 'You should have trained as a concert pianist.'

'Oh, I'm not musically inclined, boss,' said Dougal. 'I think I was at the back of the line when they were handing out rhythm.'

'Then you would have made a fine jazz musician. Have you managed to find anything yet?'

'I have,' said Dougal, 'and not just for you. Prepare yourself for what you might call "a web of intrigue".'

Dougal clicked a tab on the browser and opened the online edition of a local newspaper.

'This is the Dumfries and Galloway! What's Going On? newsletter.'

'Aye, I'm familiar with that.'

'This edition goes back a while but the article we're interested in… is here. See the headline: "Entrepreneur to breathe new life into old hotel". It doesn't tell us anything we don't already know but it does have a wee photo of Rebecca Barlow, I needed that to make sure I was looking at the right Rebecca Barlow in my other finds.'

'Excellent,' said Munro. 'And what of your other finds?'

'Okay, you said her family were in Penrith, in the Lakes, right?'

'Correct.'

'Well,' said Dougal as he opened another tab, 'this photo is years old but it's definitely the same Rebecca Barlow.'

Munro took his spectacles from his breast pocket and studied the screen.

'Aye, no doubt about it,' he said. 'That's the same girl, younger mind, but definitely the same. The folk she's standing with, the man and the woman, are they friends of hers?'

'Aye. And this is where it gets interesting,' said Dougal. 'This photo appeared in another newspaper, *The News and Star* which covers Carlisle and the surrounding area.

Dougal gave Munro a moment to read the headline, "Local businessman to open a fourth office".

'The businessman in question is an estate agent by the name of Daniel McIntyre.'

'But is that not the fellow Charlie's been looking for?'

'Aye. Now get this. The other girl in the photo is one Emma Riley.'

Munro slumped back in his seat and drew a short, sharp breath.

'By jiminy! That's astounding!' he said. 'Aye, that's the word, astounding. You'd best check the cupboards for something alcoholic, laddie. I know it's 7:00am but when Charlie hears of this she'll be wanting a drink.'

'Hears of what?' said West as she barged through the door. 'Dougal, why are you here so early?'

'I had to break the news myself, miss.'

'For crying out loud, don't tell me someone else has died.'

'No, no,' said Dougal. 'I've been doing some research on Rebecca Barlow for the boss.'

'The girl in Auchencairn?'

'Aye, and I found a couple of folk she used to work with.'

'Sorry, Dougal,' said West, 'I'm not being rude, and no offence, Jimbo, but Barlow's not my case. That's for D&G to sort out.'

'I'd reserve judgement on that,' said Munro. 'Let Dougal finish.'

'Barlow started out as an estate agent, miss. That's where she caught the bug for doing up properties and selling them on.'

'So?'

'The agent she worked for had four offices, three in Scotland; Dumfries, Ayr, and Falkirk. And one in Carlisle. That's where Barlow was based and one of the girls she used to work with is Emma Riley.'

West stared at Dougal and dropped to her seat.

'You have got to be kidding me,' she said. 'That woman's got more bleeding skeletons than a graveyard.'

'There's more,' said Dougal. 'The fella who owned the chain of estate agents is one Daniel McIntyre.'

Cherishing one of the rare moments when West was actually lost for words, Munro sat back and smiled as he waited for the penny to drop.

'That does it,' said West. 'I need some Nurofen and a large whisky. Just a flipping moment! If he's got four blooming offices dotted around the country then why is he so difficult to find?'

'He rolled the business,' said Dougal, 'nearly two years ago. I looked at the returns he filed with HMRC and it looks as though he was heading for bankruptcy anyway.'

'But what about his address?' said West. 'If he's listed as a director with Companies House then they'd have his address!'

'They have,' said Dougal. 'I've already followed it up. He lived in Carlisle but the house he owned was sold nine months ago so his current whereabouts remain unknown.'

West threw back her head, ruffled her hair, and groaned.

'Do me a favour,' she said, 'check online, see if there's any jobs going at Tesco. I think I've just about had enough of this.'

* * *

As proven by the medical profession, an irrefutable fact of life is that a lack of sleep will undoubtedly have a detrimental effect on the body's physical and cognitive ability to perform at peak levels, and for those who endured the agony of a restless night the cause was either buried in the realms of the deep subconscious or a direct result of emotional or anxiety-related stress but for Duncan, it was the irritating niggle that something surrounding the investigation was awry.

Returning to the office in the hope that an hour on his own might evoke an epiphany, he paused in the doorway with a look of weary disappointment on his face.

'I wasn't expecting a full house,' he said.

'There's breakfast there,' said West, waving towards the kitchenette, 'tuck in before it gets cold. I thought you were having a lie-in.'

'I couldn't sleep.'

'Heavy night?'

'No, no,' said Duncan, snatching a bacon toastie, 'it's just… you know what it's like when you hear a record on the radio and you can't remember the name of the artist even though at the back of your mind you know damn well who it is?'

'Aye,' said Munro, 'and when I do remember I often wish I hadn't.'

'Is this a personal thing?' said West. 'Or is it something to do with work?'

'It's work,' said Duncan. 'Definitely work.'

'Do you want to talk about it?'

'No, you're alright. It'll come to me sooner or later.'

'Nice job on Drennan by the way. Well done.'

'All in the line of duty,' said Duncan. 'I'm not being funny, miss, but should you not be downstairs with Riley?'

'Been there, done that.'

'Well the clock's ticking so are we charging her or letting her go?'

'Neither,' said West. 'Not yet anyway. I spoke to Elliot earlier and he's agreed to let us hold her for another twelve hours.'

'You spoke to The Bear? At this hour? I bet he's not happy about that!'

'He wasn't, but given the circumstances he soon calmed down.'

'So what's the story?'

'Well, on the one hand,' said West, 'she's more than willing to co-operate because she wants McIntyre off her back, but on the other, as far as Drennan's concerned, she's claiming it's his word against hers and she's refusing to talk to a brief because she sees that as an admission of guilt.'

'So she's planted herself between a rock and a hard place.'

'Exactly.'

'Well, is there anything else we can throw at her to seal her fate?'

'Aye, there is,' said Dougal. 'If we could find the homeless fella Drennan assaulted, get him to identify her, and then admit he'd taken drugs he never paid for, then would that not substantiate Drennan's claim?'

'I think it just might,' said West. 'Can we get a decent still off the CCTV to circulate? Then we can ask uniform to keep an eye out.'

'Aye, I'll give it a go,' said Dougal, 'I'll finish with MacDuff first, I've just the second phone to go through now.'

'Did you get anything off the first?'

'Not much, miss. The usual texts and contacts but they're all business related. Oh, and he had the same creepy apps we found on his laptop, the ones he used to access the cameras. I'm guessing he had the second phone for personal use.'

'He should've upgraded and got himself a dual SIM,' said West, 'it would've saved us all a lot of bother. So, Jimbo, are you going to visit your mate Byrne in Dumfy now?'

'I am indeed,' said Munro. 'I shall finish my tea then wee Murdo and I will–'

Munro stopped at the shrill tone of West's phone.

'Oh, Gawd,' she said. 'It's Andy.'

'Dr McLeod? Then you best take it, lassie. It's no doubt important.'

'I know but after what happened the other night, when I lost it over dinner, it's just a bit awkward, isn't it?'

'No offence,' said Duncan, 'but you're both adults, miss, and we have to work with the fella too. The chief's right, you need to answer it.'

West scowled at Duncan, laid the phone on the desk, and took the call.

'Andy. You alright?'

'Charlie. Yourself?'

'Yeah, all good. Listen you're on speaker and everyone's here so let's stick to business, shall we?'

'If there was another reason for my call, Charlie, I'd have phoned you on the landline later this evening.'

'That's me told,' said West. 'Sorry, mate, I'm just a bit wound up at the moment. So, what have you got?'

'Alan MacDuff. Have you time to talk?'

'Yup. Fire away.'

'Okay, I'm not one for conjecturing but my initial hunch was correct. As you know, the victim was exhibiting a large contusion on the fossa jugularis sternalis and, having opened him up, I can confirm that the hyaline cartilage was forced back under pressure thereby severing the larynx and the trachea. As a result, I've been able to attribute the cause of death to asphyxiation.'

'Forgive me for interrupting,' said Munro, 'but would you hold the line while I fetch an interpreter?'

'Sorry,' said McLeod. 'In layman's terms, James, extreme pressure was exerted just below his Adam's apple, probably by a thumb, this effectively ruptured the windpipe thereby blocking his airways. The amount of blood present was also a contributing factor.'

'So tell me,' said West, 'I mean, this all sounds a bit specialist, would whoever did this be trained in anything like martial arts or survival techniques, maybe?'

'No, I doubt that,' said McLeod, 'it's a common enough hold even for street brawlers, the only difference being they usually stop when the victim blacks out. Nine times out of ten they're not even aware of the damage they're causing and for that reason alone I'd have to say that finding a fatality as a result of this kind of injury is actually a rare occurrence.'

'How rare?'

'Rare enough for me to backtrack to see if any other similar cases had been reported.'

'And had there?'

'Aye,' said McLeod. 'One. It happened a few days ago. A lady by the name of Rebecca Barlow.'

Munro, smiling at the prospect of a double murder to solve, hooked Murdo to his leash and stood.

'Tell me,' he said, reaching for his coat, 'to inflict this kind of injury, would the perpetrator have to be particularly strong?'

'No,' said McLeod, 'they'd simply need the determination to continue exerting pressure until the job was done.'

'So anyone could've done it?' said West. 'I mean, even a girl?'

'I don't see why not, Charlie. And if she had the element of surprise on her side it would make it even easier. Don't go getting any ideas now, will you.'

Munro paused by the door.

'I fear I already know the answer to this question,' he said, 'but tell me, Dr McLeod, in your professional opinion, would you say these two deaths are related?'

'Going by the post-mortem report on Barlow and what I've seen of MacDuff, I'd say yes. Whoever killed the girl definitely killed MacDuff as well.'

Chapter 12

When faced with the trials and tribulations of everyday life there are those who possess the admirable if not irritating ability to laugh in the face of adversity and soldier on with the dogged determination of a salmon swimming upstream, but for those burdened with the stress of a demanding job or trying to cope with the loss of a beloved spouse the answer to their woes sometimes lay atop a high-rise building or at the bottom of a fast-flowing river.

With his collar up against the cold and a crushing sense of pessimism weighing heavy on his shoulders, DI Byrne, oblivious to the scores of people milling along the river bank, contemplated the icy waters of the Nith as a spritely gent with a dog in tow approached from his left.

'The only upside to jumping,' said Munro, 'is that you'll probably have a cardiac before you drown.'

Byrne turned his back to the railings and smiled.

'Mr Munro,' he said, 'it's good to see you.'

'Likewise, I'm sure.'

'I hope you don't mind coming here. I thought if we met at the office it would only raise a few eyebrows.'

'Right enough,' said Munro. 'So, are you making progress?'

'To be honest, I'm muddling through,' said Byrne. 'Truth be known, I preferred life as a DC. I'm not one for dishing out orders, I think I'm better off taking them.'

'Och, away and stop your havering, laddie! It's all a question of adjustment. You have to give yourself time to settle in. You'll get there.'

'Aye. Maybe. So, will we walk?'

'Aye, my car's up the way,' said Munro, 'by Dock Park. I suggest we fetch ourselves a coffee and get out of the cold.'

* * *

Byrne, sitting silently with his arms folded, gazed vacuously through the windscreen towards a group of adolescents lounging about the playground as Munro popped the lid on his latte and tore through a cheese toastie.

'Are you sure you're not hungry?' he said.

'I've no appetite just now,' said Byrne. 'I'll have some supper later.'

'As you wish. So come on, laddie, what have you got?'

'Not very much, I'm afraid. We went back to Barlow's house and ran over it with a fine-tooth comb. Nothing. SOCOs managed to lift a few prints from her office but they're not hers, and they're not on the system, so that's another dead end.'

'Your optimism is inspiring,' said Munro. 'Can your GP not prescribe you something to lift your mood?'

'I'm fine. Really.'

'I'd have a word with those lads on the swings, if I were you. They could probably set you up with ketamine. I hear it's quite the tonic when it comes to raising your spirits.'

Byrne smiled and reached into his pocket.

'We got copies of Barlow's missing bank statements,' he said, handing Munro a memory stick. 'I've been over them twice, as have two other members of the team.

We've double-checked all the transactions and can't find anything amiss. Maybe your lads will have better luck.'

'It's never easy when you dinnae have a clue what it is you're looking for,' said Munro. 'Still, we can but try. Anything else?'

Byrne cast a sideways glance, took a deep breath, and sighed.

'No,' he said. 'Door-to-doors in the village drew a blank. The gardener who was at the hotel knows nothing. And the lady in the shop gave us a wide berth so I'm sorry to say, Mr Munro, we're still at square one.'

'I suggest you go back to the shop,' said Munro. 'According to the owner Miss Barlow had a boyfriend, or a partner. I'd stroll along that avenue, if I were you.'

'Duly noted,' said Byrne. 'I'll nip back later.'

'And what about the hotel? Did the SOCOs not find anything there?'

'Not a sausage,' said Byrne, 'and that's why it's so annoying. I mean, if Rebecca Barlow was killed indoors and then carried out to the garden you'd think we'd have something but there's not so much as a footprint.'

Munro leaned over the seat, tossed Murdo the crust off his toastie, and sipped his coffee.

'Speaking of Rebecca Barlow,' he said, 'were you not a wee bit surprised at the results of the post-mortem?'

Byrne cleared his throat and said nothing.

'You've not read it, have you?'

'It's on my list,' said Byrne. 'I've just not got around to it.'

Wary of exacerbating the dithering detective's sense of despair by raising his voice, Munro spoke softly and offered some backhanded encouragement.

'See here, Mr Byrne. I'm more than willing to help you out. And if you find yourself in a wee hole, I'll happily nudge you in the right direction, but I'm not here to do your job for you. Do I make myself clear?'

'Aye,' said Byrne, nodding. 'Sounds like a deal. Thanks.'

'Good. Now then, our friend MacDuff. I'm sure you'll agree his passing was, to say the least, unexpected.'

'Aye, you're not wrong there,' said Byrne. 'I don't mind saying seeing him sprawled out on the kitchen floor fair took the wind out of my sails.'

'The pathologist's ascribed the cause of death as asphyxiation, with a wee bit of blood drowning thrown in for good measure.'

'So he was strangled?'

'In a manner of speaking, aye. But without a ligature, and with just the one hand. A thumb was placed on his throat and forced back until his windpipe ruptured.'

'Would it not have been easier to use a knife?'

'Possibly,' said Munro, 'but the problem you'd have there, Mr Byrne, is that MacDuff would have screamed. Think about it. Nae windpipe. Nae larynx. Nae chance of speaking.'

'Clever. I'll make a note of that.'

'Something else you may like to note. Rebecca Barlow died of the same injuries. *Exactly* the same injuries.'

Byrne turned to Munro and frowned.

'So, are you saying the same fella killed both Barlow and MacDuff?'

'Aye,' said Munro. 'Just one thing though, it's not necessarily a he. You dinnae have to be a Mike Tyson to inflict an injury like that, a wee lassie could have done it.'

Byrne rubbed his forehead and moaned.

'I'm not sure if that's a good thing,' he said. 'Or bad.'

'At the very least it narrows your horizons,' said Munro. 'It gives you something to focus on.'

'Sorry?'

'Good heavens, man! Do I have to spell it out? You're looking for someone who's known to both MacDuff and Barlow! Someone who knew where they both lived! And as there are no signs of a forced entry at either of their addresses, it would be someone they trusted enough to let in! Someone they were not afraid of!'

Byrne, looking like a wean who'd won a reprieve from the naughty corner, glanced at Munro with a glimmer of hope in his eyes.

'Thanks,' he said. 'That's just what I needed.'

'A kick in the pants?'

'No. Something to focus on.'

'Well, if you're being sincere,' said Munro as he reached for his phone, 'then I've done my job. Oh, and take my advice, next time you take a walk by the river, make sure you've got your water wings with you.'

* * *

Endeavouring to enhance an image of the homeless man on his computer whilst simultaneously attempting to unlock MacDuff's second mobile phone, the normally ambidextrous Dougal McCrae was left unable to concentrate by Duncan's persistent pacing of the floor accompanied by the muffled mumblings of someone who'd spent too long in the cuckoo's nest.

'Are you still thinking about that record?' he said, brusquely.

'There was no record! I was speaking metaphorically.'

'Aye. I get that. So was I.'

'Oh. Well in that case the answer to your question is yes. How are you getting on?'

'Slowly,' said Dougal, 'but I'm nearly there with the image of the homeless fella. It's not the greatest angle, and it's not exactly passport quality, but it will have to do. Is Westy still downstairs with Riley?'

'Aye. Since you uncovered that wee photo of her with McIntyre and Rebecca Barlow, she's keen to find out what their relationship is so she's grilling her like a well-done steak.'

'I'm not sure she'll get anywhere with that,' said Dougal, 'Riley seems like a tough nut to crack.'

'I agree, but Westy's got a plan. I think her tactic is to wear her down so when she comes to question her about getting Drennan to hammer the roofless fella she'll crumble like the walls of Jericho.'

'Well I hope it works,' said Dougal, 'but my money's on Riley keeping quiet. She knows if she says nothing then sooner or later we'll have to let her go and that means…'

Dougal paused mid-sentence and stared at the mobile with a look of consternation on his face.

'What's up?' said Duncan. 'Have you found more porno pics?'

'No, no. This phone, Duncan, it's not MacDuff's at all. It belongs to Rebecca Barlow.'

Not normally given to overt displays of elation, Duncan, experiencing the same buzz of excitement as a lovestruck lassie on Valentine's Day, stood behind Dougal and grinned like the proverbial cat.

'Wait until the chief hears of this!' he said. 'MacDuff must've lifted that from the hotel!'

'Aye, maybe,' said Dougal, pragmatic to a fault. 'The question is: why?'

'What?'

'Why would he steal her phone? I mean, he's got one of his own and this one's no different, it's the same model. And he was making good money so if he wanted to, he could've bought a new one.'

'Well there has to be a reason,' said Duncan. 'Unless he was a kleptomaniac as well as a peeping Tom.'

Dougal lay the phone on his desk, leaned back in his chair, and stared pensively at the ceiling.

'What are you playing at?' said Duncan. 'Are you not going to delve into that?'

'I'm thinking,' said Dougal. 'I'm thinking that under different circumstances, him having this phone would have put him right in the frame for Barlow's murder.'

'Well it doesn't exclude him.'

'But he's dead.'

'And your point is?'

'Simple,' said Dougal, 'they were both killed by the same perp, that's what McLeod says anyway, and as MacDuff didn't commit suicide, it couldn't be him.'

'Not necessarily,' said Duncan. 'You're thinking's too logical. See here, Dougal, what if MacDuff wasn't alone at the hotel? What if he turned up with a pal or a workmate? MacDuff could have murdered Barlow then his pal could've topped him a day or two later, only he was clever enough to make it look like one fella had killed the pair of them.'

'I never thought of that. It's possible, but if MacDuff did murder Barlow, then why did he call it in?'

'Have you not learned anything?' said Duncan. 'It's a textbook diversion technique. Right, that's enough theory, let's move on to the practical, get that phone open and let's see who she knows.'

* * *

Dougal, swiping slowly through the contacts lest he should miss any abbreviations, acronyms, or nicknames, jumped as Duncan slapped him on the shoulder.

'There!' he said. 'Make a note of that one – "Dan". That has to be McIntyre. We're going to need that before you hand this over to the boys in Dumfries.'

'Calm yourself,' said Dougal. 'I'll copy all the contacts before we release it.'

'Well whatever you do, make sure you don't accidentally dial that number or we're humped.'

'Give me some credit; as if I'd do that. She's not got what you might call a wide circle of friends.'

'Who's that?' said Duncan, pointing over his shoulder. '"Dante". Is she in league with the devil?'

Dougal cross-checked the number on his computer and laughed.

'Aye, of sorts,' he said. 'It's a takeaway in Dumfries. Fish and chips and kebabs.'

'That's plenty. I could go a chicken shish myself, just now. Who else?'

'No-one we know,' said Dougal, as he continued scrolling, 'I'm guessing they're... jeez-oh! I know some folk are friends for life but I wasn't expecting this!'

Duncan leaned over his shoulders and peered at the phone.

'Emma Riley! I'm not kidding, pal, the chief's going to have kittens over this, and as for DI Byrne, he'll be wanting to open a vein! Quick, let's see the call log.'

'The most recent call she made,' said Dougal, 'was to Dan at 7:33 on the day she was murdered. Seven minutes before that, she called MacDuff.'

'Maybe that was to check he was on his way. Who else?'

'That's it.'

'Are you joking me? That can't be right, I've a history on my phone that goes back weeks! She must have more than that!'

'Nope. She must've deleted them.'

'What about incoming?'

'One,' said Dougal. 'MacDuff at 7:49.'

'Texts then?'

Dougal shook his head and frowned.

'They're not here, Duncan. It looks like she's wiped those, too.'

'Aye. Or MacDuff did. What the hell was he after?'

'Or what was he trying to hide?'

'Good point, pal. Well, I suppose we'll never know, now.'

'Don't be daft,' said Dougal. 'I can get them back.'

'How?'

'If she's got back-up enabled, I can log in to iCloud and download them from there.'

'And if she hasn't?'

'Not a bother,' said Dougal. 'She may have wiped them from the SIM but there'll be something on the phone memory. Trust me, there's always a way.'

'How do you fit so much information in that wee head of yours?'

'It's not so wee,' said Dougal. 'It's like the Tardis.'

'Right, you call the chief and fill him in. With any luck he'll still be with Byrne. I'm away to fetch Westy.'

Chapter 13

With the diligence of a teacher and the patience of a saint, James Munro had spent his latter years nurturing the hidden talents of his protégés with the same care and dedication he afforded his rhododendrons, however, despite his best efforts, trying to find even one redeeming feature in the blundering DI Byrne was proving to be an uphill struggle.

Relieved to be back in the office and feeling the strain of the ninety-minute drive from Dumfries, he hung his coat on the door and eased himself into a chair as Murdo scoured the floor for any stray crumbs.

'If it's not too much trouble,' he said, loosening his tie, 'I could do with a brew just now.'

'No bother,' said Duncan. 'You look shattered, chief. Was DI Byrne doing your nut in?'

'Och, I admit the man's a balloon,' said Munro, 'and I'm really not sure what his superiors make of his performance to date but if it was up to me I'd give him a chance if for no other reason than he's probably got the Samaritans on speed dial.'

'That bad?'

'Worse. The poor chap's floundering like a flatfish on the deck of a trawler.'

West, feeling equally fatigued from a two-hour session with an unresponsive Emma Riley, checked her watch.

'Did you tell him about the connection between Barlow and McIntyre and Riley?' she said.

'I most certainly did not. That would only muddy the waters.'

'Thanks. The last thing we need right now is someone like him sticking his oar in.'

'It's not the oar that troubles me, Charlie,' said Munro. 'It's his complete inability to pilot a boat let alone row one.'

'I need a break. We should have some supper, Jimbo. I'll give Riley another going over once we've eaten.'

'I'll be with you in a moment,' said Munro. 'There's something I have to deal with first. Dougal, this is a memory stick courtesy of our friend Byrne. Apparently it contains Rebecca Barlow's missing bank details. Be so kind as to take a wee peek when you have a moment. See if you can find anything untoward. Byrne seems to think there's nothing amiss but frankly his judgement leaves a lot to be desired.'

'No bother,' said Dougal. 'I'll get onto it soon enough.'

'So, where do we go from here?' said West. 'I know we've got a number for McIntyre but it's not as if we can call him up and ask for his address.'

'Triangulation,' said Dougal, as he copied the bank files to his computer.

'You what?'

'Triangulation, miss. Every time a mobile's used it sends out two signals to the phone masts, one to identify the SIM, the other to identify the phone. The signals are picked up by the three nearest masts. Using that trajectory we can pinpoint his location to within a square mile, or just under.'

'Blinding,' said West, 'but I'm assuming we'll need him to pick up so what are we going to say? PC Plod here, can you come in for a chat?'

'The council,' said Duncan as he handed Munro a mug of tea. 'We can say his vehicle's been reported as abandoned and if he asks, we could tell him we got his number from the DVLA.'

'One day,' said West, 'I'm going to come up with ideas like that. So, shall we give it a go?'

'Not tonight,' said Dougal. 'I'll have to set things up so we can track it in real time plus we'll have to organise a couple of cars to help locate him once we know roughly where he is.'

'Okay, tomorrow morning, then,' said West. 'I can't see there's any real rush right now anyway. Did you get anywhere with the mugshot of the tramp? Anything we can hand out yet?'

'Aye, miss,' said Dougal, waving a sheet of A4 in the air. 'Here's a print out. It's not brilliant but it's the best I can do.'

West cocked her head as she squinted at the photo.

'Not bad,' she said. 'Not bad at all. We'll need quite a few copies to distribute amongst the–'

West, cut short by Duncan jumping from his seat, watched as he grabbed the sheet of paper from Dougal's hand.

'Did your mother not tell you it was rude to snatch?'

'Sorry, pal,' said Duncan, 'but this is important. Remember that record I was thinking about? It's just come to me.'

'Bing Crosby?' said Munro. 'Or Perry Como, perhaps?'

'The beggar under the ATM at the supermarket.'

West gazed at Duncan and shrugged her shoulders.

'Have you got short-term memory loss, miss? When we were tailing Riley, she came out of the supermarket and while she was waiting for the Lexus to turn up, she handed this fella a twenty pound note.'

West stood, took the photo from his hand, and studied it closely.

'You're right!' she said. 'You're only bleeding right! Well done, mate.'

'Oh, don't thank me yet,' said Duncan as he returned to his seat. 'It's actually not a good thing.'

'What the hell are you on about? Of course it's a good thing! How can it not be good?'

Duncan folded his arms, rested a hand on his chin, and stared at West.

'If we're to believe Drennan,' he said, 'and we've no reason not to, then Emma Riley had this fella beaten up because he owed her money for drugs he hadn't paid for, right?'

'Yeah, so, what's wrong with that?'

'Simple. If *he* owed *her* money, then why did *she* hand *him* a twenty pound note?'

West thought for a moment, glanced at Munro, and reached for her coat.

'Jimbo,' she said, 'do you mind if we skip supper and head straight for the pub?'

* * *

Were it not for the need to return to the office to question a stubborn suspect as well as cater for a house guest whose dietary requirements revolved around anything fried, bland, or bovine, then West – desperate to avoid another late night – would have crashed on the sofa with a chicken jalfrezi, half a dozen poppadums, and a large Balvenie.

However, with the clock ticking and a ravenous Munro poised like a vulture at the dining table, she was forced to rummage through the cupboards for something that hadn't exceeded the use-by date.

'There's a takeaway down the street,' she said, 'I could nip out and get a couple of kebabs.'

'I'd rather chew on my own leg,' said Munro. 'Besides, by the time you've been there and back we could've cooked something edible ourselves.'

'Yes, but the problem is, Jimbo, we're missing one vital ingredient.'

'And what, pray, would that be?'

'Food. Christ, I feel like Old Mother Hubbard,' said West as she unearthed a loaf. 'Oh, here we go, we're in luck. Right, how about beans on toast?'

'Fail.'

'Cheese on toast?'

'Double fail.'

'Just toast?'

'There's a half a pie left, Charlie, we can reheat that.'

'Steak and haggis again?' said West, as she popped two slices into the toaster. 'You're on your own, Jimbo. I think I'll stick with beans.'

'Are you really in that much of a hurry?'

'No, but there's a method in my madness. The sooner I get going, the sooner I'll be back, which means the sooner I can dive into that bottle of Beaujolais.'

'Och, a wee spot of temperance willnae harm you.'

'You're joking, it'll be the death of me,' said West, as she slipped the pie into the oven, 'but if I'm not drinking, then neither are you. I'm not going to sit here and watch you quaff, not unless you fancy giving me a lift again.'

'If I ran a taxi service,' said Munro, 'I'd have a meter on the dashboard. You can have your fill when you get back.'

'Spoilsport.'

'So, it's Emma Riley again?'

'Yup.'

'She must be sick of the sight of you.'

'I hope so, Jimbo. I really hope so. I've got a mountain of stuff to run through with her but I've got a funny feeling all I'm going to get is "no comment" until the bell rings.'

'And then?'

'And then,' said West, 'I'll have to charge her or let her go.'

'And it's not the latter you're after.'

'No, it isn't, but I might not have any choice. All we've got on her is art and part but we've no evidence to support the charge. It's Drennan's word against hers.'

'Well, you cannae back a winner all the time,' said Munro. 'You'll get a second bite of the cherry, I'm sure. Folk like Riley have a habit of leaving banana skins about the place.'

West pulled up a chair, slid the pie across the table, and wired into her beans on toast.

'I would have asked Duncan to do the honours,' she said, glancing at her phone, 'but he's carrying more than his fair share of the workload as it is.'

'Count your blessings you've got him and not DI Byrne.'

'It's Dougal,' said West, answering the call. 'Better see what's up.'

'Are you okay to talk, miss?'

'Yes, mate, everything alright?'

'Aye, I've just received an email from Kay,' said Dougal, 'she's detailed everything she found at MacDuff's house.'

'Come on then, I could do with some cheering up.'

'That's not going to happen just now,' said Dougal, 'I'm afraid there's nothing of any significance apart from some fingerprints she lifted from the inside of the door.'

'Well, that's good, isn't it?'

'Yes and no,' said Dougal. 'The good news is they're already on the system, the bad news, they're not a match to anyone, but here's the thing, the reason they're on the system in the first place is because the same set were lifted from the office in Rebecca Barlow's house.'

West laid her cutlery on the table, sat back, and took a large sip of water.

'So,' she said, 'it seems like McLeod was right after all. It's obviously the same bloke who's killed both of them.'

'Aye,' said Dougal, 'and whoever it is, is clearly new to the game because he's utter crap at covering his tracks.'

'Anything else?'

'Aye, I've a wee question for the boss.'

'I have to warn you,' said Munro, 'if it's anything to do with football, I'll not be able to help.'

'It's DI Byrne,' said Dougal, 'have you any idea who he has working for him?'

'I have not. Why?'

'Because whoever it is needs to book an appointment with Specsavers. I've just been through Barlow's bank records and there's plenty of interest here.'

'I'm not surprised,' said Munro. 'Let's have it.'

'Right,' said Dougal, 'Barlow's made a number of irregular transfers over the past few years to one Daniel McIntyre. Not standing orders, not direct debits, but transfers direct to his account.'

'And you say they're irregular? How exactly?'

'Both the amounts and the dates, boss. Sometimes there's two a month, sometimes there's none at all. And all the amounts vary but there's nothing less than ten grand in any single transaction.'

Munro left the table, walked to the window, and stared at his reflection with his hands clasped behind his back.

'Why?' he said, ponderously. 'Do you think he was extorting money because he had some kind of a hold over her?'

'I don't think it's as sinister as that,' said Dougal. 'You see, boss, two months before Barlow made the first payment to McIntyre, *he'd* transferred a substantial amount into *her* account. Two hundred thousand pounds, to be exact. Four days later, one hundred and forty-three thousand went out.'

'Back to him?'

'No, to a firm of solicitors in Carlisle. I've checked with Land Registry and the sum and the date seem to coincide with the purchase of her first property. Now, I may be wrong, but all this happened after she quit the estate agency so I'm guessing McIntyre lent her the money to buy that property and the subsequent sums to him were repayments of the loan.'

'Well, I cannae fault your thinking,' said Munro, 'but as you know, we need to verify it. As you now have McIntyre's bank details I suggest you request copies of all his transactions for the same period.'

'Already on it, boss.'

'Good,' said Munro, 'and tell me, Dougal, as far as McIntyre's concerned, is it a savings account or a current account?'

'Current account.'

'Then no doubt he'll have some sort of a debit card. Put a trace on it, then if he goes shopping or withdraws any cash, we'll have another way of locating him instead of relying on his mobile phone.'

'Brilliant,' said West, 'I was just about to suggest that myself.'

'Aye, I'm sure you were, Charlie. I'm sure you were.'

'Right,' said Dougal, 'I'll let you get on. Are you heading back here, miss?'

'I sure am. Before you go, is Duncan still there?'

'I am,' said Duncan, 'but I'm out the door, why?'

'I was just wondering, I don't suppose…'

'If this has anything to do with clocking up more overtime, miss, the answer's no. I'm not that keen on becoming a millionaire.'

'Oh, well, can't blame me for trying.'

Chapter 14

Like the hundreds of health workers, school teachers, vets, and fellow officers who regarded their occupations as more of a vocation than just a job, West, though dedicated to bringing the perpetrators of even the most petty of crimes to justice, was also painfully aware of the fact that the takeaway closed at 10pm and that surviving on less than six hours' sleep without a decent meal for two nights on the trot was, by anyone's standards, going above and beyond the call of duty.

Seated at the desk with her phone and a bulky, brown envelope laid out before her, she glanced at the clock on the wall as the door eased open and a bedraggled Riley, looking more rough than diamond, entered the room with bags under her eyes and a blanket wrapped around her shoulders.

'Take a seat,' said West, as she pressed the voice recorder. 'The time is 7:09pm. I'm Detective Inspector West. For the benefit of the tape would you please state your name.'

'Again?' said Riley. 'Are you joking me?'

'Name!'

'Emma Riley.'

'Are you still waiving your right to legal representation?'

'I am. Aye.'

'Have you had something to eat?'

'Aye.'

'Alright for some,' said West. 'Can I get you anything to drink?'

'No.'

'Blinding. Then let's crack on. I take it you're still keen to get McIntyre off your back?'

'Definitely. Aye.'

'Then it's time you started answering some questions,' said West, 'or you'll be going straight back inside and he'll be right behind you. So, down to business, let's have a quick recap. A Mr John Drennan, one of your regular punters, has been charged with assault for attacking a homeless man. He claims he carried out the assault because you paid him to do so. Do you still deny the allegation?'

'I do, aye.'

'Mr Drennan also claims that the reason you orchestrated the attack is because the person in question owed you money for drugs he received but never paid for. Again, do you deny the allegation?'

'Again. Aye.'

'You were recently convicted for possession and intent to supply. Since your release from jail have you, at any time, been involved with the sale, supply, or possession of any banned substances?'

'No.'

West slipped her hand into the envelope and retrieved an A4 sheet of paper.

'For the benefit of the tape,' she said, 'I am now showing Miss Riley a photograph of the gentleman assaulted by Mr Drennan. Do you recognise this man?'

Riley gave a lingering blink and slowly shook her head.

'No,' she said, lethargically. 'I've never seen him before. Never. Never. Never.'

'Take another look,' said West. 'Are you absolutely sure?'

'Aye! What's your fixation with this fella? I've told you a hundred times, I've not seen him before!'

'That's funny,' said West, 'because I have. He was squatting beneath a cash machine outside the supermarket.'

'Common practice,' said Riley. 'They all do. You'll be telling me next he's got a wee doggie, too.'

'It was the same supermarket you were shopping in.'

'Big deal. It's a free country. He can sit where he likes.'

'The same supermarket McIntyre picked you up from.'

Riley shivered at the sound of a nail being driven into her own coffin.

'You're guessing,' she said. 'How could you possibly know it was Dan picking me up? It might have been a mini cab.'

'In a spanking new Lexus?' said West. 'I don't think so. But here's the interesting thing: while you were waiting for McIntyre to arrive, you gave this homeless bloke twenty quid.'

'Prove it.'

'Okay, I'll get the dashcam footage, if you like. So, can you explain why you gave him twenty quid?'

'I was being charitable,' said Riley. 'He's a beggar, he's skint.'

'Yeah, I get that,' said West, 'but why twenty quid? I mean, you've just come out of jail, you haven't got a job, and you're not signing on. Strikes me as being a bit generous for someone with no income. Most people would be hard-pushed to part with a pound.'

'It's just the way I am. It's better to give than it is to receive.'

West leaned back in her seat and smiled.

'That's exactly what the judge says when he's handing out sentences,' she said. 'He's very altruistic like that. Let's move on, shall we? You had quite a good job a few years back, didn't you?'

'I've had several jobs,' said Riley. 'They've all been good.'

'Yeah, but working for an estate agent's pretty cushy though, isn't it? I mean, you sit around all day waiting for the phone to ring, show a few buyers around a house or two, job done. Why'd you pack it in?'

Worried that line of questioning was turning away from John Drennan and the alleged assault and appeared to be focusing on a part of her life she believed to be a closed chapter, Riley hesitated and slowly pulled the blanket tight around her shoulders.

'Carlisle,' she said, clutching at straws. 'I left because I didn't like living in Carlisle.'

'So what happened?' said West. 'Did McIntyre give you a helping hand? Did he transfer you to another office?'

'No. I just left.'

'But you stayed in touch. You must be good mates because you still work together. If you can call it that.'

Riley stared blankly at the desk and said nothing.

'Who else was there?' said West. 'In the office, I mean, apart from McIntyre? Did you have any mates you hung out with?'

'No,' said Riley. 'I'm not that sociable.'

'Really? So, there's no-one you used to go to lunch with? No-one you'd have a drink with after work?'

'No!' said Riley, getting agitated. 'I went to work! I went home! I didn't mix with anyone!'

'Not even Rebecca? Rebecca Barlow?'

West watched as Riley tightened her grip on the blanket.

'I don't know who you're talking about.'

'Oh, come on!' said West. 'I'm getting bored of this now! You worked in the same office together. You were under each other's feet five days a week! The difference is she got bored before you. And she left before you. She started her own business doing up tatty flats and selling them on. Before you. Did that make you jealous?'

'No.'

'So you didn't stay in touch?'

'No! Alright, look,' said Riley, 'I knew Rebecca, I admit it, but we worked together and that was it. It was years ago. I've no idea where she is or what she's doing!'

'I find that hard to believe,' said West. 'I find that really hard to believe.'

'Why? It's not that strange, folk move on. I moved on. We don't all cling to the past.'

'Yeah, I couldn't agree more,' said West as she reached into the envelope. 'This is your phone, isn't it?'

'Aye. What of it?'

'Well, if what you say is true, then there's something that bothers me.'

'What?'

'We've had a look at your list of contacts,' said West as she switched it on, 'and it makes for quite interesting reading.'

'You're not allowed to do that!'

'Says who? Anyway, what I can't figure out is, if you haven't seen Rebecca Barlow in years, in fact so long that phones like this hadn't even been invented, then how come you've got her number on it?'

As the sagacious James Munro had once pointed out, suspects in the line of questioning who proffered the truth rarely changed their body language whilst those attempting to slide a lie or two past the interrogator would subconsciously fidget, blink, and glance furtively around the room or, as in the case of Emma Riley, look the interviewer square in the eye and exhibit what they believed to be a reassuring if not utterly sincere smile.

'I probably forgot to delete it,' said Riley, smugly. 'It's not exactly top of my agenda just now.'

'No, and it clearly hasn't been for some time,' said West. 'Tell you what, why don't we give her a quick call and see what she's been up to. Let's see what she's got to say about your friendship, shall we? Oh no, I forgot, pointless exercise really. She won't answer anyway.'

'I know,' said Riley. 'Like I told you, she's probably moved on. She's probably got a new job, a new phone, and a new number.'

'Oh, it's nothing to do with that,' said West. 'The reason she won't answer is because she can't. She's dead. Dead as a dodo. She was murdered three days ago. Now, what have you got to say about that?'

Riley rolled her eyes and looked to the ceiling.

'What do you want me to say?'

'Well, you don't look very surprised,' said West, 'or shocked, even. It's almost as if you already knew.'

'People die,' said Riley. 'It's a fact of life. I've not seen her for years, we weren't close, so why should I show any remorse? Now, if I'm not mistaken, your time's almost up so can I have my things, please.'

'Your watch must be fast,' said West, 'you're not going anywhere for at least another twelve hours except back to your cell.'

'No, no,' said Riley, indignantly. 'See here, Inspector, I may not be across the law like you but one thing I do know is you either have to charge me or let me go, so that's me away.'

'Dream on,' said West. 'Emma Riley, I'm arresting you–'

'Again?'

'–under Section 1 of the Criminal Justice Act on suspicion of art and part in the murder of Rebecca Barlow. The reason for your arrest is that I suspect you have committed an offence and I believe that keeping you in custody is necessary and proportionate for the purposes of bringing you before a court or dealing with you in accordance with the law. Do you understand?'

Chapter 15

Despite his anxiety at having to relinquish the late shift and consequently suffer the interminable distraction of clattering coffee cups, idle banter, and probing questions on the state of his love life, Dougal thought there were, nonetheless, occasions when the office had more in common with a reference library than a hub of criminal investigation.

With nothing more than the sound of Munro leafing through a newspaper to disturb him, Dougal, preparing for the call to McIntyre, happily set about configuring the tracking software on his computer when West's theatrical entrance caused him to shudder in his seat.

'I'm all over the shop!' she said, as the door slammed open. 'Jimbo! Why didn't you wake me? I was going to make breakfast!'

'What with, Charlie?'

'I stopped at the corner on the way back last night; eggs, bacon, tomatoes, and black pudding.'

'Well, you were sleeping,' said Munro, 'I didnae want to drag you from your pit. Far be it for me to comment on beauty sleep, lassie, but you could certainly do with a few more hours.'

'Thanks very much.'

'The chief's right,' said Duncan. 'No offence, miss, but you look like you've swallowed a wasp.'

'It's that flipping takeaway,' said West, licking her lips. 'I can still taste the chilli sauce.'

'Well, if you dine with the devil,' said Munro, 'you've only yourself to blame.'

'I need a cuppa.'

'I'll do it,' said Duncan. 'I gather you played a blinder last night, miss, getting Riley locked up for another twelve hours.'

'Yeah, God knows how that happened,' said West, 'it just came to me out of the blue but if I'm honest, I think I'm winging it a bit.'

'How so?'

'Because we've still got nothing on her! I need to see The Bear and make sure he's onside with it, there's a chance he might say we have to let her go.'

'I can't see that happening,' said Duncan, 'you re-arrested her on suspicion of a different offence, that resets the clock and gives us another twelve hours at least.'

West took her mug and made for the door.

'Even so,' she said, 'I'd best make sure. Wish me luck, I'll be back in a bit.'

'Before you go,' said Dougal, 'can I just–'

'Not now, Dougal. Be back in ten.'

* * *

Munro, who despite his retirement still considered himself to be the patriarch of the team, folded the newspaper, returned his spectacles to his pocket, and crossed his arms.

'Dougal,' he said, mustering the gentlest of smiles, 'you're more of a night owl than an early bird, how are you coping with these early starts?'

'Oh, I'll survive, boss, I mean it's not for long. Once we've stitched this up I can get back to normal.'

'Has it not played havoc with your sleep patterns?'

'No, no. To be fair, I think I'm getting used to it.'

'Good. I imagine you're quite enjoying having the evenings to yourself.'

'Well I have to admit,' said Dougal, sheepishly, 'there is an upside to finishing at a reasonable hour.'

'And what's that?'

'A foxy wee SOCO by the name of Kay!' said Duncan. 'You can tell by the colour of his cheeks.'

'Is that so?' said Munro.

'No! Aye. Maybe. The bottom line, boss,' said Dougal, 'is she doesn't work the same hours as us, so I gave her a key. Sometimes she's there when I get back.'

'Oh, aye?' said Duncan. 'It didn't take her long to get her feet under the table!'

'Away!' said Dougal. 'It's not like that! She's a decent girl, not like some I've met.'

'I'm pulling your leg, pal! I'm made up for you, we all are. It's about time.'

'He's right,' said Munro, 'I for one am glad you've finally found something other than druggies, dealers, and dead bodies to occupy your time. Now, if we could only find a suitor for Charlie, we'd be one big happy family.'

'Don't hold your breath,' said Duncan, 'she's not hooking up with Redbeard, if that's what you're thinking. In fact she's not hooking up with anyone. I think she's enjoying her freedom just now.'

'Och, you're probably right,' said Munro, 'unless of course she happens to meet the owner of a distillery or a vineyard, then that could all change in the blink of an eye.'

* * *

West, one hand in her pocket with the other clutching her mug, stood in the doorway and glanced first at Munro, then at Duncan, and then Dougal, her curiosity roused by the suspicious smiles plastered across their faces.

'I don't know what you lot are up to,' she said, 'but you can stop it right now.'

'How'd it go, miss?'

'Sorted,' said West, 'we're in the clear. Right, shall we start?'

'Before we do,' said Dougal, 'can I just–'

'Let's get McIntyre out of the way first,' said West. 'Are you ready?'

'Aye, I'm all set.'

'Is it not a bit early to be calling him?' said Duncan. 'He's probably still asleep.'

'I disagree,' said Munro. 'In my experience folk are more likely to answer an unexpected call, especially if it wakes them. If you leave it any longer he'll probably ignore it and wait for a voicemail.'

'In that case,' said West, 'let's crack on. So, who's going to do the honours? Dougal?'

'No, no. Not me, miss. I'll be tracing the call.'

'Duncan, you then?'

'Aye okay, but to be fair I think the chief sounds more like a council jobsworth than me.'

'Another quip like that,' said Munro, 'and you'll find out what your job's really worth.'

'Jimbo? What do you say?'

'Nae bother, lassie. Dial him up and hand me the phone. You'd best put it on speaker, a wee bit of echo never goes amiss.'

Munro, adopting the poise of a bored civil servant, waited for the call to connect as West hovered silently beside him.

"You have dialled an incorrect number. Please hang up and try again."

'Butterfingers.'

'For crying out loud,' said West, 'I could have sworn…'

"You have dialled an incorrect number. Please hang up and try again."

'Something's not right,' said Dougal. 'The number starts with 07949, that's the EE network, I'll make a quick call and see what I can find out.'

'Well, that's just brilliant,' said West. 'Talk about an anti-climax.'

'That number,' said Duncan, 'was it taken from Riley's phone?'

'Yup.'

'Then it has to be right. Was there a log on the phone of when she last called him?'

'Nope, and he certainly hasn't called her.'

'Maybe that explains why she's on tenterhooks, being cooped up in that house all the time would be enough to drive anyone mad.'

'Okay,' said Dougal, 'according to EE that was definitely McIntyre's number.'

'Was?' said West. 'What do you mean *was*?'

'He used to have a pay-monthly contract but it was terminated three months ago.'

'Why? Did he screw up on the payments?'

'No, miss, he cancelled it himself.'

'Why would he do that?'

'Who knows,' said Dougal, 'but if he'd gone bust maybe he didn't need it anymore.'

'Is there anything else we can try?'

'Aye, but–'

'Oh, forget the *buts*, Dougal! Just give me the options!'

'Well, we could try using GPS. Or I've got some software which would allow me to hack his SIM, and if it's an iPhone I could always log in to iCloud and access the "find my phone" feature.'

'So, what's stopping you?'

'Simple, miss. I need a number.'

'So, we're stuffed?'

'Temporarily, aye.'

'Not so,' said Duncan, 'we do have two other options that don't involve technology and I hate to say it but they're blindingly obvious.'

'Come on then, clever clogs, let's have it.'

'Well,' said Duncan, 'we could use Riley as bait.'

'You mean let her go?'

'Aye. She's bound to meet with McIntyre at some point, but there is an easier option.'

'Go on.'

'He's still not collected the Lexus, miss. Assuming he's not going to leave a car like that sitting around too long we could sit it out. He's bound to pick it up sooner rather than later.'

'If it's not gone already,' said Dougal. 'He may have gone knocking for Riley then legged it when she's not answered.'

'There is that,' said Duncan, 'but there's only one way to find out. It just means sitting in a car and slowly freezing to death while we wait.'

'Not necessarily,' said Dougal. 'We've got her keys, you could wait in the house.'

'Can we do that?' said West.

Munro looked up and smiled.

'Are you familiar with the phrase "turning a blind eye", Charlie?'

'Yes,' said West. 'And I'm also familiar with the phrase "collect your cards".'

'That's me away, then,' said Duncan. 'I'll give you a call as soon as he shows up. If he shows up.'

'Just watch your back,' said West, 'he may have a set of keys, too.'

* * *

West strolled to the kitchen, filled the kettle, and rummaged through the sandwich bags in search of some leftover breakfast.

'Why,' she said, tucking into a cold bacon roll, 'is nothing in life ever easy?'

'If everything was easy, Charlie, we'd all be bored. Think of it as nature's way of avoiding dementia.'

'Speaking of which,' said West, 'Dougal, did you remember to put a track on McIntyre's debit card?'

'I did, miss, aye. Nothing's happened yet.'

'Well at least we've still got that to fall back on. Anyone else for coffee?'

'Much obliged,' said Munro. 'Milk and three, if you will.'

'Listen, miss,' said Dougal. 'There's something I've been trying to tell you all morning, can we do that now?'

'Yes, alright, let me get my coffee.'

'You might want a drop of whisky in that.'

'Why?'

'I've been going through the last bag of bits and bobs Duncan brought back from MacDuff's house.'

'I thought you'd done all that.'

'The laptop and the phones, aye, but there was also this.'

Dougal grabbed a large, plastic bag containing a collection of goodies normally found down the back of a sofa and held it up.

'This lot was in a bowl on the sideboard.'

'What is it?'

'Just stuff,' said Dougal. 'Stuff Duncan thought might be useful. There's about fifteen quid in loose change, a second set of house keys, six first class stamps, an old credit card, an unopened letter with a telephone number scrawled on the back, two biros–'

'And Duncan thought that would be useful?'

'–and this.'

'A key fob?' said Munro. 'It might have been useful to MacDuff, laddie, but not us. It's probably for that wee white van of his.'

'I'm afraid not,' said Dougal. 'This, boss, is for a Lexus.'

Contrary to popular belief, the stoical Charlotte West was neither as hard as nails nor as cold as a reptile but, despite barely batting an eyelid during *The Blair Witch Project*, the unexpected revelation had much the same effect as cattle prod wired to the mains.

'Working with you, Dougal,' she said, trying to keep calm, 'is like waiting for the bleeding Enola Gay to perform a flyby. You, my son, are the king of the bombshells.'

'I do my best.'

'What the hell, *just what the hell* is MacDuff doing with a key to the Lexus?'

'Maybe it's not McIntyre's,' said Dougal, apologetically. 'Maybe he's got one himself, tucked away somewhere, in a garage maybe.'

'Nice try,' said West, 'but it's too late for sticking plasters, Dougal.'

'The only logical explanation,' said Munro, 'is that McIntyre was known to MacDuff.'

'Talk about stating the bleeding obvious,' said West. 'The question is, Jimbo, why? What's the connection? And how do we prove it?'

'One step at a time, Charlie. Start at the beginning. Think about it.'

'I am! MacDuff knew Barlow. Barlow knew Riley. And Riley knows McIntyre. So what's the link between the first and the last?'

'You've already got a link, Charlie. Prove it and you're on your way. What do you need when you drive a car?'

'Oh, you're great help today,' said West. 'A key. You need a flipping key, and we've got the key!'

Munro, unimpressed, scowled at West then opened his newspaper and said nothing.

'Okay. We've got the key,' said West. 'What else do you need. Petrol? An MOT? Insurance? Of course! Jimbo, you're a genius! Dougal, can we check if McIntyre's got any named drivers on his policy?'

'Easy, miss,' said Dougal, as he logged into the Motor Insurance Database. 'Just give me a minute.'

'Far be it for me to interfere,' said Munro, 'but if this proves fruitful you'll have to have another wee chat with Miss Riley.'

'Already done that, Jimbo. She claims never to have heard of MacDuff.'

'What she claims and what she knows,' said Munro, 'is the difference between reality and fantasy. I'm sure that key will jog her memory.'

Not wanting to interrupt, Dougal, like a wean wanting to be excused, raised his arm and waited politely.

'Got something?' said West. 'Please tell me you've got something.'

'McIntyre's policy was taken out on the twenty-third of October last year, miss, and Alan MacDuff is down as a named driver.'

'Thank you, God!' said West, as she grabbed the key. 'I'm off to see Riley, you two do something useful while I'm gone. And if you hear any banging, that'll be my head against the wall.'

Chapter 16

Unlike a junior detective who'd wallow in the glory of a facile conviction based on overwhelming evidence and a suspect's admission of guilt, Munro – rankled by the lack of intelligence concerning Rebecca Barlow's ill-fated transition from property developer to hotelier – preferred the challenge of searching for chinks in the armour of a suspect's testimony or a witness's statement in order to bring the perpetrator to justice.

Embroiled in a case with more missing pieces than a charity shop jigsaw puzzle, he leaned back, closed his eyes, and sat with his hands clasped behind his head as he quietly contemplated the conundrum, his furrowed brow causing Dougal a degree of consternation.

'Are you okay, boss? Will I fetch you an aspirin?'

Munro smiled and shook his head.

'I've an itch,' he said, 'and I cannae scratch it.'

'Sorry?'

'The old Commercial Hotel. It was owned by a gentleman called Jack Muir. He and his wife had lived there for decades.'

'And?'

'He was older than me,' said Munro, 'but we're both cut from the same cloth. We're what some folk might call "the make do and mend" generation.'

'Aye well, there's nothing wrong with that,' said Dougal. 'I'd take it as a compliment. So, what's the problem?'

'If I'd lived in the same house for forty, fifty, sixty years, I'd not give it up that easily, especially if I was in my twilight years, so why did Jack? Why did he readily accept an offer on his house? The house where he'd raised a family. I cannae fathom it just now, but I will.'

'Maybe he just fancied a change,' said Dougal.

'Wait until you're my age, laddie. Trust me, the last thing you'll be wanting is change.'

'Is there anything I can do?'

'As a matter of fact,' said Munro, 'there is, aye. Jack Muir, you've got his address, see what you can find on him, the obituaries might be a good place to start–'

'I'm on it.'

'–and he'd have needed a solicitor to complete the sale of the old Commercial, follow the trail from Land Registry and find out who it was. With any luck he may have used the same firm to draft his Last Will and Testament. I'll make us a brew while you crack on.'

* * *

Reminded of the comfort and security he derived from his own home where every room, nook, and cranny was filled with indelible memories of his late wife, Munro, smiling wistfully, filled the mugs, his musings cut short by the piercing warble of the landline.

'Duncan, it's yourself,' he said. 'Are you okay?'

'Aye, chief. I tried Westy but she's not picking up.'

'She's with that Riley woman,' said Munro. 'Can I help or would you rather speak with Dougal?'

'No, no. You'll do.'

'Flattered, I'm sure.'

'It's McIntyre's Lexus,' said Duncan. 'It's gone.'

'And you're sure it was he who picked it up?'

'No. But I've called the council and it's not been towed so it must have been him.'

'Perhaps if you'd been an hour earlier, thirty minutes, maybe.'

'Aye well, there's no point dwelling on "ifs" and "maybes", is there, chief?'

'Quite right,' said Munro, 'I stand corrected.'

'I had a wee swatch inside Riley's house, it doesn't look as though anything's been disturbed, not so far as I can tell, anyway.'

'So have you a plan of action?'

'I have,' said Duncan. 'I've given control details of the Lexus so uniform can keep an eye out for it. I told them to alert traffic too. I don't know why but I've a feeling he might head back towards Carlisle. If he's on the motorway then their ANPR might pick him up.'

'Well, I've got to hand it to you,' said Munro, 'you're on the ball this morning, you'll not be needing my help, that's for sure.'

'Thanks very much.'

'Is there anything in particular Charlie should be made aware of?'

'No, just fill her in, please, chief. I'm away back to MacDuff's house just now, it's the only other place he could possibly go. I'll be a while yet.'

* * *

Munro, feeling a flush of pride at Duncan's progression from an errant DC into a DS capable of controlling his own destiny, handed Dougal his tea and pulled up a chair.

'Any luck?' he said.

'Oh aye,' said Dougal. 'This, boss, has been a breeze.'

'Maybe it's my age,' said Munro, 'but everyone seems to be firing on all cylinders this morning. I'm beginning to think my days are numbered.'

'Well I can't speak for the others, boss, but so far as I'm concerned it's probably the after-effects of the Irn-Bru I had for breakfast.'

'If you carry on drinking that stuff,' said Munro, 'you'll not need a tanning salon. So, what's the story?'

'Okay, I'll get more details and verification on this in an email later this afternoon,' said Dougal, 'but so far, we're here – the solicitors used for the conveyancing in the sale of the old Commercial Hotel were Cox, Latham, and Hines of Dalbeattie and you were right, they also drafted Jack Muir's will and they acted as executors of his estate.'

'So we're off to a cracking start. What else?'

'Well, I had to wheedle it out of them ahead of their email but I did manage to find out that Jack Muir was good to the tune of £212,786.'

'Good grief!' said Munro. 'No disrespect to the dearly departed but the man must have been a penny-pinching miser. Did they tell you anything else about the will?'

'They did, aye. Everything was left to his wife but in the event that she should pass before him, then it would all go to his son, Fraser. They gave me an address for him. He's in Perth, western Australia.'

'And did she?' said Munro. 'Did his wife pass before him?'

'Aye. By four days.'

'And his daughter, Barbara? Was she not mentioned in the will?'

'No, boss. She got hee-haw. Nothing. Not a penny.'

Ruminating on the vagaries of family life and how greed, jealousy, and sibling rivalry had the potential to drive a wedge between members of the same household, Munro, relieved to have no offspring of his own, took a moment and sipped his tea.

'Why?' he said, softly. 'Tell me, Dougal, why would he do that? If his son's away and his daughter's here, why did he not split the inheritance between them? Why was she cut out of the will?'

'Oh, you're asking the wrong fella,' said Dougal, 'my family's tighter than a hangman's noose. We don't even argue.'

'Well, this has all the hallmarks of a family rift,' said Munro, draining his cup. 'See what you can find on his daughter, Barbara, maybe we'll discover the reason there. Now, it might be cold but the sun's shining. I'm of a mind to take a wee drive in the country.'

'Somewhere near Auchencairn, no doubt.'

Munro hooked Murdo to his lead, turned to Dougal, and smiled.

'You know me too well,' he said. 'I'll be back after lunch.'

* * *

Like a boxer who'd taken one too many blows to the head, Riley, sitting with her shoulders hunched and her hands dangling between her knees, barely flinched as West, regarding her dishevelled state as an indication that her ploy to wear her down was about to reap some dividends, gently closed the door and pulled up a chair.

'How are you feeling?' she said. 'Can I get you anything?'

'Emma Riley.'

'You what?'

'I'm pre-empting your first question,' said Riley. 'Let's get this over with, I'm pure shattered and I need to sleep.'

'You and me, both.'

'So, what is it this time?'

'Alan MacDuff.'

'Did you not mention him before?'

'I did,' said West, 'and you claimed not to know him.'

'Did I? Well in that case, I still don't.'

West, not averse to fabricating the truth if the ends justified the means, sat back and folded her arms.

'We've still got several hours on the clock,' she said, 'and if we run out of time I've two more charges I can throw at you. Two more *separate* charges. You could be here that long we'll have to start charging you rent.'

'You're pulling my leg,' said Riley. 'I don't believe you.'

'There's only one way to find out. It's up to you.'

West reached into her pocket, retrieved the key fob, and laid it on the table.

'This,' she said, 'is a key for McIntyre's car. The Lexus. *How did we get it?* I hear you ask. *Have we found McIntyre?* No. This key belonged to Alan MacDuff. So, last chance, what's the deal with McIntyre and MacDuff?'

Believing that anything she said could only further the case against McIntyre without incriminating herself, Riley, head bowed, conceded defeat and spoke without looking up.

'They've not known each other long,' she said, heaving a sigh. 'They met when MacDuff was going through his divorce.'

'Where?'

'Glasgow, I think. Some seedy pub Danny used to like.'

'Seedy, how?'

'Low lives. Wheeler-dealers. Everyone on the make.'

'And?'

'Well, they're two of a kind,' said Riley, 'a couple of chancers with an eye for the ladies.'

'Go on.'

'They got on like a house on fire. Two single fellas in the pub with nothing to do but leer at the women, talk about football, and drink until they could barely stand. Danny took a shine to MacDuff and when he told him his wife was about to kick him out of the house, that was it. Danny answered all his prayers in one.'

'I never realised he was so generous,' said West. 'So, what did he do? Bung him a few quid or something?'

'Aye. And the rest. Danny gave him an empty rental property to stay in until he got back on his feet.'

'Taylor Street?'

'Aye.'

'And McIntyre,' said West, 'did he kip there too?'

'Sometimes. Normally after they'd got hammered in the pub.'

'And when he wasn't with MacDuff, where did he stay?'

'He had a wee flat above the agency,' said Riley. 'In Dumfries.'

'Does he still have it?'

'No. He let it go when the business folded.'

'And his relationship with MacDuff,' said West. 'This great friendship of theirs. I'm assuming it all started before he went under.'

'Aye. How the mighty fall, eh?'

'So, how come he went bust?' said West. 'I mean, estate agents earn a packet for doing bugger all. He must've been minted.'

'The market went flat,' said Riley. 'He's not a big chain or a firm of solicitors, he was an independent businessman. If the houses weren't selling, he wasn't earning. So that was him humped.'

'Even so, surely he had something tucked away. Savings?'

'Not Danny. He liked to look the part. He spent a wee fortune on anything that made him look good. Fancy suits, flash cars, expensive watches.'

'And when he lost it all, what did he do, then? I mean, he had to earn a living somehow.'

'What do you think?' said Riley. 'I'd not be sitting here if he'd got himself a job in McDonald's now, would I?'

'Right. So McIntyre gave MacDuff the run of the place on Taylor Street. Was that it, or did he do anything else for him before he ended up skint?'

'Plenty,' said Riley. 'He threw some work his way to keep him busy, to earn his keep, as it were.'

'What kind of work?'

'Replacing the security cameras in the Falkirk office, then the ones in Dumfries, and when he'd finished that…'

Riley paused, slowly raised her head, and stared at West.

'What?'

'Well, he had him,' said Riley. 'Danny had MacDuff in the palm of his hand, he could get him to do anything he wanted and MacDuff wasn't in a position to refuse. Now I think about it, I reckon that was his plan all along.'

'Get to the point,' said West. 'What did he do?'

'He gave him a wee job. A wee driving job.'

Experiencing the same rush of relief as someone who'd struggled for days to release the lid on a jar of marmalade, West, allowing herself the subtlest of smiles, left the table and stood with her arms folded in the corner of the room.

'It was MacDuff, wasn't it?' she said. 'When you came out of the supermarket, it was Alan MacDuff who picked you up.'

'Aye,' said Riley with a nod. 'It was him.'

'So, apart from acting as your own personal chauffeur, what else did he do with this little driving job?'

'Parcels. He delivered parcels.'

'We're not talking FedEx here, are we?'

'No,' said Riley, 'it was the same sort of parcels I used to handle.'

'So, he did you out of a job?'

'Aye, but that never bothered me,' said Riley. 'The fact of the matter is, I was glad to be shot of it.'

'But you were still working for McIntyre. What did you do?'

'I kept the local punters happy.'

'Local, like John Drennan?'

'Aye, just like John…'

'Oops, looks like you just slipped up, Miss Riley. You really should learn to concentrate when you're answering these questions. Now, is there anything else you'd like to add before I charge you?'

* * *

In contrast to the view from the village square which, though easy on the eye, was limited to rows of whitewashed cottages and the local garage, the nearby Shore Road offered the spectacle of Hestan Island's snow-covered slopes shimmering in the low, winter sunshine as the incoming tide battered its rugged coastline.

Smiling at the sight of a lovelorn pheasant gamely pursuing a clearly uninterested hen, Munro turned his back on the sea, brought Murdo to heel, and returned to the car as he answered the call.

'Dougal,' he said, as he slammed the door shut, 'you've caught me just in time.'

'I'm not holding you up, am I, boss?'

'No, no. I've just arrived. Have you some news for me?'

'Oh aye. And if you're not sitting down, I suggest you do. I've spent the last ninety minutes researching that Barbara Muir for you. Have you spoken to her yet?'

'Not yet,' said Munro, 'but it sounds as though you're about to pass the ammunition.'

'I am, boss. I've trawled through everything I can lay my hands on – the National Records, the General Register Office, births, marriages, deaths, the lot – and it seems that Barbara Muir, née Cassidy–'

'Ho! Just a wee moment there, laddie! What do you mean, *née*?'

'She's not Jack Muir's daughter,' said Dougal. 'According to the Adopted Children's Register she was taken in by the Muirs at age fourteen after her parents, Gary and Kerry Cassidy were both killed.'

'Killed? Dear God,' said Munro, 'to lose one parent is hard enough but two? How on earth did that happen?'

'It was a rail accident, boss. Invergowrie, 1979. They were on their holidays. Barbara and her brother were two of three lucky ones to be pulled alive from the wreckage.'

'And her brother? Was he adopted too?'

'Aye, but by a different family.'

'Well, I'm much obliged,' said Munro. 'It seems I shall have to tread lightly. After a loss like that I'm sure she's still suffering. Was there anything else?'

'Aye,' said Dougal, 'the village shop, it used to be a residential premises, a ground floor flat.'

'If you're telling me that, it must be relevant. How exactly?'

'It was owned by Jack Muir, too. He converted it to retail twenty-odd years ago. When he died his son, Fraser, got that as well.'

* * *

Not wanting to have his conversation stifled by the presence of any other customers, Munro glanced up and down the street before stepping briskly through the door and greeting the lady behind the counter with a disarming smile.

'It's James, isn't it?'

'None other,' said Munro. 'And yourself, Barbara, how are you?'

'Better now the sun's shining.'

'Aye, it's a beautiful day,' said Munro, reaching for the chiller cabinet. 'In fact, it's feeling positively tropical.'

'Oh, I'd not go so far as that!' said Barbara, eyeing the sausage roll in his hand. 'Will I heat that up for you? I can pop it in the microwave if you like.'

'Very kind but not necessary. It's for the journey back, just in case I get peckish.'

'Well if you're hungry now I could fire you up a bacon roll, or a cheese toastie, perhaps?'

'No, you're alright,' said Munro, 'I had something before I came out although if it's not too much trouble a cup of hot, strong tea wouldnae go amiss.'

'No bother,' said Barbara. 'Milk?'

'Aye, full fat and three.'

'So, are you up at your house, then?'

'I'm still waiting for the sale to go through but the agent's been kind enough to let me in so I can measure up for a few wee bits and bobs.'

'That'll be carpets and curtains, then.'

'Aye, something like that.'

'Get ahead of the game,' said Barbara, 'that's the way to do it. That way when you pick up the keys you can crack right on.'

'Quite right,' said Munro, 'and I've plenty to do.'

'That's all part of the fun, making the place your own – you'll enjoy it. I hope you've saved your pennies, have you seen the price of carpets these days?'

'I have not,' said Munro. 'You make it sound as though I'm in for a wee shock.'

'Aye, you are! They're not cheap, that's for sure.'

'Perhaps I should have fought for my inheritance after all!'

Like an avaricious widow-chaser at the wake of a wealthy landowner, Barbara, unable to conceal her interest, placed the tea on the counter and smiled at Munro with a covetous glint in her eye.

'So, you're a man of means, then?'

'Quite the opposite,' said Munro. 'I didnae get a penny.'

'Oh. I must've misheard you. I'll not pry, it's personal.'

'Och, it was a long time ago,' said Munro. 'I had, for want of a better word, a falling-out with my father. Succinctly put, my sister got everything.'

'And you got nothing?'

'Correct.'

'You have my sympathy,' said Barbara, 'the same thing happened to me.'

'Is that so?'

'Aye, the other way around, of course. It was my brother who hit the jackpot and he's ten thousand miles away. He emigrated years ago and he's never been back. Not once. Not even for the funeral.'

'I get the impression you didnae see eye to eye.'

'No,' said Barbara, 'we did not. See here, James, as far as my father was concerned, Fraser was the blue-eyed boy and I... well, I was never good enough.'

'I'm sorry to hear that,' said Munro, 'but I'm sure he must have had his reasons.'

'Let's just say I wasn't of the same stock, but I'm not fussed, I'm over it now. What you've never had, you never miss.'

'Right enough,' said Munro, as he reached for his wallet. 'I suppose it's true what they say after all – you can choose your friends but you cannae choose your family. How much do I owe you?'

'One pound and seventy-nine pence. Still, I take solace in the fact that Fraser never got his hands on the old Commercial. I might have felt different about things if he had.'

'Och, that's right,' said Munro, 'I remember you saying, it was sold to the woman who... who died.'

'That's right, so Fraser didn't get a penny.'

Munro, looking mildly inquisitive, handed over a five pound note.

'Forgive me for asking,' he said, 'but I'm a wee bit confused, would your brother not have got the proceeds from the sale of the house?'

'Ordinarily, aye, I suppose he would,' said Barbara, but my father was canny with cash. He didn't want that amount of money just sitting in the bank doing nothing so he opened a saving account in my mother's name and put it all there.'

'That was very shrewd of him,' said Munro, 'but why not a joint account?'

'He didn't see the point. He was convinced he'd go before her. That way she'd have the lot without having to go through all those legal wrangles and all that waiting around before she could get her hands on it but as it turned out she went just before him.'

'It's a shame she didnae get to enjoy it.'

'Aye, right enough, but neither did Fraser. By the time the executor got his hands on the paperwork the account was all but empty.'

'Is that so?'

'Aye, but my folks, James, for all their foibles, they loved their charities, their wildlife. They were soppy like that. I'd not be surprised if they gave it all away.'

'How very philanthropic of them.'

'Phil and who?'

'Generous.'

'I see.'

'Well, I've kept you long enough,' said Munro, smiling as he slipped the sausage roll into his pocket. 'It's been a pleasure. You can let me have the next instalment of your life story the next time I'm in.'

'Aye, I look forward to that, James. I look forward to that very much indeed.'

* * *

Unfazed by flashing lights, sudden movements, or loud noises, Murdo, had he been conscripted into service by Police Scotland, would have been described as 'bombproof', however, belying his ability to sleep through the fiercest of thunderstorms or the deafening bang of a barrage of fireworks, he possessed the uncanny knack of waking at the sound of anything edible being unwrapped.

Stirred by the crinkle of a cellophane wrapper, he raised his head, sniffed the air, and pawed at Munro until a half a sausage roll landed on the seat beside him.

Munro, polishing off the rest, reached for his phone and called the office.

'Dougal,' he said. 'Have you a moment?'

'All the time in the world, boss. What's up?'

'Jack Muir,' said Munro as he started the engine, 'I need everything you can possibly find pertaining to his estate. I'm particularly interested in what he did with the proceeds from the sale of the Commercial Hotel. Is that possible?'

'More than possible,' said Dougal, 'it's all detailed in the email from the solicitors in Dalbeattie. How'd it go with Miss Muir?'

'It was interesting. She's a nice enough lady but my instinct's telling me there's more to her than meets the eye.'

'Well, while we're on the subject, you might be interested to learn that–'

'Sorry, Dougal, it'll have to wait,' said Munro, 'I'm driving now. Save it for when I get back.'

Chapter 17

For the majority of the working population there came a point in the day when the tedium of tackling the mundane was replaced by the expectation of an evening filled with the frivolity of socialising, dining, or simply vegging in front of the television, but for those beset with the emotional stress of a virtuous occupation and whose selfless commitment compelled them to toil relentlessly until the job was done, there was often little to look forward to but a stiff drink and a relaxing soak in a steaming hot bath.

Pacified by the leisurely drive back to base through the unspoilt environs of the Galloway Forest Park, Munro – touched by the plight of Miss Barbara Muir who, despite her outward appearance, seemed to be hiding her grief beneath a veil of contentment – paused in the doorway flabbergasted at a scene reminiscent of an under-staffed care home with West, mouth agape, reclining in a chair with her feet propped on the table, Duncan slumped over a desk with his head in his arms, and Dougal, normally a hyper-active bundle of nervous energy, yawning as he struggled to stay awake.

'Dear God,' he said. 'Did somebody leave the gas on?'

Duncan opened one eye and looked towards the door.

'We're pure shattered, chief.'

'It's hardly surprising,' said West, stretching her arms. 'It's been a bit full-on recently, hasn't it?'

Munro closed the door, unclipped Murdo from his leash, and placed a carrier on the table.

'Your dedication to duty is to be commended,' he said, 'but you've nae stamina.'

'I think you'll find sleep deprivation has something to do with that.'

'Nonsense, lassie. You simply need to keep your strength up. I suggest you start the day with a hearty bowl of porridge, get plenty of protein down your neck and maintain a healthy intake of antioxidants.'

'Sorry,' said West, 'but there's only so much tea a girl can take.'

'Actually,' said Munro, 'I was referring to wine. The red variety of course. Now then, Charlie, you'll be pleased to know you no longer have to go scavenging behind the cooker for something to eat. I stopped along the way and picked up some provisions.'

'Please tell me it's not haggis again.'

'Certainly not. It's fillet steak, some ready-to-roast potatoes, and a not inexpensive bottle of Bordeaux but you'll not get your paws on any of it until the day is done.'

'I'll say this for you, Jimbo, you certainly know how to dangle a carrot.'

'So what's with all this fatigue? You're not telling me that Riley woman's worn you out?'

'Pretty much,' said West, 'but you'll pleased to know we got there in the end. She made an almighty gaff when I was questioning her about MacDuff. She let slip that she knew John Drennan after all.'

'So you've charged her?'

'Yup. But what I really need now is to find that homeless bloke. If we can get him to verify Drennan's story then we'll be one hundred per cent watertight.'

'Well despite that loose end, it sounds to me like you've a cause for celebration.'

'Don't put the champagne on ice just yet,' said Duncan. 'Riley's only a part of the problem, chief. We've yet to locate McIntyre and we've still no idea who killed MacDuff.'

'Well that's where our worlds collide,' said Munro. 'If I can find Rebecca Barlow's assassin, then we'll have MacDuff's killer, too.'

'Good luck with that,' said West. 'It's a tall order, even for you, especially if that doughnut DI Byrne's still on the case. I hear you went back to Auchencairn.'

'I did indeed. And I'm not ashamed to say I feel for Miss Muir. She's certainly had more than her fair share of grief to bear.'

'But?' said West. 'I feel a "but" coming on.'

'But without wanting to sound callous, I get the distinct impression she's not quite as innocent as she seems.'

'How exactly?'

'I'm not entirely sure,' said Munro. 'She showed little remorse for the passing of her parents but was clearly elated by the fact that her brother didnae get a penny from the sale of the old Commercial Hotel.'

'Some people are like that,' said West. 'Self-centred and selfish.'

'Perhaps,' said Munro, 'but it was her attitude, too. She was too flippant, too blasé about where the money actually went when most folk in her situation would be inclined to harbour a grudge.'

'Sorry, chief,' said Duncan, 'but you're losing me. If her brother didn't get the money, then who did?'

'Nobody,' said Munro, 'and that's my point. Apparently the funds were placed in a savings account which was opened in her mother's name and according to Miss Muir, when she died her father gave it all away.'

'Who to?'

'A handful of charitable causes. But I'm not convinced.'

'How so?'

'Because,' said Munro, 'for somebody like Jack Muir who was of a certain age and acting under the guidance of his solicitors it would have made more sense to specify the beneficiaries in his will, not just fritter it away to anyone who took his fancy. No, no, mark my words, Duncan, my instinct tells that the money went somewhere else.'

With the bored nonchalance of a Mensa candidate answering the tie-break in the final round of a pub quiz, Dougal, stifling a yawn, sat back and raised his hand.

'I can tell you where it went,' he said. 'I tried explaining on the phone, boss, but you cut me short.'

'Sometimes,' said Munro, 'you need to be more forceful and stand your ground! Well, dinnae keep me in suspense, laddie! Let's have it!'

Dougal took a large swig of Irn-Bru, wiped his mouth with the back of his hand, and opened the email on his computer.

'She was telling the truth about where the money went,' he said, 'it was an online savings account and as you know it was opened in her mother's name but here's the thing, boss; can you guess what her name is?'

'By jiminy!' said Munro, rolling his eyes. 'It's not the time for twenty questions, laddie! Enlighten me!'

'It's Barbara,' said Dougal. 'Barbara Muir.'

Munro glared across the room, cocked his head, and frowned.

'Are you telling me they share the same name?'

'Aye, and that's the beauty of it,' said Dougal. 'You see, boss, with this kind of account, money can be deposited from pretty much any source and by any means *but* in compliance with the anti-money laundering legislation, money can only be taken out by transferring it into one other account, and that account must bear the same name as the savings account holder.'

'So Barbara Muir was able to take the money from her mother's account, place it in her own, and the bank was none the wiser?'

'Aye. And I've all the evidence here to prove it,' said Dougal. 'There's a daily limit to the amount that can be transferred which is currently twenty grand but even so, it didn't take much more than a week for her to get her hands on the lot.'

'It's true what they say,' said Munro, 'the female of the species is deadlier than the male. The woman's as shrewd as a snake but tell me this, how did she manage to enter her details on her mother's account without her knowing?'

'I'm guessing,' said Duncan, 'because her mother didn't open the account herself. It sounds to me like Barbara Muir opened it for her.'

'What makes you think that?' said West.

'Muir senior was in her nineties, right? Most folk that age haven't a scooby about online stuff let alone bank accounts. They'd rather have a chequebook or a mattress that needs stuffing.'

'Okay, I'll go along with that,' said West, 'but why would they open it in the first place? What, at their time of life, made them think they needed an online account?'

'The word "coerced" springs to mind,' said Duncan. 'Maybe Barbara Muir convinced them it was the right thing to do but the question still remains – why?'

'Oh, keep up,' said West, 'that's easy, to get her hands on the money, of course.'

'No offence, miss, but that's not adding up.'

'Why not?'

'Because when that account was opened the old Commercial Hotel wasn't even up for sale.'

West gazed at Duncan with the vacuous expression of a waxwork dummy while Dougal, smiling blithely, stared at Munro with a mobile phone hanging limply from his wrist.

'I've a feeling,' said Munro, 'that the answer to this particular puzzle lies with the brains of this organisation.'

'Duncan's right,' said Dougal. 'The property wasn't on the market but Barbara Muir knew it would be sold.'

'How?' said West. 'Are you telling me she had a sixth sense?'

'No, but she did know how to send a text. This is Rebecca Barlow's iPhone. I managed to retrieve most of the deleted messages and it seems she didn't make an offer on the Commercial out of the blue, Barbara Muir contacted her and asked if she'd be interested in acquiring the property at a reasonable price.'

'The scheming cow,' said West. 'So she orchestrated the whole thing?'

'Aye, it certainly seems that way,' said Dougal. 'She might be a lot of things but she's clever, I'll give her that.'

* * *

Disappointed that somebody like Muir who appeared to be a compassionate pillar of the community could in reality be so cold and calculating, Munro, with his faith in human nature on the back burner, placed a hand on his chin and gazed ruefully into space.

'What's up?' said West.

'People, Charlie. People. They were put on this earth to disappoint. I'm sticking with dogs from now on.'

'It's not all bad. At least you know how Barlow got her hands on the Commercial.'

'It's not enough,' said Munro. 'Agreed, the string of messages on the mobile phone explains how the hotel came to be sold and if nothing else they cast a bleak shadow on Miss Muir's sense of morals, but they contribute nothing as far as Miss Barlow's untimely death is concerned.'

* * *

Conscious of a dinner date with Kay looming on the horizon, Dougal, keen to convey as much information as possible in the shortest space of time, grabbed a wodge of papers, coughed politely into his hand, and waved them at Munro.

'These are all the other messages and emails I recovered, boss. You can read them when you get a chance.'

'Much obliged,' said Munro, 'but I'm not sure that will help.'

'Oh, it will, boss. Trust me, it will. You see, there's a few here from Daniel McIntyre.'

West jumped from her seat and swept the sheaf of papers from the table.

'McIntyre!' she said. 'Why didn't you bleeding well say so!'

'I was getting to it, miss.'

'Charlie,' said Munro, softly, 'there's a time to speak and there's a time to listen. I suggest you do the latter. Go on, Dougal.'

'Okay, we know they have a history, right? We know from her bank records that she received a large sum of money from McIntyre, probably a loan of sorts, and we know she'd gone some way to repaying it.'

'Yeah, yeah, been there, done that,' said West. 'What's new?'

'It seems she still owed McIntyre twenty-three thousand pounds and he'd been hounding her for it.'

'Sounds like he was desperate.'

'She replied several times saying he'd get it soon but that's when he starts getting nasty.'

'Nasty how?'

'He sent a couple of messages demanding interest on the loan and when she refused he started hassling her for a slice of her business instead.'

'Charming,' said West. 'They're as bad as each other. One's a thug and the other's a walking compulsory purchase order.'

'Can you date these messages?' said Munro. 'Precisely, I mean.'

'Oh, aye,' said Dougal, 'no bother at all.'

'Were they before or after Mr McIntyre lost his business?'

'Long after,' said Dougal. 'In fact, they were relatively recent.'

'How recent?'

'The last message received from McIntyre was two days before she died. It reads: "Meet you in Auchencairn, you'd better be there". There's no reply.'

'Sounds like you've got yourself a suspect, Jimbo,' said West. 'Looks like our worlds have collided after all.'

Munro raised his head at the kerfuffle in the corridor and watched in mild amusement as a red-faced DCI Elliot blundered through the door struggling to slide an arm into the sleeve of his overcoat.

'George,' he said, 'are you okay?'

'Aye, but I'm not stopping, James. Mrs Elliot's got a vegetarian lasagne in the oven so I need to get myself a sausage supper before I get home or I'll starve to death. Charlie, you're after a white Lexus, is that right?'

'Certainly is,' said West. 'Why?'

'One's been spotted on the northbound carriageway of Allison Street, details are downstairs.'

'Bang goes my evening,' said Duncan, leaping to his feet. 'Right, that's me away, then, Allison's not far from MacDuff's house, maybe he's heading there. Dougal, get me some back-up, pal, just in case.'

West zipped her jacket and tucked her hair beneath her cap.

'Well, for once,' she said, 'it looks like we're going to get an early night, Jimbo.'

'Hold your horses,' said Munro. 'I need a wee word with DI Byrne. I'll not keep you long.'

Chapter 18

Questioning the wisdom of the council's planning department which, like many up and down the country had introduced one-way systems and pedestrianised precincts under the misguided belief that it would lower air pollution despite increasing the taxpayers' daily commute by forty-five minutes, Duncan – forced to negotiate queues of traffic and blocked thoroughfares like an Uber Eats driver a sat nav short of a destination – huffed as he finally cruised to a halt on Taylor Street.

Buttoning his battered leather coat against the cold, he approached the patrol car parked on the opposite corner, rapped the roof with his knuckles, and pressed his badge against the window.

'DS Reid?' said the constable behind the wheel.

'Aye. Do you know why you're here?'

'You're after some nutter in a Lexus, is that it?'

'Close enough,' said Duncan. 'Listen, I have to check on a house up the street, you sit tight, I'll not be long.'

'No bother,' said the constable, nodding towards his partner, 'if it all kicks off, Geordie here is an STO so we can always stun the numpty if it comes to it.'

Duncan, unimpressed, leaned down and poked his head through the window.

'See here, pal,' he said, menacingly, 'I've already had a day of it and I'm not in the mood for waiting on paramedics if you fire anything so you'd best keep that Taser in your pocket, understand?'

With his cap pulled snugly over his ears and his hands buried deep in his pockets, Duncan, astounded that a trigger-happy Specially Trained Officer should be deployed to assist in the search for a stolen vehicle rather than patrol the pubs and clubs of the town centre, trudged up the street, crossed the lawn in front of the block of flats, and peered through the reinforced glass of the communal entrance.

Satisfied that the blue and white tape draped across the door to MacDuff's apartment was still intact, he walked to the front of the building and cupped his hands against the blackened windows where, in the absence of any light, he concluded that McIntyre was probably already on his way to Carlisle.

Resigned to the fact that he'd no doubt be woken at 2:00am with a phone call informing him that his quarry had been stopped for a speeding offence on the southbound lane of the A74, Duncan, intent on telling his back-up to stand down, ambled along the street and, safe in the knowledge that West would be cavorting with a glass of red rather than tucking into her steak supper, reached for his phone when the shrill sound of an impact driver emanating from a lock-up over the road stopped him in his tracks.

Deeming it far too late for anyone with a modicum of respect for their neighbours to be embarking on a DIY project, he crossed the street and, like a moth to a flame, peeked through the gap between the dilapidated doors where the glow of an inspection lamp hanging from the ceiling was bouncing off the bonnet of an unidentified white vehicle.

Citing the serendipitous discovery as second only to meeting Cathy, a witness in a murder inquiry who later became his partner, he smiled as he beckoned the constables from their car instructing them with a downward wave of the hand to approach with caution.

Raising a finger to his lips, he gestured for them to wait to one side and eased open the door to find the Lexus up on blocks with the wheels and the seats stacked neatly against the wall.

'Danny?' he said, boldly. 'Is that you?'

A middle-aged man sporting a severe crew cut with a well-established beer belly straining against the seams of his ill-fitting coveralls scrambled from beneath the car and scowled.

'You're in the wrong place, pal,' he said, struggling to get to his feet. 'On your way.'

'Danny sent me,' said Duncan. 'I'm a mechanic. I could have that thing stripped in no time.'

'Are you deaf, son? I've no idea who Danny is. Now, do one.'

A substantially slimmer second man who clearly patronised the same barber as his ageing partner, emerged from the rear of the vehicle brandishing a wheel brace.

'Better do as he says. We're busy and you're holding us up.'

Raised on a scheme where trouble was often courted by the runt of the gangs, Duncan, unperturbed by his threatening behaviour, smiled as he produced his warrant card.

'See here,' said the beer belly, wheezing as he jabbed his finger in the air, 'I'm not bothered if you're the police! I'm not bothered if you're the effing SAS! I'll do you. It's two against one.'

Duncan, raising his eyebrows, casually swung the door aside with the heel of his foot to reveal one officer wielding a baton and an STO standing legs akimbo with his Taser drawn.

'I think you'll find the bookies just revised the odds,' he said as he drew his cuffs. 'It's two against three. I'm arresting you under Section 1 of the Criminal Justice Act on suspicion of theft and TDA. You're not obliged to say anything but anything you do say will be noted and may be used in evidence. Now turn around and place your hands on the roof of the vehicle.'

* * *

Whilst the loners of the country relished the thrill of whipping up a culinary masterpiece with no-one for company but the thumping sound of their iPod, cooking for those unfortunate enough to have had solitude foisted upon them was often a chore of necessity where appetites were sated with factory-produced fodder in fancy packaging labelled with the promise of an authentic Tuscan recipe and the assurance of no artificial additives.

Lounging on the sofa with a large glass of red balancing on her chest and Murdo curled at her feet, West, grateful for the opportunity to be a guest at her own table, watched as Munro checked on the tatties before dropping two thick-cut fillets into a searing hot pan and seasoning them with a sprinkling of salt.

'Fifteen minutes,' he said, 'unless you're wanting yours swimming in a pool of blood.'

'I'm not French, Jimbo. Burnt to a crisp will do me fine. Cheers.'

'Health, wealth, and happiness,' said Munro, raising his glass. 'You look troubled.'

'Not really,' said West. 'I'm just thinking.'

'What about?'

'Your woman in Auchencairn.'

'Barbara Muir?'

'Yeah. All that stuff about the money, can't you nick her for theft or fraud or something?'

'I'd be averse to doing any such thing, Charlie. It's her business and no-one's been affected by her actions.

Besides, we'd have to prove she took the money without her father's consent and given his present circumstances there's nae chance of that happening. Not unless we hold a séance.'

'I'll take that as no, then. Oops, hold on, phone. I wonder who's calling at this time of… Duncan, you alright, mate?'

'Aye, miss, not bad. I'm not interrupting your supper, am I?'

'No, chef's still in the kitchen. What happened with McIntyre?'

'Nothing,' said Duncan, 'it was a false alarm, of sorts. McIntyre's nowhere to be seen but we did find the Lexus.'

'Top man! Where?'

'In a garage opposite MacDuff's house.'

'Hold up, that's a bit of a coincidence, isn't it? I mean to find it on Taylor Street?'

'Makes sense to me,' said Duncan, 'besides, you've seen Taylor Street yourself. I bet if you opened every workshop, lock-up, or garage up there you'd find something not quite legal going on. I believe it's what they call the black economy.'

'Whatever,' said West. 'And you're sure McIntyre wasn't in the flat?'

'Aye, I checked. The place is secure.'

'And what's happening with the motor? Are you getting a flatbed to pick it up? I think SOCOs should take a look, don't you?'

'It's not worth the effort,' said Duncan, 'and we'll not need a flatbed, just a few carrier bags.'

'What?'

'It's in pieces, miss. A couple of neds were stripping it for parts.'

'Were they anything to do with McIntyre?'

'No, just a couple of chancers who'd nicked the vehicle.'

'Any trouble?'

'Nothing we couldn't handle,' said Duncan. 'Uniform are taking them in as we speak. I've a wee bit of paperwork to sort out before I charge them then that's me away. I'm needing a pie and a pint.'

'You deserve it,' said West. 'Have one on me and I'll see you in the morning.'

Called by the clattering of cutlery, West shot to the table with Murdo in hot pursuit as Munro served supper and topped up their glasses.

'I take it that was Duncan,' he said.

'Yup, he found McIntyre's motor,' said West as she wired into her steak. 'Dougal was right, it'd been nicked after all.'

'And McIntyre?'

'Gawd knows. He could be anywhere.'

'Well, given he's a suspect,' said Munro, 'should you not be informing the authorities over the border?'

'It's all in hand, Jimbo. The thing is, without the Lexus, it's going to be difficult, isn't it?'

'How so?'

'Because the only likeness we've got of him is the mugshot off his driving licence and a press photo that's years old. The words needle and haystack spring to mind but he did have a flat in Dumfries so maybe your mate Byrne should keep an eye out for him.'

'He already is,' said Munro.

'You mean he's not resigned yet?'

'He's surviving, Charlie. Just. I've brought him up to speed on what we know so with any luck he'll soon start to allay the fears of his superiors.'

'Well, I wish him luck,' said West. 'I was cacking myself when I was in his shoes, until you dragged me out of the mire.'

'All in a day's work, lassie. All in a day's work.'

* * *

Having demolished her meal in record time, West sat back, sipped her wine, and eyed the last of the potatoes sitting on Munro's plate.

'Any news on the house?' she said. 'In Auchencairn?'

Munro raised his eyebrows and smiled.

'Your very asking suggests you've changed your mind,' he said. 'Are you warming to the proposition?'

'Maybe,' said West, coyly. 'I must admit, the thought of having a garden is quite appealing.'

'Not to mention no mortgage,' said Munro, 'or two reception rooms. Or a bedroom big enough to host a performance of *Riverdance*.'

'Yeah, yeah, alright, there is that as well. So? Any news?'

Munro cleaned his plate, raised his glass, and winked.

'You're forgetting,' he said, 'estate agents and solicitors are driven by greed, Charlie, not efficiency. It'll be a few weeks before we hear anything yet.'

'Even so, there's a chance we might be in by summer?'

'Och, there's every chance, lassie. And we'll not be needing a wing or a prayer.'

'Can we take another look?'

'Aye. We can. I'll call them in the morning and arrange a visit. Now, I suggest you retire to the sofa so I can do the dishes in peace.'

Chapter 19

Bewildered by the empty chairs, the dormant computers and more worryingly the mystifying absence of his punctilious colleague whose obsession with cyberspace drew him to his desk with the infallible punctuality of the Shinkansen railway, Duncan, attributing Dougal's tardiness to an overnight encounter with a besotted SOCO intent on dusting his dabs, grinned slyly, snatched a sandwich from a bagful of breakfast and filled the kettle as the patter of paws scampering across the floor echoed around the room.

'Alright, wee man?' he said as Murdo begged for a bite of his bacon toastie. 'Miss, chief, how's it going? Did you get plenty of antioxidants last night?'

'I think I got my RDA,' said West. 'How about you?'

'Well I managed to make it to my pit before twelve so I'm not complaining.'

'Where's laughing boy? It's not like him to be late.'

'I'm not sure,' said Duncan. 'I've tried calling him but he's not picking up.'

'Och, the poor chap's probably overslept,' said Munro. 'You cannae blame him for that, his brain's been working overtime recently.'

'Gawd, it's not as if he's been lugging bricks around a building site all day,' said West. 'He's on his backside most of the time.'

Munro helped himself to a fried egg roll, looked at West, and smiled.

'Do you know why you get so irritable, Charlie?' he said. 'It's mental fatigue. The stress of dealing with the turmoil in your head. It can burn more calories than a workout in the gym which explains why young Dougal is built like a stick insect.'

'Well, if you're right,' said West, 'that would explain why my ex was built like a Christmas pudding.'

'Actually,' said Duncan as the phone rang, 'if he's overslept then it's nothing to do with his brain. I'm guessing it's because he had Kay stay over. She's probably worn him out.'

'Maybe that's a good thing, he needs to build his stamina. Any coffee on the go?'

'Aye, on the way, I'll just answer… it's Dougal. Are you alright, pal?'

'Aye, not bad. Sorry I couldn't answer your call.'

'No bother. I'll pop you on speaker. Are you enjoying your lie-in?'

'I'm not having a lie-in!' said Dougal, indignantly. 'I'm at the hospital.'

'Bloody hell!' said West. 'Are you okay? What happened? Did you fall off your scooter?'

'No, no…'

'Is it Kay, then? Did you cook last night? Have you poisoned her?'

'Calm your jets, miss! We're both fine! I got a call last night. Some homeless fella was picked up suffering from hypothermia. They thought it might be the same fella we're looking for.'

'And is it?'

'I've no idea,' said Dougal, 'I've not seen him yet. They're still checking him over and making sure he gets some rest. They reckon I can see him in an hour so, so I'm stopping here.'

'Perfect,' said West, heading for the door. 'I'll come over. If it is him and he's up to it, then maybe he can verify Drennan's story. That'll sort Riley out once and for all.'

* * *

Smiling as a stillness descended on the room, Munro took his breakfast to the table, sat down, and loosened his tie.

'I'm not being rude,' he said, 'but there are times when I think that woman swallowed the Blarney Stone.'

'Aye, right enough,' said Duncan. 'Is she like that after hours, too?'

'If by that, you mean talkative, excitable, stubborn, irrational, and argumentative, then aye, the answer's yes. So, what's on your agenda today?'

'Top of the list, chief, is a report for the fiscal. I've still got the neds who lifted the Lexus sitting downstairs. And yourself? Are you heading back down south again?'

'No, no,' said Munro. 'I intend to make the most of the peace and quiet and catch up on some reading.'

'Is that not something for bedtime?'

'Ordinarily, aye, but this,' said Munro, waving a bundle of pamphlets, 'is not for the faint-hearted.'

'Oh?'

'I picked these up in the village shop. They're newsletters published by the Auchencairn Historical Society. They offer a fascinating insight into what really goes on in that village.'

'You're not telling me it's a den of iniquity, are you? All massage parlours and wife-swapping?'

'Och, that's tame by comparison,' said Munro. 'We're talking smuggling, theft, murder, and betrayal. Not to mention the odd haunting or two.'

Duncan sat back, cradled his coffee in both hands, and smiled at Munro.

'Alright,' he said. 'You've got me. What's the story?'

'Rebecca Barlow. She was found tied to a stake next to a dead tree. A rowan tree.'

'Sorry, chief, I'm not a gardener, you'll have to explain.'

'I'll keep it brief. In Celtic mythology it's considered bad luck to fell a rowan. For want of a better phrase, *hell hath no fury like a rowan downed.* The repercussions could be fatal.'

'Like a black cat crossing your path?'

'If it's a panther, aye.'

'Okay,' said Duncan, 'I'm all for a bit of folklore, what else?'

'The Hass Burn runs through the village, in fact, it runs right behind the old Commercial Hotel. Not too long ago a woman, unknown to anyone in the village, was found dead on the banks. Cause of death unknown.'

'You mean she didn't drown?'

'The post-mortem found her to be in rude health. There was no evidence of drowning or heart failure. Not even a bump to the head.'

'Well, that's odd, I'll give you that,' said Duncan. 'What else?'

'John Graham, happily married to Janet Newbigging, killed his wife by blasting her in the head with a shotgun.'

'Why?'

'It's a question he was asked many times,' said Munro, 'and the answer was always the same. He simply didn't know. Then there's the case of–'

'That's plenty,' said Duncan, 'I get the picture, chief. It sounds like the place is full of fruit-loops, Westy will fit in well but I have to say, and no offence, all this superstitious stuff, is it not a bit far-fetched? I mean, I think we saw the back of satanic cults and pagan rituals some years ago.'

'Never dismiss a possibility because of your own personal presumptions, Duncan. There has to be a reason for Rebecca Barlow being left as she was and in the absence of any pentangles at the scene of the crime, I intend to get to the bottom of it. Now, if you'd be so kind, I've some reading to do.'

* * *

For those in need of medical attention, University Hospital – a state-of-the-art facility catering to the needs of the frail and the elderly, the clinically obese, and those inexperienced enough to be handling a chainsaw – offered the reassurance of expert care and imminent relief from fractured hips, mild strokes, and severed limbs but for others, the sterile stench of phenolic disinfectant and the sight of gurneys littering the corridors held all the appeal of a terminal prognosis.

Seated on a blue, plastic chair designed for stacking rather than comfort, Dougal – fearing he'd be an admission himself as his scooter twitched uncontrollably along the icy roads – sat recovering from his sub-zero ordeal with his helmet in his lap.

Shaken by the sound of footsteps squeaking down the corridor, he slowly raised his head as West, carrying two cups of burnt coffee from the vending machine, approached from his right.

'On your own?' she said, handing him a cup. 'I thought you'd have Kay with you.'

'We're not joined at the hip, miss. Besides, I could say the same for you, is the boss not coming?'

'You've got to be joking,' said West, scalding her lips on the tasteless brew, 'you know what he's like. As far as he's concerned, "infirmary" is just a euphemism for "God's waiting room".'

'Aye, right enough,' said Dougal, 'although I had thought he might have changed his mind after his bypass.'

'If anything, I think it's made him more determined to stay away. So, any news on our homeless chum yet?'

'No,' said Dougal. 'I'm waiting on the nurse, he said he'd shout me when he's ready.'

'How long have you been here?'

'Hours.'

'Have you had any breakfast?'

'A can of pop.'

'You,' said West, 'are bleeding unbelievable. Carry on like that and you'll end up in a bed next to him. I'll get you something from the canteen, be back in a…'

West paused as a jaded-looking nurse emerged from the room.

'DS McCrae?' he said.

'Aye, is he okay?'

'He's getting there, he still needs plenty of rest and rehydration but I'll give you five minutes.'

'That's all we'll need,' said West, 'as long as he's able to talk we won't keep him long.'

The nurse raised a hand and mustered a sympathetic smile.

'Sorry, miss,' he said, 'no family just now, only the officer.'

'You're alright,' said Dougal, 'this is DI West, she's with me.'

The nurse thought for a moment and heaved a sigh.

'Okay,' he said wearily, 'in that case, come away inside, but take it easy, okay?'

* * *

Whilst never the easiest of tasks, the trauma of interviewing suspects, victims, and witnesses as they lay in their hospital beds was somehow alleviated when the injuries sustained could be directly attributed to an assault with a deadly weapon or a road traffic collision, but when the wounds were the result of nothing more than prolonged exposure to the elements it made the ordeal seem all the more harrowing.

Struck by the reddish tinge of his peeling, cracked skin, his blistered lips, blackened fingertips, and grubby, matted beard, West – waiting silently by the door – could have been forgiven for thinking that the dozing victim had been hauled from the summit of K2 rather than the streets of Ayrshire.

Dougal, acknowledging the patient as their missing man, stood beside the bed and smiled as the drowsy down-and-out opened his eyes.

'Alright, sir?' he said. 'How are you feeling?'

'I'm warm, and I've a bed. What's not to like?'

'We're police officers. I'm DS McCrae and this is Detective Inspector West. Are you up to answering a few questions?'

'As long as they're not on geography, aye. Okay.'

'I see you've a wee bruise on your face, there. Have you any idea how that happened?'

'No. Maybe I tripped and fell.'

Dougal thrust his hands deep into his jacket pockets and smiled.

'No, you know that's not true, sir. Is it?'

The beggar glanced at Dougal, took a deep breath, and slowly exhaled.

'It goes with the territory,' he said. 'Folk have no idea what it's like for a rough sleeper, or how we got there. They see us as losers and wasters.'

'There's always a reason why people end up on the streets.'

'Aye, there is. And therein lies the irony. We don't get benefits. We don't get social housing. We rely on the charity of the kind-hearted.'

'Right enough,' said Dougal. 'So, that bruise, would you like to tell us what happened?'

'Nothing to tell. It was just some kid. He was probably blootered, and bored.'

'Well, you can relax,' said West. 'He won't be doing it again. We know who it was and we've got him.'

‘Is that so?’

‘Yup. Fortunately there was a camera in the doorway where you were trying to get some kip. We managed to ID him from that.’

‘Well don’t be too hard on him,’ said the beggar. ‘Like I say, he’s a youngster, he’s probably got problems of his own.’

‘Maybe, but the law’s the law, and you wouldn’t be here if it wasn’t for him.’

‘You mean I’d not be warm and dry with a hot meal on the way? That’s a pity.’

West, bemused that somebody who’d taken a kicking and almost frozen to death could be so compassionate, took a step forward and crossed her arms.

‘I need to ask you something,’ she said. ‘Don’t worry, you’re not on trial or anything, and I’m not going to berate you for having any bad habits, but the man who assaulted you, he says he was paid to do it.’

‘Paid?’

‘Aye, that’s right,’ said Dougal. ‘Can you think of a reason why anyone would want to do that?’

‘None at all,’ said the beggar. ‘I keep myself to myself. I get enough grief on the streets as it is.’

‘I get that, but here’s the thing – are you on drugs of any sort? You know, a bit of weed, maybe? Or something stronger, perhaps?’

‘No, no. Definitely not. That’s a mug’s game. The hardest thing I’ve ever touched is lager and I’m even off the booze now.’

‘How come?’ said West with a grin. ‘Are you on some kind of a health kick?’

‘Are you joking me?’ said the beggar, laughing. ‘I can’t afford it, hen. It’s as simple as that. So why are you asking? About the drugs, I mean? Was this fella some kind of a junkie?’

‘He was,’ said Dougal, ‘and he says he was paid to assault you because you had a drug debt.’

'Oh, aye. Of course I have. I've also got a mansion in the south of France and a Bentley in the garage.'

Whilst safe to assume that a number of homeless people were there through eviction or addiction, there were those whose predicament, through no fault of their own, was a direct result of a mental, marital or business breakdown.

Categorising the beggar as one of the latter, West, touched by his ability to laugh in spite of his circumstances, made a mental note to ensure he was transferred to suitable accommodation upon his release rather than being left to fend for himself on the streets.

'Once you're back on your feet,' she said, 'you should consider a career doing stand-up.'

'I think you'll find lying-down is more my thing.'

'Well, we're nearly done. Just a couple more questions and we'll let you get some rest.'

'You're alright,' said the beggar, 'no rush. It's actually quite nice to have a conversation with someone.'

'The bloke who attacked you,' said West, 'his name's Drennan. John Drennan. Does that ring any bells?'

'No.'

'Okay. He says the person who paid him was his dealer. She goes by the name Riley. Do you know anyone called Emma Riley?'

The beggar looked at West and gave a wry smile.

'Aye,' he said, as he closed his eyes. 'I know a Riley.'

'But she wasn't your dealer?'

'Like I said, hen. I don't do drugs.'

'I think that will do for now,' said the nurse. 'He needs to rest. Come back this afternoon if you need to.'

'Right you are,' said Dougal. 'Just one last question. It's an easy one. Is that okay with you, sir?'

The beggar answered without opening his eyes.

'Aye. Go on, then.'

'Can we have your name?'

'No bother. It's Daniel. Daniel McIntyre.'

Chapter 20

As an advanced nurse practitioner attached to the ICU with a wife, five children, two Labradors, and a hefty mortgage to support, it was little wonder that Derek Fisher, a harried forty-eight-year-old with a shiny, bald head and more wrinkles than a bed sheet in a brothel, looked fit to drop.

Yearning for a strong cup of coffee, an energy-boosting cereal bar, and a wee sit down, he hovered in the corridor as he waited for Dougal and West to vacate the room.

'Right,' he said, 'I've a million things to do and none of them are here, so that's me away. If you've any more questions you'll have to wait until this evening.'

'No bother,' said Dougal, 'we appreciate your help.'

'You look knackered,' said West, 'still, I suppose your shift will be over soon.'

'Are you joking me?' said Fisher. 'I only came on an hour ago.'

'Well listen, I know you're busy but before you run off, can I ask you for one small favour?'

'You can ask,' said Fisher, 'but it doesn't mean you'll get.'

'We need some background on our victim here.'

'What kind of background?'

'An address.'

'Address? But the fella's homeless.'

'He is now,' said West, 'but we don't know how long he's been living on the streets. Now that we know his name, I was hoping you might be able to tell us if he was registered with a GP somewhere, that way we can find out where he used to live.'

'Can you not just ask him?'

'He's under investigation,' said Dougal, butting in. 'If we start asking questions like that then guaranteed, we'll get nowhere fast.'

'So, you want me to take a look at the PIP?'

West looked at him pleadingly, raised her eyebrows, and smiled.

'If you wouldn't mind.'

'Okay,' said Fisher, sighing as if it were a habit. 'Come on then.'

* * *

Forced to wait in the doorway of the tiny office which also housed a couple of mops and a month's worth of janitorial supplies, West, smarting from the lingering smell of chemicals, watched in silence as Fisher squeezed himself behind a desk and logged onto the Patient Information Platform.

'Right,' he said, muttering as he typed. 'Name; McIntyre. Daniel. Date of birth?'

'No idea. Sorry.'

'Off to a good start. Have you any idea how many McIntyres there are here?'

'A few, I dare say.'

'Well, do you know where he might have lived? Roughly, even?'

'Aye,' said Dougal, 'we know he used to own a flat above a shop in Dumfries. On the High Street somewhere.'

'That must have been a while ago,' said Fisher. 'The nearest I've got to the town centre is a Donald McIntyre in Heathall and a Denise McIntyre in Cargenbridge.'

'Well, it's definitely neither of them.'

'Then it seem to me you've no option but to ask him yourself, after all.'

'Hold on,' said Dougal, 'forget Dumfries, can you try Taylor Street in Ayr?'

'Aye, okay,' said Fisher. 'Do you happen to have a postcode?'

'Kilo-Alpha-Eight, Eight-Alpha-Uniform.'

'You're in luck. But I can't guarantee it's the same fella.'

'Oh, it's him alright,' said West. 'Is there anything else you can tell us?'

'There is,' said Fisher, 'but I can't. Patient confidentiality.'

Under normal circumstances, Dougal, a respecter of red tape, rules, and regulations, would have thanked the nurse for his time and politely walked away but with McIntyre all but in his grasp he refused to take no for an answer.

'See here, Mr Fisher,' he said, brushing West aside, 'I'm not being funny but that fella's under investigation for a serious crime and we need to know if we're putting him or ourselves in danger by bringing him in, so if he's got a wee bit of a temper or a heart condition then you'd be doing us all a favour by telling us now. And a date of birth would be useful, too.'

Visibly shaken by Dougal's volatile if not threatening behaviour, Fisher pondered the penalty for breaching the code of confidentiality before finally relenting.

'This goes no further,' he said, turning to the screen. 'Do you understand?'

'I promise,' said West. 'So, what have you got?'

'Date of birth: third of the tenth, seventy-seven. A couple of years ago he was prescribed… oh.'

'Oh what? You look surprised.'

'I am,' said Fisher. 'He was prescribed amitriptyline.'

'What's that?'

'An anti-depressant.'

'That would coincide with his business going bust,' said Dougal. 'What's it like?'

'I told you, it's an anti-depressant.'

'Aye, I get that! But you said it was prescribed so it must be strong, am I right?'

'It's strong, aye.'

'Then there could be serious side effects.'

'Maybe.'

'Well?'

Fisher focused on the keyboard, typed in a few choice words, and sighed as he reeled off a list of possible symptoms.

'Confusion,' he said, 'drowsiness, blurred vision, vomiting, headaches, irregular heartbeat, muscle spasms, suicidal tendencies, seizures, and hallucinations.'

'Bloody hell!' said West. 'And that's a licensed drug? I think I'd rather see a vet.'

'There's more,' said Fisher. 'Before starting that particular course of treatment he was on Clopixol. He had four jags over a two month period.'

'And is that an anti-depressant, too?'

'No. It's an anti-psychotic drug administered intravenously.'

'So basically what you're saying is, our man next door has some serious mental health issues?'

'Has, or had. Aye.'

'And now?'

'I'm not a psychiatrist,' said Fisher, 'I wouldn't know. Clearly he's not had any medication for a while now so maybe he's doing okay. Maybe he isn't.'

'Well, he certainly seems chirpy enough,' said West. 'Right, one more thing before we go. When he was brought in he was obviously stripped and given a gown to wear. Did he have any personal belongings with him, like a–'

'Like a phone, you mean? And a wallet?'

'Yeah, exactly.'

'They're in the locker by his bed,' said Fisher, 'but I'm telling you now, Inspector, if you're thinking of taking them, you can't. And the rooms are monitored so don't even go there.'

'I wouldn't dream of it,' said West. 'We'll leave you in peace, you've been blinding, thanks very much.'

* * *

Dougal, aware that his breakfast was fast becoming brunch, waited impatiently in the corridor while West, adopting the look of someone who'd lost their car keys, rifled frantically through her pockets until Fisher, counting the loose change in the palm of his hand, wandered out of sight towards the vending machine.

'Wait here,' she said, as she slipped into McIntyre's room, 'I'll be two ticks.'

Unlike Duncan who'd graduated with a degree in rule-bending, Dougal, worried that Fisher might return at any moment, shuffled nervously on the spot and breathed a sigh of relief when West eventually reappeared.

'No offence, miss,' he said with a scowl, 'but you do realise you're on film, don't you?'

'You worry too much,' said West, handing him a plastic beaker, 'take this, wrap it in your handkerchief, and get it to Kay. Tell her we need it dusted and the dabs up on the system as soon as she can.'

'You've done this before, haven't you?'

'Once or twice,' said West as she moved away from the door, 'now, look at this.'

Dougal frowned as he peered at a photo on her phone.

'This was in his wallet,' said West, 'tucked inside a neatly-folded twenty pound note with a couple of hundred in fifties.'

'You opened his wallet? Jeez-oh, miss! You can't do that!'

'I already have.'

'Did he not clock you going through his things?'

'Nope, he's out like a light, sleeping like a baby.'

'So why are you showing me a receipt from a supermarket?'

'This,' said West, 'is not just any old receipt. Emma Riley handed it to McIntyre when she came out of the shop. It's a top-up voucher for a pay-as-you-go phone.'

'So, that's why his mobile wasn't working when we called him! He ditched it for one of those!'

'Exactly.'

'But why?'

'There's only one way to find out,' said West, 'I need to have another chat with Riley before they whisk her off to court. Sorry about breakfast, you'll have to get something yourself.'

Chapter 21

Although she'd forsaken the pocket sprung mattress with Egyptian cotton sheets for a slither of plastic-coated foam, the deep pile carpet for a resin floor, and the luxury en-suite for a stainless steel pan, life in the holding cell for Emma Riley was no different to the suffocating confinement of her own home where she'd waited on tenterhooks for the domineering Daniel McIntyre to advise her of her next move.

Relieved that she was finally on her way to court, she stood up straight, dusted herself down, and cocked her head at the unexpected sight of Detective Inspector West standing in the doorway.

Dismayed at the prospect of having to spend another night in the custody suite she fell back on the bed and ruffled her wayward hair.

'For God's sake!' she said, despondently. 'I thought I was out of here!'

'You will be,' said West, 'any minute now. But first we need a chat.'

'What is it this time?'

West leaned against the door and folded her arms.

'It's about McIntyre,' she said. 'You'll be pleased to know we're going to get him off your back.'

'What? How?'

'We've found him.'

Caught off-guard by the startling revelation, Riley's brief moment of elation was swiftly followed by an overwhelming urge to make use of the toilet facility.

'Where?' she said. 'I mean, shite! Did he mention me?'

'You've nothing to worry about,' said West. 'He's in the hospital. A bit the worse for wear from roughing it on the streets but he'll survive.'

'Danny? Sleeping rough?'

'Yeah. But you knew that anyway, didn't you? After all, you pointed him out to Drennan.'

With enough subconscious signals to make a body language expert blush, Riley, following a fleeting glance, a casual sniff, and a subtle cough, stared at West and brushed imaginary fluff from her thighs.

'That's rubbish,' she said. 'I told you before, I've not seen Danny in ages so how could I know he was sleeping rough?'

Exhausted by Riley's recalcitrant behaviour, West took a deep breath, slipped her hands into her pockets, and pushed herself off the door.

'You know what, Miss Riley?' she said, as she began pacing the width of the cell. 'There comes a point in everyone's life when they have to admit defeat. For Napoleon it was Waterloo. For the Jacobites it was Culloden. And for you, it's Wallacetown. Whitletts Road to be precise. That's where we got the dashcam footage of you leaving the supermarket and handing McIntyre a twenty pound note–'

'That wasn't Danny,' said Riley, 'that was just some tramp.'

'–and inside that twenty pound note was a top-up voucher for a mobile phone. How do we know this? Because McIntyre has the note and the voucher in his wallet. Now, here's the score. In a few minutes' time you'll be on your way to court and instead of getting the sentence you deserve you'll probably get off with a slap on the wrist because I've mentioned how co-operative you've been throughout the course of this inquiry, but here's the thing – it's not too late for me to change my mind. I can make sure you get the maximum sentence possible. So, last chance, why was McIntyre sleeping rough and why were you giving him vouchers for a mobile phone?'

Alarmed at the thought of returning to an over-crowded prison where the only way to avoid being locked in a cell for thirteen, fourteen, or fifteen hours a day was to take a job in the laundry or the kitchens or sign up for an Open University course in chemistry, computing, or social science, Riley, without even a visit from friends or family to look forward to, relented for the sake of her own well-being.

'It was his idea,' she said, glumly. 'He said he had to keep his head down, keep a low profile, and slumming it was the perfect disguise.'

'Oh, come off it!' said West. 'At this time of year? No wonder he's in the bleeding hospital, he should've bought himself a balaclava. Why didn't he stay at your place, or check into a hotel?'

'In case he was spotted,' said Riley. 'He said if questions were asked then he could be traced.'

'He's bonkers,' said West. 'Stark raving bonkers. So tell me, if you wanted him out of your life so much, why were you keeping him sweet?'

'Like the saying goes, keep your friends close, but keep your enemies closer.'

'So what exactly were you doing for him?'

'Not that much, really. I'd take him food and drink, get his phone credit sorted, that kind of thing.'

'Am I missing something here?' said West. 'You said McIntyre was Mr Flash, he liked his cars and his jewellery, he liked to make his presence known, so why did he feel the urge to keep his head down?'

Riley glanced at West and shrugged her shoulders.

'Someone took a dislike to him.'

'Who?'

'I don't know who exactly. Just someone.'

'Well it's obviously someone he saw as a threat.'

'Aye, you could say that.'

'I'm waiting.'

'Look,' said Riley with a sigh, 'all I know is someone was after him.'

'Why?'

'He'd started peddling gear on somebody else's patch. He was scared.'

'McIntyre? Scared? I'm surprised.'

'I'm not,' said Riley. 'Let's face it, Danny was small fry compared to these fellas.'

'And that's what I'm struggling with here,' said West. 'You see, even the dumbest of criminals knows you don't go treading on someone else's toes, you don't try and muscle in on their territory. He's not that stupid, so why did he do it?'

'Desperation,' said Riley. 'He was skint. He needed the money.'

'And is that why he was hounding your pal, Rebecca Barlow?'

'I don't know anything about that.'

'Oh, stop playing games!' said West. 'I'm beginning to lose my patience!'

'It's the truth! Listen, I know the two of them had a thing going back in Carlisle and when they split up he was like a dog without a bone, he'd not leave her alone.'

'Is that why he helped her out? To keep close?'

'He said he knew the market better than she ever would. He used to go see properties with her but I don't know anything about the money you're talking about. Really.'

West paused for moment, stared at Riley's swollen, red eyes, and sighed.

'Alright,' she said. 'I believe you.' 'Alright,' she said. 'I believe you.'

'That's a first.'

'Right. Let's go back a bit because there's something else that's not quite adding up. McIntyre's in the hospital, he looks a state because he's got a touch of hypothermia but for someone who claims to be homeless, he's remarkably clean. There's not an ounce of dirt on the bloke, in fact, he doesn't even have grubby fingernails so he must've been going somewhere for a good scrub-up. Where was it? Was he going to your place?'

Riley took a deep breath and hung her head in her hands.

'MacDuff's house,' she said, softly. 'He used to pop into MacDuff's house when he was out but…'

'But what?'

'He stopped. He stopped doing that when…'

Rattled by Riley's inexplicably poignant pause, West suddenly stopped pacing the floor as a flash of realisation smacked her in the face like a gardener stepping on an upturned rake.

'You knew, didn't you?' she said as a smile crept across her face. 'You knew MacDuff was dead. No. Hang on, let me rephrase that. You knew MacDuff had been murdered.'

Riley, unusually still, simply nodded.

'Was it McIntyre?'

'Aye.'

'Why?'

'He was afraid MacDuff might shoot his mouth off.'

'About what?' said West. 'His dodgy dealing habits?'

'No. Worse.'

'Well, what could be worse?' said West. 'He's got some nutter coming after him for… hold on. It's Barlow, isn't it? Are you saying McIntyre killed Rebecca Barlow as well?'

'Aye. He did.'

'Why?'

'Same reason,' said Riley. 'Money.'

West slid down the wall and squatted on her haunches.

'Bloody hell,' she said, 'no wonder you've been wanting him off your back. You must have been crapping yourself.'

'Aye. So now you know.'

'And that's why you paid Drennan to give him a good hiding? To scare him off?'

'It was worth a try.'

Feeling a pang of sympathy for the put-upon Riley, West gave her a moment to compose herself before continuing.

'You've known McIntyre long enough,' she said, 'in all that time has he ever been violent to anyone? Anyone at all.'

'The occasional punch-up at the football,' said Riley, 'but nothing else. Nothing I know of. I think his tablets calmed him down.'

'That's what worries me,' said West, 'because he's not had them for a while. Right, you wait here, I'll be back in ten, then you're coming with me.'

'Where to?'

'The interview room. We're going to do this all over again and don't even think of holding back or changing your story because if you do, I'll charge you with art and part in the murders of Barlow and MacDuff and if you're found guilty then trust me, your sentence will be as long as McIntyre's.'

Chapter 22

With nothing but the tick of a clock and the rustle of a newspaper to punctuate the idyllic silence, the office – despite the lack of an open fire or the scent of a vintage Pauillac breathing on the sideboard – had the tranquil ambience of a members-only gentlemen's club.

Attributing his new-found fondness of a peaceful working environment to either a natural part of the ageing process or the onset of chronic hyperacusis, Duncan – who'd battered his ear drums with more decibels than a jumbo jet as a younger man – completed the report for the fiscal, sipped his tea, and nearly fell off his chair as West, arriving with the grace of a gas explosion, blew through the door.

'Bloody hell,' she said, 'it's like a flipping morgue in here!'

Munro closed his paper, looked to the door, and sighed.

'Never underestimate the quiet folk,' he said, 'no-one ever planned a murder out loud.'

'Is Dougal back yet?'

'No,' said Duncan, bluntly. 'Where have you been?'

'Downstairs with Riley.'

'Again?'

'I had to,' said West. 'Breaking news, our friendly tramp in the hospital *is* McIntyre and wait for it… he's our man! He's the one who…'

'Take a breath!' said Munro as he returned his spectacles to his pocket. 'Now then, Charlie, in a clear and concise manner, what on earth are you havering about?'

'Riley spilt the beans,' said West. 'McIntyre was on skid row, he lost everything when his little property empire went bust, that's when he fell back on his dealing to eke out some kind of a living.'

'Aye, no offence, miss,' said Duncan, 'but that's yesterday's news.'

'Hear me out,' said West. 'When he failed to rake in the cash he needed, he decided to spread his wings and tried dealing a little farther afield but he over-stepped the mark and ended up crossing swords with some bloke a bit bigger than himself. That's why he ducked out of sight, he didn't fancy staring down the barrel of a shotgun.'

'There's nothing wrong with a little self-preservation,' said Munro. 'Longevity is to be embraced.'

'Maybe,' said West, 'but when his drug-dealing rival put the kybosh on his plans he went after Rebecca Barlow to get the rest of his cash back and when that wasn't happening, he topped her.'

'Is that not a bit extreme?' said Duncan. 'Could he not have taken an IOU?'

'Not when he was on amitriptyline,' said West, 'and he was taking plenty of it.'

'Amitriptyline?' said Munro. 'Is that not used for treating depression?'

'Aye, it is,' said Duncan, 'and it'll mince your head, too. Did Riley tell you that, miss?'

'Nope. The nurse at the hospital.'

'So our pal, McIntyre, is a closet psycho?'

'I'm not sure we can say that anymore but that's pretty much the gist of it, yeah. And that's why Riley's been cacking herself, in case he turned on her. That's why she paid Drennan to give him a good kicking, she was hoping it'd be enough to make him disappear.'

Recognising West's desire to utter the phrase 'case closed', Munro, not wanting to dampen her enthusiasm, was nonetheless compelled to ask the inevitable.

'Apart from Miss Riley's testimony, Charlie, do you have the evidence to back this up?'

'Not yet, Jimbo, but we soon will have. Dougal's taking care of it now.'

'How, exactly?'

'We've got a set of unidentified prints at Barlow's place, right? If we match those to McIntyre, then bingo, we're there.'

'So you've taken his prints?'

'Not exactly,' said West, 'he wasn't in any fit state and besides, we didn't have the kit with us, but we did get the next best thing.'

'Oh?'

'A plastic beaker from his bedside cabinet.'

'You mean you took it?'

'Of course not! It just sort of fell into my pocket–'

'You've been with Duncan too long.'

'–and Dougal's taken it to Kay for dusting. We should have them up on the system soon.'

Munro stood, straightened his tie, and checked his watch.

'I should inform DI Byrne,' he said, 'this'll be the feather in his cap he's so desperately been needing but unfortunately for you, Charlie, it still leaves the riddle of MacDuff unsolved.'

'That's where you're wrong,' said West, beaming. 'The same unidentified prints were found at MacDuff's place too, remember? According to Riley, he knocked him off as well.'

'And what would his motive be?' said Munro. 'I'm assuming MacDuff wasnae indebted to him financially?'

'You're right, he wasn't, but MacDuff knew what McIntyre had done and wanted to distance himself from him. That's why he nicked Barlow's phone and wiped all the messages. McIntyre, however, wasn't taking any risks. He knew they had a history and he was worried MacDuff might blab if he was questioned so he polished him off.'

'The fella's demented,' said Duncan.

'That's one way of putting it. Right, I can't stand here gassing all day, I've got to get Riley on tape so, Duncan, I need you to get over to the hospital and arrest McIntyre.'

'Roger that, miss.'

'And listen, he's not well enough to travel so we'll need uniform on the door until he's back on his feet, got that? We certainly don't want him going anywhere.'

'No bother,' said Duncan, 'I'll sort it on the way. Chief, are you up for a ride?'

* * *

Whether through bravery, stupidity, or a misplaced sense of invincibility, James Munro, during his varied and often precarious career, had pulled dismembered bodies from railway lines, tracked down serial killers, and courageously confronted armed criminals in the belief that he would triumph over adversity but if there was one thing, apart from vegetables or curry, that was guaranteed to instil a sense of fear, it was anywhere with the word 'infirmary' by the entrance.

With an elevated BP and slow, measured strides he followed Duncan tentatively through the automatic doors and reeled at the abundance of lilies positioned around the foyer which, he mused, were more suited to adorning a headstone rather than welcoming visitors to a place of recovery.

'Don't worry, chief,' said Duncan as they approached the desk, 'you'll not be leaving by the back door.'

'Dinnae count your chickens,' said Munro, 'one slip on a hastily discarded sterile wipe and they could be fighting over my organs before you can say haggis supper.'

The lady on reception, trying not to flinch at Duncan's dishevelled state, glanced around the lobby in search of security and smiled nervously.

'Hello,' she said. 'Can I help?'

'Alright, hen?' said Duncan, waving his warrant card. 'We're here to see a patient of yours, a Mr Daniel McIntyre. He's in the ICU.'

'Okay,' said the lady, sighing with relief. 'Bear with me and I'll fetch someone for you.'

* * *

Derek Fisher, too tired to make it across the hall for a formal introduction, waved from the end of the corridor and beckoned them over.

'Are you anything to do with the two officers who were here this morning?'

'We are indeed,' said Duncan. 'DS Reid, and this is James Munro. How's he doing?'

'Aye, okay,' said Fisher. 'He's responding well to treatment and he's been resting all day which is what he needs just now.'

'What was his condition like,' said Munro, 'when they brought him in?'

'Just as you'd expect with hypothermia. He looks worse than he is, but it's nothing to worry about. Human skin has a great habit of repairing itself.'

'Right enough,' said Munro, 'it's a shame the bits on the inside cannae do the same.'

'Right, that's you,' said Fisher pointing at the door. 'Don't be long, I'll wait for you here.'

No stranger to the paraphernalia used to keep someone in the land of the living, Munro was struck not by the stack of monitors displaying the patient's vital signs, nor by the ventilator, the IV lines, or the pillows which, as he recalled, were as comfortable as a sack of cement, but by the unusual silence and the empty bed.

Unlike Dougal who would have panicked at the thought of losing a suspect, or West who would have turned the air blue with expletives as she demanded to know who was in charge, Munro simply turned to Duncan and shrugged his shoulders.

'He's probably gone to fetch himself a brew from the canteen.'

'Aye,' said Duncan, 'or maybe he's in the gents. I'll find security and take a look at the CCTV.'

'Right you are,' said Munro. 'I'll have a wee word with the nurse and get you in reception.'

* * *

Barely blinking as Duncan breezed down the corridor, a distraught Derek Fisher sat staring at the opposite wall, his mind awash with thoughts of defending an allegation of negligence and more worryingly how he'd tell his wife that he'd been suspended pending the results of a full investigation.

Munro, hands clasped behind his back, stood to one side and proffered a reassuring smile.

'The look on your face,' he said, 'is that fatigue or fear?'

'Both,' said Fisher. 'If I have to face disciplinary sanctions for this, that's me humped. No job, no pay, no wife.'

'Och, dinnae fret,' said Munro, 'it's not your fault.'

'That's not how they'll see it.'

'Nonsense. You've obviously been in the job a wee while, has anything like this ever happened before?'

'Not on my watch. I've got a clean sheet,' said Fisher. 'I've never put a foot wrong.'

'Well there you are, then. If anything you'll get a written warning and everything will be back to normal.'

'I wish that were true.'

'The gentleman who's disappeared, have you any idea who he is?'

'Aye! Of course. His name's McIntyre!'

'Sorry, I didnae phrase that correctly,' said Munro. 'What I meant was, have you any idea what he's done?'

'Done? You've lost me,' said Fisher, 'I thought he was the victim here.'

'Aye, of course he is. I'm wondering,' said Munro, 'how did he manage to leave his bed without being noticed?'

'It's not difficult,' said Fisher, 'I mean, we can't watch him twenty-four-seven. A wee check in-between meals, that's about it.'

'Was he not hooked up to a heart monitor or some other piece of equipment?'

'He was, aye.'

'Surely that would have made a sound if he took his wires off?'

'Ordinarily, aye, unless they were switched off first and as you can see, the screen's blank so I'm guessing that's exactly what he did.'

'So he was fit enough to do that?'

'It doesn't take much to pull a plug, does it? It's not as if he was an invalid or incapacitated, just cold and tired.'

'I see the bedside cabinet's open, did he have anything in there?'

'Aye, not much, just a phone and a wallet and he's obviously taken them with him.'

'Well he'd not get far without them,' said Munro. 'Listen, I've taken up too much of your time already, I apologise for all the questions, I didnae mean to give you a grilling.'

'You're alright,' said Fisher, 'you've got your job to do. I just hope you're better at it than I am.'

* * *

Mystified as to why anyone in their right mind would choose to stand in the freezing cold rather than the warmth of a foyer or a patrol car, PC Clive Mullen, an opinionated thirty-year-old with more attitude than aptitude, shivered outside the hospital as he waited with Munro for Duncan to arrive.

'The fella inside,' he said, 'is he an armed robber or something?'

'No,' said Munro. 'He is not.'

'It's pure Baltic out here. Are you sure I can't fetch us a drink? A hot cup of tea, maybe?'

'No.'

'I don't agree with experienced officers like myself being used for jobs like this, we should be on the front line. If you asked me, they should have sent you a Special. You're not one for a blether, are you?'

Munro turned to Mullen and scowled.

'With the amount of hot air coming out of your mouth, it's no surprise you're feeling the cold. Now wheesht!'

'Seven minutes past one,' said Duncan as he barged through the door and joined them outside. 'He didn't hang around. He came here, cut across the car park, and turned left up the street.'

'Sorry,' said Mullen, 'I'm not being funny but should I not be inside?'

'Aye, you should,' said Duncan, 'but not anymore. I'll be with you in a minute.'

'Right, no bother. Just as long as I know where I stand.'

'It'll be out here if you dinnae show some respect for a senior officer, I'll not tell you again,' said Munro. 'Duncan, you were saying?'

'Unless he's a fitness fanatic, he'll not get far on foot, it's miles into town, he'll be needing the bus.'

'I cannae see him doing that,' said Munro. 'If he'd booked a taxi, it could have met him on the street.'

'Aye, right enough. You, what's your name?'

'Mullen. Sir.'

'I need you to ring the local taxi firms and see if anyone did a pick-up here between one-ten and one-thirty. There's a place in Doonfoot, not ten minutes' drive away, start there. The passenger's about five-ten, scruffy with a bushy beard.'

Gritting his teeth as Mullen wandered towards his car, Duncan glanced at Munro and shook his head.

'He'd not last five minutes if he was with me,' he said, 'the fella needs a belt up the bahookie.'

'If I'm not mistaken,' said Munro with a grin, 'you've had a few of those yourself.'

'Aye, and I've still got the bruises. Just a thought, chief, if McIntyre did jump a taxi, how would he pay for it?'

'He's got his phone and his wallet,' said Munro, 'the problem you've got is finding out where he went.'

'Well, he'd not go to Riley's or MacDuff's, that's for sure, so there's only one place he could go, and that's back to Carlisle.'

'You're not thinking like a killer,' said Munro, 'at the risk of sounding like a cliché, there is most definitely somewhere else he could go. Somewhere nobody would think of looking for him.'

'Oh, you're not suggesting that old chestnut about returning to the scene of the crime, are you?'

'It's a compulsion criminals have. Besides, he'd know the police would be long gone by now, he knows how to get in, it's warm and dry, and there's probably food in the fridge.'

'Aye, maybe,' said Duncan, 'but a taxi? He'd have to be daft.'

'How so?'

'You know as well as I do, chief, it'd take him at least an hour and a half, not to mention a couple of hundred quid.'

Duncan rolled his eyes as Mullen stepped from the car and paused to check his phone.

'Ho! You! Are you familiar with the phrase "a sense of urgency"?'

'Aye okay, just coming,' said Mullen. 'It's the lads, they're meeting in the Black Bull later. I was just saying I might be late.'

'Carry on like this and there's a good chance you might not make it at all. So?'

'You were right about the cab company. They picked your man up on the main road.'

'And where did they take him?'

'Kilmarnock.'

'Did you get the address?'

'The train station.'

'And did he go inside or wander off?'

'No idea,' said Mullen. 'I didn't ask.'

'They've cameras there,' said Duncan, 'but it's too late for that. If he did board a train then he has to be heading south. Constable Mullen, do something useful and check the train times from Kilmarnock to Carlisle. Now!'

Of the opinion that logic and intuition were not mutually exclusive but rather the strangest of bedfellows, Munro, a skilled oarsman when it came to paddling his own canoe, reached for his phone and scrolled through the list of contacts.

'Are you calling Westy?' said Duncan.

'No, no. DI Byrne. It's an hour by train to Dumfries. Too late for a welcoming party, I'll give you that, but he could meet us in Auchencairn. Unless, of course, you fancy a wee drive across the border?'

'No, you're alright, chief. I'll come with you. Just give me a minute to–'

As a firm believer in the tenet that manners maketh the man, Munro, though riled by the constable's irreverent behaviour, politely refrained from commenting as he interrupted their conversation.

'There was a train at 13:51,' said Mullen, 'that arrived into Carlisle at 15:40–'

'If he was on that,' said Munro, 'he'd be long gone by now.'

'–and the next was at 14:28, that gets in at 16:47.'

'Then we're in with a shout,' said Duncan. 'Right, Mullen, that's you away. Chief, let's go. I need to make a quick call.'

Munro slipped into the passenger seat and buckled-up as Duncan clipped his phone into the dashmount and fired up the Audi.

'Dougal,' he said, 'are you back in the office, pal?'

'Aye, we're waiting on McIntyre's fingerprints to appear on the system, should be any second now. What's up?'

'I need BTP at Carlisle station, quick as you like.'

'No bother, but why British Transport Police?'

'There's a chance McIntyre might be on the next train from Kilmarnock, it gets in at ten to five.'

'Jeez-oh, that's tight! Leave it to me but don't hang up, someone's wanting a word.'

'Where the bloody hell are you two?' said West, bellowing down the phone.

'Where do you think, miss? Following your instructions to arrest McIntyre.'

'So is he still laid up, or is he fit to travel?'

'Oh, he's fit to travel,' said Duncan. 'No doubt about that.'

'So are you bringing him in?'

'That's a negative, miss. He's taken himself off.'

'What?'

'He's gone. Done a bunk. Had it away.'

Duncan glanced at Munro, smiled, and rolled his eyes at the momentary silence.

'Well, he can't go far,' said West, 'he hasn't got a flipping car!'

'No, he hasnae,' said Munro, 'but he does have money and a phone. He took a taxi to the station and he's heading south.'

'Well, if you're heading for Carlisle, Jimbo, you'll have to get your own supper.'

'Relax, Charlie, we're not going to Carlisle, we're going to Auchencairn.'

'Come again?'

'The old Commercial Hotel, it's the perfect place to hide.'

'For crying out loud! Have you lost the plot?'

Not normally given to sudden outbursts of emotion, Dougal, unable to contain his excitement, leapt to his feet and yelled across the room.

'Miss!' he said, his eyes glued to the screen. 'He's right!'

'What?'

'The boss, I think he's right! The prints we lifted from the beaker, they're a positive for those in Barlow's place!'

'Oh, for God's sake,' said West, 'what's the big deal? It's just what we've been hoping for, isn't it?'

'Aye, but they're not a match to Daniel McIntyre, he's not on the system, they're a match to Daniel Cassidy!'

'Well, who the bloody hell is Daniel Cassidy?'

'If I'm not mistaken,' said Munro, 'he's Barbara Muir's brother.'

'Spot on,' said Dougal.

'Somebody fill me in,' said West, 'I feel like I'm losing my mind.'

'Barbara Muir was adopted, right?'

'Yeah?'

'Her birth name is Cassidy. She was pulled from the wreckage of the train crash with just two other survivors, her brother and an adult male. Her brother was adopted too.'

'But not by the Muirs? Is that what you're saying?'

'Correct, miss. He was taken in by a family in Carlisle.'

'Well how come he's got a record?' said West. 'If he's on the system, he must have done something.'

'Daniel Cassidy was arrested after a brawl outside a pub under Section 38, what we used to call Breach of the Peace. He was twenty-seven years old and gave his birth name, not his adopted one.'

'So,' said West, 'maybe going to the old Commercial isn't so bonkers after all? Maybe he's going to see his sister?'

'Welcome aboard,' said Munro. 'We'll call you later, Charlie. In the meantime, if you're quick, you'll just catch the butcher on the High Street. I'll take a sirloin, please.'

Chapter 23

As an incurable urbanite who craved the clamour of a crowded curry house, the convenience of late-night shopping, and the safety of a well-lit street, DI Byrne – already unsettled by a pitch black night and the distant rumble of the raging burn – jumped at the hoot of a tawny owl and raced back to his car where, fearful of an attack by a feral predator, he locked the doors and sat with his thumb poised above the speed dial button on his phone until the welcoming glare of oncoming headlights bathed him in relief.

Zipping his coat, he stepped from the car as Munro, tickled by his wan complexion, crunched across the gravel to greet him.

'Mr Byrne,' he said, smiling, 'you look like you've seen a ghost.'

'I'm not used to the countryside,' said Byrne, 'I'm hearing things I've never heard before.'

'Och, relax. There's nothing here to harm you.'

'Are you sure?'

'Well, you might get a wee nip from an adder if you dinnae watch your feet, and there's a chance you might get trampled by a herd of cows, or you might pick up a tick or two, but apart from that it's a feast for the senses.'

'If it's all the same with you, Mr Munro, I prefer my feast on a plate, thank you very much. Have you not got your dog with you?'

'Aye, he's on the back seat,' said Munro, 'and he's brought a pal with him. This is Detective Sergeant Reid.'

'Alright?' said Duncan. 'I take it you're not the nocturnal type.'

'I am not,' said Byrne. 'I like to see what I'm doing. Before we go any further, I should thank you, Mr Munro, and no doubt you too, Sergeant, for all your help.'

'Och, away,' said Munro. 'You'd have got there in the end. It may have taken you a year or two but you'd have got there all the same.'

'So McIntyre's definitely our man?'

'Aye, it would appear so,' said Duncan, 'you'll get the details soon enough.'

'And you think he's here?'

'I do,' said Munro. 'We'll check the old Commercial first and if he's not there, then there's one last place we can try.'

'Sorry,' said Byrne, 'the Commercial? Why would he go back there?'

'Because,' said Munro, 'it's the last place someone like yourself would look for him.'

'Thanks for that. There's nothing like a wee confidence boost to get you going.'

'Dinnae take it the wrong way, you're in good company. Now, as this is your territory perhaps you should be the one making the arrest.'

'No, no. I'll not steal your thunder,' said Byrne. 'If he's responsible for MacDuff as well, then he's all yours. After all, I'd not be here if it wasn't for you.'

'As you wish. In that case we'll leave it up to DS Reid to do the honours. Right, we'll not want to draw attention to ourselves so you walk on ahead and we'll get you by the hotel.'

* * *

Had he been in the town then choosing to sit on a bench beneath the glow of a street lamp like a lovestruck Lothario waiting for his date, a distrait DI Byrne may have gone unnoticed but in a small village where privacy was at a premium, the incongruous figure drew nothing but suspicion from the locals.

Unnerved by the curious gaze of an elderly gent walking his dog and the twitching curtains in the house across the square, he ducked down the darkened path to the side of the Commercial as Duncan and Munro approached at a leisurely pace.

'The place looks haunted,' he said. 'Will we try somewhere else?'

'Calm your jets,' said Duncan, 'I've a crucifix in my pocket if you want to borrow it.'

'But he's not here!' said Byrne, anxiously. 'There's no lights on!'

'Och, he'll not turn the lights on, will he?' said Munro. 'Dear God, if you cannae think straight, Mr Byrne, perhaps you should wait in the car.'

'No, you're alright. I'll stick with you.'

Duncan turned the latch on the gate and gave it a hearty shove.

'It's locked from the inside,' he said as he hauled himself over the top, 'but no bother. I'll be back in a jiff.'

Byrne shuffled nervously on the spot and glanced towards the square.

'I'm reminded of that song,' he said. '*The Night Has a Thousand Eyes*.'

'It's not the eyes I'd worry about, if I were you,' said Munro. 'It's the teeth.'

'I'll give you this, Mr Munro, you certainly know how to put a man at ease.'

'I do my best.'

'So, McIntyre. What really makes you think he'd come back here?'

'He's a relative down the way,' said Munro. 'A sister. They were separated as weans so I'll be frank, this may come to nothing. Nothing at all.'

'Well if that's the case, have you any idea where he may have gone?'

'Aye. The family home in Carlisle, which means you'll have to liaise with the Cumbria Constabulary. Duncan will give you the address if it comes to that.'

Byrne flicked his head as Duncan appeared from the front of the hotel.

'All clear,' he said. 'The place is empty.'

'How did you get in?' said Byrne. 'Without a key?'

'Trade secret. So, what's next, chief?'

'Barbara Muir,' said Munro, 'but we dinnae want to look like a heavy-handed mob come to repossess her car so, Mr Byrne, I suggest you keep your distance while Duncan and I have a wee chat.'

* * *

Unlike the suited city dwellers who thrived on the pressure of working to impossible deadlines, racing to pointless meetings, or gambling on the fortunes of a multinational corporation, Barbara Muir, whose only concern was what to cook for her tea, enjoyed a comparatively stress-free existence.

Settled in front of the TV with a jigsaw on her lap, a tin of shortbread by her side, and a cottage pie in the oven, she raised her head at the sound of the bell and, with visitors to the house something of a rarity, hurried downstairs and opened the door.

'Oh, James! This is a surprise! Are you okay?'

'Aye, remarkably well,' said Munro. 'And yourself?'

'I'm fine! I'm always fine! Wait just a wee moment and I'll fetch the keys.'

'Keys?'

'Aye, for the shop. You'll be wanting some milk, I imagine. Or is it teabags you're after?'

'No, no, I've not come for the shop,' said Munro, 'I'm here with a colleague. This is Detective Sergeant Reid.'

'Sergeant? So you're not a journalist after all–'

'I never said I was.'

'–you're the police?'

'Retired. Aye.'

'Well, what on earth would you be wanting with me?'

'It's not you we've come to see,' said Munro. 'It's Daniel.'

As the smile dropped and the laughter lines disappeared, Barbara Muir was left with a remarkably smooth if somewhat blank expression.

'I take it he's here?' said Munro.

'Aye. You'd best come in.'

McIntyre, resting in an armchair and looking much the worse for wear, glanced up as they entered the lounge, took a deep breath, and offered a resigned smile.

'Where's the two that came earlier?' he said.

'They've other fish to fry,' said Munro. 'How are you feeling?'

'I'm fair shattered,' said McIntyre. 'And I could do with my meds.'

'Well, I'm not a doctor,' said Munro, 'but you've probably done yourself more harm than good leaving the hospital like that.'

'Right enough. I don't know why I did it. I should've stayed put.'

'I dare say you panicked. We're fight or flight by instinct and you were in no state to do the former.'

'I'm in no state to do the latter either,' said McIntyre. 'I guess, as they say, the game's a bogey.'

'You give up too easily,' said Duncan, trying to lighten the mood. 'We've not even said why we're here.'

McIntyre looked at Duncan and smiled.

'Rebecca and Alan,' he said. 'Am I right?'

'Spot on.'

'There you go then.'

'Would you like to talk about it?'

'Here? Then do it all again at the station? No, no, once is enough. Let's go. Barbara, I'm sorry, hen. I'm sure these fellas will tell you where I am.'

'I will indeed,' said Munro. 'In fact, I'll be back in the morning, if that's okay with you?'

'Aye, no bother. I'll not be going anywhere.'

'Sorry,' said Duncan, 'but I'm obliged to do this by the book. I am Detective Sergeant Reid. Daniel McIntyre, I'm arresting you under Section 1 of the Criminal Justice Act on suspicion of the murders of Miss Rebecca Barlow and Mr Alan MacDuff. The reason for your arrest is that I suspect you have committed an offence and I believe that keeping you in custody is necessary and proportionate for the purposes of bringing you before a court or otherwise dealing with you in accordance with the law. Do you understand?'

'Aye, all good,' said McIntyre. 'My coat's in the hall.'

'You are not obliged to say anything but anything you do say will be noted and may be used in evidence. You have the right to have a solicitor informed of your arrest and to have access to a solicitor. Okay?'

'I'll not bother,' said McIntyre as he dragged himself from the chair. 'As far as I'm concerned you can lock me up and throw away the key. I deserve it.'

Chapter 24

Lacking the patience of the enlightened and with it the proclivity to indulge in a spot of yoga, mindfulness, or meditation to bring some order to the muddle in her head, West – still grappling with the convoluted complexities of the chain linking Riley, Barlow, MacDuff, and McIntyre – distracted herself with thoughts of lying sprawled in front of an open fire with a Balvenie in her hand and the smell of a home-cooked pie wafting from the kitchen until her daydream was dashed by Dougal's dire plea to call it a day.

'No sweat,' she said. 'There's no point in the two of us hanging around. You get going and I'll wait for them to get back.'

'I'd not normally ask,' said Dougal, 'but Kay's bringing a fish supper and I'm not keen on cold chips.'

'You're too fussy,' said West. 'I'd have them hot, cold, and anywhere in between.'

'I thought you two would have been long gone by now,' said Duncan as he booted open the door.

'How'd it go?'

'Success, but we're not done yet. McIntyre's downstairs, he's getting the once over from the doctor before I charge him.'

'I'll come with you,' said West. 'I can't let you do all the donkey work.'

'It'll not take him long,' said Munro, 'the poor fellow's just about ready to throw in the towel.'

'You mean he's not putting up a fight? Not even going to defend himself?'

'No, he is not. The man needs his medication and despite his protestations we've instructed the duty solicitor to attend, and if he does his job properly then he'll be entering a plea of diminished responsibility so if he is found guilty it will be for culpable homicide and not murder.'

'You sound like you've warmed to him,' said West. 'I must admit, he was quite the charmer when we saw him in the hospital.'

'Och, he's not a bad chap,' said Munro, 'he just cannae handle what goes on in his head.'

'I know how that feels.'

'You should take yourself off, miss,' said Duncan. 'You look shattered.'

'I look like this every day.'

'I rest my case.'

Conscious of the fact that his looming fatigue was down to a lack of sustenance rather than the intricacies of the inquiry, Munro, stifling a yawn, glanced around the office in search of a carrier bag emblazoned with a familiar logo.

'Did you manage to get to the butcher?' he said. 'If Murdo and I dinnae eat something soon, you'll have two more bodies to deal with.'

'Don't panic,' said West, 'I've got two of Scotland's finest sitting in the car.'

'Then take Duncan's advice and grab your coat. Duncan, are you sure you'll be okay?'

'Aye, no bother, chief. I'll get this wrapped up and I'll be on my way in no time. We can a get a report to the fiscal in the morning.'

* * *

In need of a hot bath, a good shave, and a decent night's sleep, McIntyre, sipping coffee from a plastic cup, glanced at Duncan as he entered the room and scratched his beard.

'I said I'd not bother with a solicitor. You've got this fella out for nothing.'

'It's for the best,' said Duncan. 'You're under no obligation to take his advice and he's not here to defend you. Right, the time is 19:22 and I am Detective Sergeant Reid. For the benefit of the tape, would you state your name please.'

'Aye, it's Dan. Daniel McIntyre.'

'Also present is the duty solicitor, Mr John Mercer. Mr McIntyre, do you understand why you're here?'

'I do.'

'Good, then let's crack on, shall we?'

'Aye, on you go,' said McIntyre. 'You ask and I'll answer.'

'Rebecca Barlow. You used to work together, is that right?'

'Spot on. A long time ago, mind, but yes, I gave her a job.'

'Doing what exactly?'

'Selling property. I used to own an estate agency.'

'And she was good at the job?'

'Aye, too good. She had a talent for it.'

'And is that why she left to set up her own business?'

'Correct,' said McIntyre, 'but not as a competitor. She had a knack of spotting potential in a property so she'd do them up and sell them on.'

'And you helped her get started?'

'I did. She was a lovely wee girl. She deserved to succeed so I helped her out, financially that is.'

'But then things didn't go so well for you, did they?' said Duncan. 'I understand your business went under.'

'It sank without a trace,' said McIntyre. 'The market crashed and that was me humped.'

'So you went after Miss Barlow to try and get your money back?'

'Aye, only she didn't have it. She'd paid back some but I was desperate, I needed the rest.'

'And when she said she couldn't pay you back, what did you do?'

McIntyre ruffled his hair and sighed.

'I flipped,' he said. 'I lost my temper. I didn't mean to but I'm not, what is it they say? I'm not right in the head.'

'How long have you been on medication?'

'A while,' said McIntyre. 'A long while.'

'And without it, you have a tendency to lose your temper, is that right?'

'Aye, but it's not intentional. It just happens. I can't control it. I can't even see it coming.'

'So when Miss Barlow said you'd have to whistle for your cash, you lost it?'

McIntyre paused, glanced across the table at Mercer, and declined his advice to keep quiet.

'I did,' he said. 'I was raging.'

'How did you kill her?'

'I didn't mean to. I was angry. I had her by the neck. I was squeezing. The next thing I know she falls to the ground like a sack of potatoes.'

'And then?'

'I got the fear,' said McIntyre. 'I left. I got as far as Dalbeattie and pulled over. I was panicking. I was thinking, what if somebody found her. What if somebody saw me leave.'

'The village is deserted at the best of times,' said Duncan. 'Chances are no-one would have seen you.'

'Maybe, but that's not how your mind works, is it? Then I thought of Alan.'

'Alan MacDuff?'

'Aye. I knew he'd been working at the Commercial and I knew he'd be back. I knew he could drop me in it.'

'I'm not across your reasoning,' said Duncan. 'Even if Mr MacDuff had gone back, how could he know you'd done it?'

'Because I told him,' said McIntyre. 'Not that I was going to kill her, that was spur of the moment, but that I was going to see her.'

'Why tell MacDuff? How was that any of his business?'

'Because if she didn't have the cash, I'd have to let him go. Kick him out of the flat. I had nowhere to stay and if that wasn't bad enough, some nutter with a shotgun was on my heels.'

'And I take it Mr MacDuff wasn't exactly enamoured with your plans?'

'He most certainly was not,' said McIntyre. 'He was fizzing.'

'That's gratitude for you. Did you not help him out, too?'

'I did, aye.'

'Quite the philanthropist, aren't you?'

'No. I just like to help folk if I can.'

'So you left Dalbeattie and headed for MacDuff's, is that right?'

'No, not right away. I went to Rebecca's place.'

'Why?'

'She had records,' said McIntyre. 'Folk like you would have seen I'd lent her money. Sooner or later you'd have tracked me down.'

'So did you find what you were looking for?'

McIntyre nodded.

'Aye. Bank statements. I burned them.'

'I have to say, Mr McIntyre, for someone who was in a wee bit of a panic, you were thinking incredibly straight.'

'I'm not stupid, Sergeant. I have a condition, that's all.'

'Sorry,' said Duncan. 'I didn't mean to offend. So, you left Miss Barlow's house and went to MacDuff's, is that right?'

'Aye.'

'And what happened next?'

'He refused to budge,' said McIntyre. 'I told him what had happened and he said the best thing I could do was hand myself in.'

'I hate to say it,' said Duncan, 'but that was some sage advice.'

'Aye. I get that. With hindsight that's exactly what I should have done.'

'But you didn't, instead you killed him, too.'

McIntyre drained his cup and nodded.

'Only this time it was intentional?'

'I had no choice,' said McIntyre, 'he knew what I'd done. What more can I say?'

'I think you've said it all,' said Duncan. 'Back to Miss Barlow for a minute, did you tell anyone else what you'd done, apart from Mr MacDuff? Any other pals, your sister, maybe?'

'No. No-one.'

'Okay, listen. We'll get you something to eat then you can rest. I'll make sure you're not disturbed until the morning then we'll go over the charge sheet together, is that okay?'

'Aye. Smashing.'

'Mr Mercer, is there anything you'd like to add?'

'Aye, I'd like to get a dossier together for the fiscal, can you give me twenty-four hours?'

'Aye, no bother,' said Duncan. 'What is it you're after?'

'I want to get your full medical history, Mr McIntyre, you're clearly not responsible for what you've done. It seems to me that without your medication your ability to control your actions was severely diminished, that will go in your favour.'

'I'm not fussed either way,' said McIntyre, 'I mean, it'll not bring them back, will it?'

'No. I'm afraid not.'

'Right, one last point,' said Duncan. 'I need you to satisfy my curiosity. After the incident with Mr MacDuff, you just left him lying on the floor, is that correct?'

'Aye. In the kitchen, that's right.'

'Good. Then why did you go to so much trouble with Rebecca Barlow?'

'I'm not with you.'

'Why did you attempt to disguise the body?'

'Sorry, I'm still not with you.'

Duncan pushed back his chair, looked at McIntyre and frowned.

'See here, Mr McIntyre, when Rebecca Barlow was found she was tied to a stake in the gardens of the Commercial Hotel. She was wearing a waterproof coat and a hat that didn't belong to her.'

McIntyre glared at Duncan with a look of utter bewilderment on his face.

'No, no, that's not right,' he said, 'I did no such thing. When I left the hotel Rebecca was lying on the floor by the back door.'

Chapter 25

Of the many tell-tale signs a devoted parent, guardian, or spouse might use to identify a loved one's malaise, for West, though neither married nor maternally inclined, it was the way Munro toyed with his supper like an eight-year-old faced with a plateful of cabbage.

'What's up, Jimbo? You've got that look, and you've not touched your wine.'

'I've a niggle, Charlie. Something's not quite right.'

'What is it?'

'McIntyre. He was at his sister's house.'

'Yeah, I know. Sometimes, I have to say, your instinct creeps me out. So what's the big deal?'

'They were separated at an early age.'

'So?'

'So how did they find each other?'

'Gawd knows,' said West, 'but there's probably hundreds of ways, like that ancestry website, or the adoption register.'

'No disrespect to Miss Muir,' said Munro, 'but I dinnae think she has the wherewithal to tackle something like that.'

'You're slacking, Jimbo, don't forget she opened that bank account then pilfered all the money from her stepmother.'

'No offence,' said Munro as the phone rang, 'but there's a world of difference between entering a string of digits on an application form and searching for a needle in a haystack.'

'Hold on,' said West, 'it's Duncan. You alright, mate?'

'Aye, all good, miss. I've just got to fill out a charge sheet then that's me away. I'll run through it with McIntyre in the morning.'

'Good man,' said West, 'have a lie-in tomorrow, you've earned it.'

'No chance,' said Duncan, 'I've yet to file the report for the fiscal and I have to wait for the solicitor to get back to us, he's getting McIntyre's medical history together.'

'You're heading for an early grave, you are. Anything else?'

'Aye, one for the chief, is he there?'

'Yup, but you'll have to shout.'

'Is there a problem?' said Munro. 'It sounds to me as if you have everything under control.'

'Not so much a problem, chief, more a mystery and it's right up your street.'

'I'm intrigued. Go on.'

'McIntyre's admitted everything, okay? But here's the thing, he says when he left the Commercial, Rebecca Barlow was lying on the floor by the back door.'

Munro set his cutlery on the table and frowned.

'Are you saying what I think you're saying?'

'Aye, he knows nothing about her being trussed up like a scarecrow, and I believe him.'

'Does it matter?' said West. 'After all, he's admitted he killed her. Surely that's all we need.'

'By jiminy, Charlie! Of course it matters!'

'I don't see how.'

'Loose ends, lassie. They have a habit of tripping you up. This investigation's not over yet!'

'Where are you going at this time of night? You haven't finished your supper!'

'There's someone I have to see. Look after Murdo, I'll not be long.'

* * *

Still reeling from her brother's astounding transformation from a handsome high-flyer to a destitute beggar ravaged by hunger and scarred by the cold, Barbara Muir, reluctant to receive any more guests, ignored the persistent rap at the door until the thought of a neighbour confronting her visitors forced her from her chair.

Pulling her gown tight around her waist, she took a deep breath and flung open the door to find Munro, hands clasped behind his back, teetering on the balls of his feet.

'James,' she said, despondently, 'I had a feeling it might be you.'

'I think we need a wee chat, Miss Muir. May I?'

Electing to stand, Munro allowed Muir to make herself comfortable and did his best to offer a reassuring smile.

'It can't have been easy,' he said, 'seeing your brother like that. Are you okay?'

'Aye, I'll get over it. Funny thing is, I'm not sure if I'll recognise him if he shaves that beard off. Can I get you a tea?'

'No, but thanks for the offer.'

'Something a wee bit stronger, perhaps?'

'Not while I'm driving.'

'Of course. Silly me.'

'About Daniel,' said Munro, 'he didnae tell you he was coming, did he?'

'No.'

'So it must have been quite the surprise when he turned up?'

'You're not wrong there,' said Muir, 'although if I'm honest, it was more a shock than a surprise.'

'I'm curious,' said Munro, 'perhaps you can help me out.'

'I'll certainly try.'

'Apart from Daniel mentioning the names "Rebecca" and "Alan", my colleague and I never actually said why we were here.'

'Oh, you're quite right!' said Muir. 'Now I think of it, no, you didn't.'

'And yet you weren't at all surprised that your brother was being arrested. Why is that, I wonder?'

Muir stared at the unfinished jigsaw and said nothing.

'I'll tell you what I think,' said Munro. 'I think you knew exactly why we were here but I need to hear it from you so you can either answer a few questions here or if you'd rather, we can do it more formally.'

'Formally?'

'At the station.'

'No, no,' said Muir. 'Here will do.'

'Good. Now, I know about your brother, Miss Muir. In fact I know everything about him. Where he lived, his occupation, what kind of motor car he drove, I even know that you and he were separated at an early age.'

'That's right,' said Muir. 'We were.'

'And it goes without saying, I'm sorry about the circumstances, they were nothing less than tragic but tell me, after all these years, how on earth did you find him?'

'I didn't. He found me. And I don't mind telling you, I took some convincing when he turned up on the doorstep.'

'I'm sure. When was that, roughly?'

'Oh, seven or eight years ago, I'd say. Maybe more, maybe less.'

'And was he a regular visitor?'

'Not at all,' said Muir. 'Once a year, regular as clockwork, between Christmas and Hogmanay. He'd always bring a card and a wee gift.'

'But this time he made a special trip, did he not? To meet Rebecca Barlow?'

Muir, beginning to feel uncomfortable, glanced furtively at Munro and fiddled with the jigsaw.

'Come, come,' said Munro, 'you know Miss Barlow, she's the one who bought the old Commercial.'

'I know who she is.'

'So Daniel, he went to see her?'

'He did. And he was quite distraught, too. No, not distraught, more *angry*. Aye, angry.'

'And do you know why?'

'Aye of course, he'd lost his business. He said Barlow owed him some money and he was here to collect.'

'Did that not strike you as a bit of a coincidence? Your brother finding an ex-colleague in the house that once belonged to your step-parents?'

'Aye, now you mention it, I suppose it was, but I never gave it much thought. It must be what they call six degrees of separation.'

'I think you might be right,' said Munro. 'So, your brother and Miss Barlow, what happened next?'

'Apparently she didn't have the money. I thought he was talking about a hundred pounds but when he told me how much exactly, I nearly fell off my chair. I told him, it's not as if she's going to be carrying that amount around her handbag. I said he'd have to give her time to arrange a transfer or something, so he went back.'

'To the Commercial?'

'Aye.'

'And then?'

'He came back,' said Muir, 'about a half an hour later. His head was mince, he was shaking, he was all over the place. He told me what had happened. What he'd done. He said he'd burn in hell.'

'So you offered to help?'

Muir nodded.

'I did,' she said. 'I sent him on his way. I told him not to worry, that I'd take care of it.'

'So you dressed her in a coat and hat and propped her up in the garden?'

'I did, aye.'

'What on earth inspired you to do such a thing?' said Munro. 'Was it village folklore? Something to do with the rowan?'

'In a way,' said Muir. 'I'm not capable of digging a grave and when I saw the tree, well, that was the best I could think of.'

Munro eased himself into the armchair, leaned towards Muir, and rubbed his chin.

'Have you any idea how serious this is?' he said, softly. 'Have you any idea at all?'

'Of course, James! I'm not daft, it's murder! He'll be away a long time.'

'I'm not talking about Daniel,' said Munro. 'I'm talking about you.'

'Me? But I've not killed anyone! I've not done anything wrong!'

'On the contrary, Miss Muir, you failed to inform the authorities about a murder you knew had taken place. You failed to inform the authorities of the location of the body. You failed to tell them that you knew who the perpetrator was and, to make matters worse, you made every conceivable effort to disguise the body and cover your brother's tracks. To coin a phrase you're no doubt familiar with, that's what we call perverting the course of justice and the penalty for that could be as severe as the one Daniel's likely to get.'

'Oh dear God!' said Muir. 'Are you joking me?'

'I'm afraid at times like these, my sense of humour deserts me.'

'I thought I was doing the right thing!'

'From where I'm standing, and no offence, you appear to get confused over what's right, and what's wrong.'

'Excuse me?'

'I know about the Commercial,' said Munro. 'I know you struck a deal with Miss Barlow to sell it. And I know you syphoned off the proceeds from your stepmother's account, and I was willing to let that go but this, this I'm afraid, is altogether more serious.'

'So, you're arresting me?'

'No, I cannae do that,' said Munro. 'I'm not a serving officer, that will be up to someone else. You have a choice. I can make a call and have someone pick you up, or if you'd rather not let your neighbours see you leaving in the back of a police car, you can come with me now.'

'Where to?'

'Dumfries. A nice chap by the name of Detective Inspector Byrne will take care of you.'

'Let's do that,' said Muir. 'Just give me a moment to put a sign in the shop window – "closed until further notice".'

Epilogue

Conscious of the fact that a steak supper with a glass or two of red followed by a whisky chaser and a large bar of chocolate on top of a twelve-hour shift would send West into a self-induced state of hibernation, Munro, nonetheless, slipped his key into the lock, gently closed the door, and padded softly down the dingy hallway towards the darkened lounge.

'Don't tell me,' said West, 'you've been to Auchencairn and back?'

'Jumping Jehoshaphat!' said Munro, clutching his chest. 'You cannae do that, Charlie! I've had a bypass!'

'Tosh, you're as strong as an ox,' said West, switching the lights on, 'you're not going anywhere.'

'I thought you'd be in your bed, Lord knows, you need the rest.'

'Not as much as you, old-timer. You look like you need a drink.'

'Aye, you're not wrong. Make it a large one.'

Munro licked his lips and raised his glass.

'Your very good health.'

'You must be hungry,' said West. 'I'll do you some cheese on toast.'

‘Much obliged. Has Murdo been behaving himself?’

‘Yup, good as gold, especially as he had your steak. I take it you went to see Barbara Muir?’

‘I did, and she’s now in the *incapable* hands of DI Byrne.’

‘Gawd, that means she’ll be released without charge come the morning.’

‘I’d not be surprised,’ said Munro, ‘as much as I like him, the man’s a balloon, but unfortunately folk like him are destined to succeed. He’d do well in government.’

‘So, what did you nick her for?’

‘Art and part,’ said Munro. ‘McIntyre ran to her after he’d killed Miss Barlow. She was the one who tried to throw us off the scent with all that jiggery-pokery about unexplained deaths and the wrath of the rowan.’

‘She’ll be going down for a while, then?’

‘Indeed she will, but it’s the folk in the village I feel sorry for.’

‘Why?’

‘They’ll have nowhere to shop, not unless someone takes it over, and that could take a wee while.’

‘Well, let’s hope they get it sorted before the sale goes through.’

‘Sale?’

‘Yup, your house,’ said West. ‘Are we going to see it again?’

‘Aye, next week, lassie. Does this mean you’re looking forward to it at long last?’

‘I think so, although the place does seem to be full of nutters.’

‘Och, away!’ said Munro. ‘McIntyre wasnae from the village, and neither was Barlow. It’s God’s acre, Charlie. Nothing ever happens there but good.’

‘Alright, then, you’re on. I’ll let you into a secret, I’m actually quite excited now.’

‘I’m glad to hear it,’ said Munro, knocking back his whisky. ‘Now, I’d start picking out some curtains, if I were you. Nothing modern, mind, you have to respect the age of the property.'

'So you're thinking something *traditional,* then?'

'More antediluvian, Charlie. Aye, that's the word, *antediluvian.*'

Character List

JAMES MUNRO (RETIRED) – Back to full health, aided in no small way by Murdo, his rescued Scottish terrier, the irrepressible James Munro has his suspicions roused by an unexplained death shrouded in folklore and superstition.

DI CHARLOTTE WEST – Now a force to be reckoned with, the headstrong Charlie West, preferring to shout rather than indulge in the gentle art of conversation, follows her instinct when a homeless man is the victim of an unprovoked attack.

DS DOUGAL McCRAE – Half man, half microchip, the technologically minded DS McCrae is torn between searching the darkest recesses of the internet to trace a suspect or sharing a fish supper with an alluring Scenes of Crime Officer.

DS DUNCAN REID – The maverick DS, whose appearance alone is enough to make people cross the street, goes it alone as he tracks down a violent drug dealer and uncovers a convoluted property scam along the way.

DCI GEORGE ELLIOT – The effervescent DCI Elliot, suffering at the hands of his wife's vegetarian cooking, finds his loyalties pushed to the limit when his lifelong friend and ex-colleague, James Munro, over-steps the mark.

DR ANDY MCLEOD – Forensic pathologist Andy McLeod identifies a link between two seemingly unconnected deaths and reluctantly relinquishes any hope of getting a date with the sassy DI West.

ALAN 'DUFFY' MACDUFF – Starting afresh after a messy divorce and a conviction under his belt, MacDuff establishes a successful security business until his past has him running for cover.

REBECCA BARLOW – A petite, attractive property developer with a knack for turning run-down rat holes into urban palaces is preyed upon by a jealous friend.

DI GREG BYRNE – Taking the helm in his first case as a DI, the hapless Byrne, floundering like a flatfish on the deck of a trawler, breathes a sigh of relief when the sagacious Munro becomes involved with the inquiry.

DANIEL MCINTYRE – A sharp-suited high-flyer with the gift of the gab and an eye for the finer things in life gets a wake-up call when his business suffers at the hands of the economy.

EMMA RILEY – Unwittingly lured into a life of crime, the down-to-earth office worker with a taste for the simpler things in life finds herself trapped in the underworld with no way out.

BARBARA MUIR – A respected shop keeper with the welfare of her customers at heart, Muir, whose uneventful life revolves around village gossip, hides a secret not even her family know about.

JOHN DRENNAN – A harmless, tattooed druggie keen to supplement his benefits with the proceeds of anything not quite legal, finds himself in deep water when a deal goes wrong.

DEREK FISHER – A harried nurse with a needy wife, two dogs, and children to support finds himself heading for a breakdown when one of his patients goes missing.

KAY GROGAN – An excitable Scenes of Crime Officer with a passion for fishing, forensics, and microfibres succumbs to the charms of the diffident DS Dougal McCrae.

If you enjoyed this book, please let others know by leaving a quick review on Amazon. Also, if you spot anything untoward in the paperback, get in touch. We strive for the best quality and appreciate reader feedback.

editor@thebookfolks.com

www.thebookfolks.com

ALSO BY PETE BRASSETT

In this series:

SHE – book 1
AVARICE – book 2
ENMITY – book 3
DUPLICITY – book 4
TERMINUS – book 5
TALION – book 6
PERDITION – book 7
RANCOUR – book 8
PENITENT – book 9
TURPITUDE – book 10
HUBRIS – book 11

Other titles:

THE WILDER SIDE OF CHAOS
YELLOW MAN
CLAM CHOWDER AT LAFAYETTE AND SPRING
THE GIRL FROM KILKENNY
BROWN BREAD
PRAYER FOR THE DYING
KISS THE GIRLS

SHE

With a serial killer on their hands, Scottish detective Munro and rookie sergeant West must act fast to trace a woman observed at the crime scene. Yet discovering her true identity, let alone finding her, proves difficult. Soon they realise the crime is far graver than either of them could have imagined.

AVARICE

A sleepy Scottish town, a murder in a glen. The local police chief doesn't want a fuss and calls in DI Munro to lead the investigation. But Munro is a stickler for procedure, and his sidekick Charlie West has a nose for a cover up. Someone in the town is guilty, will they find out who?

ENMITY

When it comes to frustrating a criminal investigation, this killer has all the moves. A spate of murders is causing havoc in a remote Scottish town. Enter Detective Inspector Munro to catch the red herrings and uncover an elaborate and wicked ruse.

DUPLICITY

When a foreign worker casually admits to the murder of a local businessman, detectives in a small Scottish town guess that the victim's violent death points to a more complex cause. Money appears to be a motive, but will anyone believe that they might be in fact dealing with a crime of passion?

TERMINUS

Avid fans of Scottish detective James Munro will be worrying it is the end of the line for their favourite sleuth when, battered and bruised following a hit and run, the veteran crime-solver can't pin down a likely suspect.

TALION

A boy finds a man's body on a beach. Police quickly suspect foul play when they discover he was part of a local drugs ring. With no shortage of suspects, they have a job pinning anyone down. But when links to a local business are discovered, it seems the detectives may have stumbled upon a much bigger crime than they could have imagined.

PERDITION

A man is found dead in his car. A goat is killed with a crossbow. What connects these events in a rural Scottish backwater? DI Charlotte West investigates in this gripping murder mystery that ends with a sucker punch of a twist.

RANCOUR

When the body of a girl found on a mountainside tests positive for a date rape drug, police suspect a local Lothario is responsible. He certainly had the means, motive and opportunity. But is this really such a cut and dry case? What are the detectives missing?

PENITENT

The shady past of a small town surfaces when a young woman is found murdered in a pool. As detectives investigate, a legacy of regret and resentment emerges. DI Munro and DI West must get to the bottom of the matter.

TURPITUDE

A murdered jeweller, a series of bungled moped robberies and several fingers found at a refuse site. What connects these events? That's what DI Charlie West and her team must find out, with a little bit of help from Munro. But will the latter be too distracted by his new friend to be of much help?

HUBRIS

When a dead sailor is found in a boat, detective Charlie West is tasked with finding out why. But getting answers from a tight-knit Scottish fishing community won't be easy, and besides, has the killer completely covered their tracks?

Printed in Great Britain
by Amazon

66999163R00142